DOUBLE MORTICE

Bill Daly

Published in Great Britain in 2015 by Old Street Publishing
c/o Parallel, 8 Hurlingham Business Park, Sulivan Road
London SW6 3DU

www.oldstreetpublishing.co.uk

ISBN 978-1-910400-13-5

10 9 8 7 6 5 4 3 2 1

A CIP catalogue record for this title is available from the British Library.

Typeset by JaM

Printed and bound in Great Britain.

For Mae, John, Ivy & Les

PROLOGUE

Sunday 13 February, 2011

Jack McFarlane grunted as he took the next punch to his solar plexus. He made no attempt to defend himself. That's what they were hoping for. That he would try to fight back and his remission would be cut for brawling. That would give them the opportunity to have another go at him. But he hadn't taken so many beatings over the years to crack now.

'Where the fuck did you stash it?' Rodgers growled, ramming both McFarlane's arms painfully up his back.

'Stash what?'

A hail of punches from McNee came hammering into McFarlane's guts, causing him to retch.

When the sound of approaching footsteps rang out in the corridor, Rodgers released his grip and McFarlane sank to his knees, throwing up all over the cell floor.

Despite the pain, McFarlane managed a wry grin. This was the last time they would be able to do this to him.

Tomorrow, he was getting out.

ONE

Monday 14 February

Brutus sprang onto the black duvet and froze on landing. His claws sank into the yielding down and he kneaded the quilt as he stared through the gloom at the two recumbent shapes. Circling twice, he settled at the end of the bed and started teasing his knotted fur, the rhythmic rasping of his tongue seemingly synchronised with Michael's regular snoring. When he'd finished grooming, Brutus rose, arched his back and stretched onto the tips of all four paws, his gaze flitting from one dormant figure to the other. Having made his choice, he picked his steps across the bed and purred noisily as he rubbed his whiskers into the nape of Michael's neck.

Michael swatted out blindly as he drifted into consciousness. Rolling over, he prodded the figure by his side. 'Anne. Wake up! Your bloody cat's pestering me.'

He heard a sharp intake of breath. 'Oh, for Christ's sake! Is it too much to expect you to remember who you were screwing last night?'

Before he could react she'd scrambled from the bed and was striding, naked, towards the en suite bathroom, the glass shower door rattling in its frame as she slammed it behind her.

Michael mouthed a curse as he sat up in bed and buried his face in his hands. The moment his head left the pillow he felt the dull throb at the base of his skull; the nagging ache that plagued his every waking minute. Mornings were always the worst.

'I'm sorry, Pippa,' he called out in the general direction of the closed bathroom door. Raising his voice caused a further stab of pain behind his eyes. 'I was half-asleep. I was dreaming. The cat woke me up,' he shouted while massaging his temples with his fingertips. 'I always associate the cat with Anne...' His voice tailed off, his lame excuse drowned by the crash of cascading water as the shower was turned up full.

Michael swung his legs over the side of the bed and groped to turn on the lamp. He reached for the pill-jar on the bedside table and spilled two paracetamol tablets onto the palm of his hand, stuffing them into his mouth and grimacing at the unpleasant taste as he crunched into the dry pills. He picked up the glass of water from the table and swallowed a long draught. Putting on his gold-framed spectacles, he squinted through them at his watch.

'Shit!' he muttered. 'Late again.' With a world-weary sigh he got to his feet and trudged over to the wardrobe. Sliding open the door, he pulled out his dressing gown and slipped it over his shoulders.

Michael Gibson was in his early forties, his once rugged features beginning to show signs of grizzled decline – his eyes puffy and faintly blood-shot, deep lines etched from nostrils to mouth, flecks of grey in his thinning, black hair.

When he pressed a concealed button beneath the window frame, a motor hummed quietly and the black-and-white striped curtains swished open. He switched off the bedside lamp and made his way along the corridor to the lounge, running his tongue round the roof of his mouth as he went in an attempt to rid himself of the lingering, bitter taste of paracetamol.

The decor in the lounge, as in all the rooms of the modern apartment, came straight from an interior designer's catalogue. The large, rectangular area was dominated by a red-leather settee and studded armchairs. Against the far wall, next to the bar, stood a bookcase replete with leather-bound volumes of Shakespeare, Dickens and Burns while, on the opposite side of the room, Anne's collection of nineteenth century porcelain figurines stared out disdainfully from their custom-built display cabinet.

There were no curtains in the lounge. As the flat was situated on the top floor of Dalgleish Tower, there was no need. From the floor-to-ceiling plate glass windows there was normally a magnificent view north, across the city, towards the Campsie Hills, but this bleak, February morning all Michael could see was dirty, grey sleet buffeting the glass, pinned against the window by the force of the northerly gale. He stopped and listened when he heard an unaccustomed noise – a high-pitched whine. It took him a moment to realise it was the howl of the wind. It was the first time he'd heard anything through the double-glazing.

Michael stared into the black void, fascinated by the shadowy shapes oozing across the outside of the pane; coursing rivulets of ice whipped upwards by the funnelling wind and back-lit eerily by the street lamps far below. As he watched, transfixed, swirling images formed, then melted away in the ever-changing patterns. Suddenly he saw two cold, blue eyes staring at him from the other side of the glass; unblinking eyes, locking onto his. His mouth went completely dry. He could feel the hairs on the back of his neck stand proud. He wanted to look away but he couldn't deflect his gaze. He felt panic building up. The palms of his hands turned clammy. Pressure was mounting inside his skull.

'McFarlane,' he mouthed. He tried to close his eyes to block out the image but, as in his nightmare, he found himself incapable of doing so. His eyelids seemed to be held open by some unseen force. His heart was thumping against his rib cage as the staring eyes grew larger and larger but, despite his anxiety, he realised there was something different. At first he didn't know what it was – then it struck him. The scarred face wasn't there – only the piercing blue eyes. When he focussed on the fine eyebrows he realised he wasn't gazing into McFarlane's eyes. These were Anne's eyes – the same pale blue. He'd never before made the connection.

As suddenly as it had appeared, the image exploded in front of his face, disintegrating in a puff of whiteness as a fresh torrent of snow slammed against the window. Michael looked away and blinked several times. His whole body was trembling. Although dreading the eyes re-appearing, something compelled him to peer again into the inky blackness. For a fleeting moment he thought he saw Anne's face looming in the shadows but before he could focus on her features, they dissolved in a grey, amorphous mass that slithered down the pane.

Michael swallowed hard, his mind in turmoil. What was happening to him? His recurrent nightmare was now invading his waking consciousness. Was he cracking up?

TWO

When Philippa Scott emerged from the bathroom she was swaddled in Michael's towelling dressing gown, her long, auburn hair swept back from her lightly-freckled face and turbaned in a bath towel. Tall and slim, she had a narrow face with high cheekbones and a slightly retroussé nose. Her eyebrows, plucked to the point of being non-existent, gave full emphasis to her large, turquoise eyes. Her skin was bright and clear and she was wearing no make-up. She exuded self-confidence. Although only twenty-four, she was one of the most gifted lawyers Michael had ever hired.

Philippa stopped in the lounge doorway and stared, tight-lipped, at Michael's back. He sensed her presence but didn't turn round. Without a word she swept on down the corridor and into the kitchen. Cutting two thin slices of brown bread, she popped them into the toaster before switching on the coffee machine.

Michael's head was thumping as he followed her into the kitchen. 'I've apologised, Pippa,' he said. 'What more can I do?'

'You can leave her,' she retorted petulantly. 'That's what more you can do.'

'I've told you a dozen times, I will leave her.'

'That is precisely the problem, Michael. You *have* told me a dozen times that you'll leave Anne, but you never do a damned thing about it. There's always some reason or other why you can't break the news to her. Well I'm not prepared to go on like this any longer. I've had a year of lunchtime assignations at my flat and the occasional weekend here. That's not enough. It has to be all or nothing.'

'Okay, Pippa.' Michael hesitated. 'I was giving it a lot of thought yesterday. I've made up my mind. I'm going to tell Anne tonight.'

Philippa's mood changed instantly, her surly expression evaporating and her eyes positively sparkling as she clasped her fingers to her face. 'That's fantastic!' Squealing with delight she ran across the kitchen and threw her arms around his neck, clashing their lips together and thrusting her tongue deep inside his mouth. Michael responded by intertwining their tongues and slipping his hand inside her dressing gown.

'And you can cut that out for a start.' She giggled as she twisted from his grasp and pushed him away. 'I don't know what your schedule's like today, Mr Gibson,' she said coyly, 'but I've got a meeting with a very important client at ten o'clock and it'll take me half an hour to dry my hair and get ready.'

Without warning she launched herself at him again, laughing hysterically as she grabbed him round the waist and waltzed him dizzily round the kitchen until they crashed into the table. She held on to him tightly to steady her spinning head as she ran her fingernails sensually up and down his spine. 'But you can come round to my place this evening,' she panted, gnawing hungrily at his ear lobe. 'After you've had your chat with Anne.'

Michael held her close. 'You can be a right little minx at times,' he said with a wry smile, kissing her tenderly on the forehead before releasing her from his grip. Sitting down at the table, Philippa spread marmalade on her toast and poured out two mugs of coffee.

'Talking of schedules, God only knows where I'm supposed to be this morning,' Michael said. 'I'd better call Sheila.'

Picking up the phone he dialled his office number. It was answered on the second ring; the smooth, cultured voice repeating the greeting he'd heard many times before.

'Good morning. Gibson & Gibson – Mr Michael Gibson's office – Sheila Thompson speaking. How can I help you?'

'Sheila, it's me. I'm running late. What's the diary like?'

'Let me see. You've got a meeting with Frank Whyte at nine to finalise the brief for the Madill case. The trial starts tomorrow and Mr Whyte's defending for us. At ten-thirty Inspector Anderson is coming across to discuss the case with you. You're playing squash with Tom Crosbie at eleven, then Madill and Frank Whyte have a meeting with you at half past twelve to finalise the defence.'

'I won't be able to get to the office before ten – and I haven't had a chance to look at the Madill papers. I brought the file home with me on Friday but I haven't even had time to open my briefcase.' Michael winked at Philippa. 'It's been non-stop all weekend.'

Philippa spluttered over a mouthful of coffee. Michael shook his fist in mock annoyance as he put his hand over the mouthpiece to try to avoid Sheila hearing the female laughter.

'Okay, Sheila. Tell Whyte to discuss the options for Madill's defence with Peter Davies – he knows the score. Schedule both of them to see me at ten o'clock to brief me on their recommendations. Keep the meeting with Anderson at ten-thirty – I don't want to ruffle his feathers. Cancel the squash – I couldn't face it. Leave the meeting with Madill and Whyte at twelve-thirty.'

'Very good, Mr Gibson.'

'What do I have this afternoon?'

'This is the second Monday of the month, so normally you would be going up to Crighton Hall. But with the weather being like this…?'

Michael paused to consider. 'If it's at all possible, I'll go. Leave it like that for now. I'll see what the weather's like in the afternoon. What else is there?'

'You've got two meetings later on. At four o'clock you're reviewing the promotion plan with Peter Davies and at six you've got a session with Ellen McMillan to discuss who should handle the Convery case.'

'I don't want to go back to the office this afternoon. Could those meetings be rescheduled?'

'I suppose so.' Sheila sounded dubious. 'But you have already deferred Mr Davies three times. The promotion plan should've been finalised last month.'

'You're right.' Michael sighed audibly. 'I can't put him off again. He was spitting blood the last time. Tell you what. Leave the slot with Davies at four but re-schedule the six o'clock meeting to later in the week. Anne'll be home around six-thirty this evening and I need to be here when she arrives.'

'Yes, Mr Gibson.'

'My father always said Sheila was worth her weight in gold,' Michael said as he replaced the receiver. 'Efficiency personified. No fuss, no hassle.' He picked up the coffee pot and waved it in Philippa's direction. 'Fancy another cup?'

Philippa shook her head as she finished off her toast. 'No, thanks. I really must get ready.'

'I'll grab a quick shower and we can leave together.'

As Philippa walked from the kitchen, Brutus padded in languidly. Fixing his stare on Michael, he jumped up onto the table and started miaowing noisily. Michael lifted him off and put him back down on the floor. 'Bloody nuisance,' he muttered. 'First you land me in the shit – then you expect me to feed you.'

Opening the cupboard beneath the sink, he took a tin of cat food from the shelf and tugged open the ring-pull, forking the contents into a bowl. Brutus's tail stiffened as he followed Michael down the hall towards one of the guest bedrooms. Michael placed the bowl on the floor, between the sleeping basket and the litter tray, and Brutus greedily devoured the contents, purring contentedly.

Michael adjusted the temperature of the shower until it was as hot as his skin could bear. He closed his eyes and, as the water poured down his body, he tried to rehearse how he would break the news to Anne. He was dreading the confrontation. He'd been close to broaching the subject several times during the past couple of months but had always ducked the issue. Tonight, he knew he'd have to go through with it.

His thoughts drifted back to their university days, when he and Anne had met and fallen in love. It seemed such a distant memory. The early years of their marriage had been blissful with hardly a cross word – until they started bickering over how to deal with Paul's behavioural problems. Things had never been the same after that.

His relationship with Pippa was totally different. This wasn't just a casual fling. Every day for the past year he'd become more and more besotted with her. She was like a drug to him. He needed to be with her all the time. He realised he'd have to leave Anne in order to keep her, but he knew Anne wasn't going to accept that without a fight.

When he'd finished showering, Michael stropped his razor before shaving. He found the ritual therapeutic. He'd used the same ivory-handled, cut-throat blade since he'd first started shaving. Several times he'd tried to switch to an electric razor because wet shaving was so time-consuming, but no matter which one he tried it brought his skin out in a rash.

Lathering his face, he peered short-sightedly at his reflection in the steamed-up bathroom mirror. The dark-grey bags under his eyes and the heavy jowls were now permanent features – as were the puffy, bloodshot eyes – ever since the headaches had started. He knew he should have been to see a doctor months ago, but his fear of the diagnosis outweighed the pain of the headaches.

Michael shaved quickly, his practised hand running the blade over his skin without once nicking the flesh. When he'd finished, he splashed his face with cold water and then with the Azzaro aftershave Philippa had given him for Christmas, catching his breath and wincing from the astringent sting. Having squeezed toothpaste onto his electric toothbrush, he brushed vigorously before rinsing out his mouth. Yawning and stretching, he wandered back to the bedroom.

The motif of the sparsely furnished room was Charles Rennie Mackintosh, designed around the wide double bed and the reproduction bedside tables. The decor was black-and-white throughout, apart from the dressing table, also a reproduction in the Rennie Mackintosh style, carved from mahogany and inlaid with satin-wood. The walls were lined with white fabric, a suitably neutral backcloth for the two Rennie Mackintosh watercolours that hung on the wall facing the bed.

Michael went through his customary routine of covering up the evidence of Philippa's visit; smoothing the sheet at Anne's side of the bed and plumping up her pillow, then emptying the contents of the waste bin in the bathroom into a plastic carrier bag.

He often wondered about Anne. Did she ever have affairs? If so, she'd never given herself away. To the best of his knowledge, she'd never brought a man back to their house when they'd lived in Bearsden, nor to Dalgleish Tower. But did she really go to Aberdeen every month? And if so, did she always stay overnight at her parents' cottage? Perhaps she had a secret assignation on the way there or on the way back? When she went on tour with her amateur dramatic society, was she never involved in anything more exhilarating than theatre production, make-up and costume design? And her bridge congresses – did people *really* take the ferry across to Rothesay and spend the weekend in a hotel – just to play bridge?

Crossing to the wardrobe, Michael selected one of six identical white shirts hanging on the rail. He rejected his blue cashmere suit as the waistband was getting uncomfortably tight. He had always prided himself in keeping fit – jogging regularly and playing squash several times a week. However, during the past six months, since the headaches had started, he'd taken little exercise and had put on almost a stone in weight, most of it around the midriff. Having decided on the more generous-fitting, grey pin-stripe, he selected a matching silk tie and a pair of highly-polished black shoes.

When he'd dressed, he returned to the bathroom and combed his hair carefully in front of the mirror. Although he'd never considered tinting his hair, his vanity was such that he still tried to hide the grey flecks.

Picking up the empty champagne flutes from the bedside tables, he carried them through to the kitchen and tipped the dregs down the sink. He washed and dried the glasses, along with Philippa's coffee mug and plate and put them away in the cupboard, then put his own coffee mug into the dishwasher. He dropped the champagne bottle, along with the empty red-wine bottle, into his carrier bag and left it by the front door to take down to the dustbin on his way out.

Slumping down at the kitchen table, he switched on Radio Scotland to catch the news headlines while waiting for Philippa to emerge.

Just after nine-thirty they descended together in the lift, Philippa impeccably dressed in a white silk blouse, a tight black mini-skirt and matching jacket, her auburn locks cascading down her back almost to her waist. She was carrying her overnight bag and her briefcase.

When the lift doors slid open in the underground garage, Michael dropped the carrier bag into the nearest dustbin, then stopped in his tracks. His Mercedes was missing and in its place stood a Ford transit van, painted in psychedelic colours, with the motif *Citizens Band* daubed in bright blue letters across the side.

'I'll throttle him!'

'What happened?'

'Paul came round here yesterday afternoon while you were out shopping and cadged fifty quid because he was broke.'

'You've given him a job, for goodness sake. And, I suppose, a half-decent salary. Why does he need to cadge off you?'

'I don't know. He seems to be broke most of the time.' Michael shook his head. 'God knows what he does with his money. Then he asked to borrow my car for the evening to impress his new girlfriend. Apparently his *Citizens Band* van isn't the thing to be seen in on a first date.'

Philippa burst out laughing. 'I can see his point. I don't think I'd fancy going out with someone in that heap.'

'I told him he could have the Merc on condition he brought it back before eight o'clock this morning. That's the last bloody time I'll ever let him borrow my car.'

'Don't be such an old fuddy-duddy. He probably had more important things on his mind last night than bringing your car back. Remember what it was like when you were young?' Philippa smirked. 'Jump in. I'll give you a lift to the office.'

Michael shook his head. 'It's too risky. Someone might see us together.'

'Hardly any great risk,' Philippa pouted, 'considering that you're going to tell Anne tonight that you're leaving her.'

Michael ignored her comment. 'I can take Anne's car.' He nodded towards the black Volvo in the adjacent parking bay. 'She went up to Aberdeen by train on Friday. She didn't want to risk driving because the weather was so lousy. I'll have to nip back upstairs to get the spare key.'

'Have it your own way.' Philippa flung her bag and her briefcase onto the passenger seat of her red Peugeot 207 GTi. Wiggling her hips provocatively, she slid her tight skirt up her thighs before clambering in behind the wheel. She lowered her driver's window as she fired the engine. 'I may bump into you at the office this morning, Mr Gibson. If not, I'll be waiting for you at my place tonight with the champagne on ice. We'll have a special celebration.' She winked. 'Just the two of us – after you've had your chat with Anne.'

Michael forced a smile as he pressed the button on his remote control to operate the garage doors. Blowing an extravagant kiss from her fingertips, Philippa dropped the car into gear and accelerated violently up the ramp. Michael blew back a kiss and waved, watching her car until the garage doors shuddered down and clanged shut.

THREE

Jack McFarlane pulled his scarf tight around his neck and zipped his anorak up to give himself some protection from the sleety drizzle as he walked through the doors of Peterhead prison. He slung his tartan holdall over his shoulder and waved in the direction of the white Rover parked along the street. The headlights flashed once in recognition as the engine burst into life and the car came smoothly towards him. When it pulled up alongside, the driver leaned back to fling open the rear door. McFarlane threw his holdall onto the back seat and clambered in after it.

'Thanks for the reception committee, Malky,' McFarlane said, wiping the sleet from his shaven head.

'Compliments of Mr Robertson.' Malky leaned over the back of the seat to proffer his hand which McFarlane clenched in a painfully firm grip.

'Fancy a fag?' Malky asked, producing a packet of Benson & Hedges and a book of matches and holding them up.

'Thanks.' McFarlane stretched forward to take the cigarettes. Having lit up, he inhaled deeply, then unzipped his anorak and settled back in his seat to gaze out of the window as the car accelerated away from the kerb.

Jack McFarlane was in his late-forties; tall, thickset, with shrewd, pale-blue eyes. His nose, twice broken during amateur boxing bouts, was crooked and permanently puffy. His face was indented with pock marks but his main distinguishing feature was the jagged, purple scar running from the corner of his left eye to just under his ear – the legacy of a Glasgow razor fight.

'Mr Robertson said to give you these,' Malky said, picking up an envelope and two small packets from the passenger seat and handing them across. McFarlane ripped open the envelope and pulled out the single sheet of paper. He scanned the hand-written note:

> *'Jack, I realise we've got unfinished business to sort out but it would make sense for you to steer clear of Glasgow for the time being. The cops will be sticking to you like glue. I've got a flat in London you can use. I've told Malky to drop you off at the station. The address of the flat and the keys are in one of the parcels I sent you, as well as a train ticket. Don't try to get in touch with me by phone – the cops are razor sharp on intercepts these days. There's five grand on account in the other package. That should tide you over till we get together. I'll send you the usual signal when I reckon it's okay for you to come up north.*
>
> *If you do get any hassle from the cops when you're back in Glasgow, give Frank Morrison a bell.*
>
> *Larry.'*

'Give Morrison a bell?' McFarlane mused, raising an eyebrow. If Larry had the top lawyer in Glasgow on his payroll, business must be going well. Having split open one of the parcels, he riffled the wad of new notes. Counting off two hundred pounds, he stuffed it into the hip pocket of his jeans and zipped the rest of the money into the inside pocket of his anorak. He tore open the second packet and checked the address of the flat before pocketing the keys and the train ticket.

The traffic was light as they headed towards Aberdeen city centre.

'We've got bags of time before your train, Jack,' Malky said. 'Do you fancy a swally?'

'I could fair molocate a pint.' McFarlane glanced at his watch. 'But the pubs won't be open yet.'

'Some of them are,' Malky said. 'A few things have changed for the better since you went inside.'

'Lead me to it, then. I've got one hell of a drouth on me,' McFarlane said, smacking his lips.

'What are you for, Jack?' Malky asked as they walked into the quiet bar.

'A hauf and a pint o' heavy.'

Malky ordered two Lagavulins and two pints of Belhaven at the bar and carried the drinks on a tray over to the table by the door where McFarlane had installed himself.

'What was it like in Peterheid?' Malky asked, sipping at his pint.

'Have you no' done time yersel'?'

'Just six months, like, in the Bar-L.'

'Then you ken fine weel what it's like.'

'Aye, but twelve years. That's no' like six months.'

McFarlane picked up his whisky glass and threw back the contents in one gulp. 'At first I fair missed the bevvy,' he said, grimacing as the neat whisky burned at the back of his throat. 'But you get used to that after a while. Funnily enough,' he said weighing his pint in his fist, 'the thing that really got to me was not being able to walk. You get to dauner roun' the exercise yard, of course, but that's no' walkin'. Walkin' means grass and mountains and, aye, pissin'-doon rain.'

Raising his pint to his lips, McFarlane poured the beer down his throat in one long, slow, gurgling swallow. 'Twelve years inside sure builds up a helluva thirst.' He licked his lips. 'That hit the spot. Same again?' he asked, getting to his feet.

Malky shook his head. 'I don't think I'll try to keep up with you, Jack. Not if you want me to get you to the station in one piece.'

McFarlane crossed to the bar and ordered another whisky and another pint of Belhaven. When he returned to the table he sipped his drinks slowly, savouring every mouthful, as his eyes travelled round the bar, studying the faces of all the other customers. 'Take a shuftie at that one over there,' he whispered in Malky's ear. 'The punter in the blue pullover with his heid buried in the newspaper. My money's on him. He came in just after us and ordered a half-pint shandy. He's hardly touched it.'

When they'd finished their drinks, McFarlane gave the signal and they got to their feet and strode out of the pub. As soon as he got behind the wheel, Malky swivelled his rear-view mirror so he could see the pub door.'

'Spot on, Jack. Your man came out right behind us and crossed the road to a silver-grey Ford Focus. He's our tail all right.'

'Good to know twelve years inside haven't dulled the auld senses. I could always smell a pig a mile aff.'

As they headed towards the city centre the traffic was heavier, Malky continually checking his rear-view mirror. 'He's still there. About five cars back. Do you want me to try to lose him?'

'Not at all, Malky. You wouldn't want to get booked for speedin', would you? He's welcome to follow me anywhere he wants. I'll bore the fuckin' arse off him over the next few days.' McFarlane guffawed.

Anne Gibson drained her coffee cup and dabbed delicately at the corners of her narrow mouth, taking care not to smudge her lipstick. Folding her linen napkin neatly, she slipped it back into its silver ring. 'I really think we should be making a move, Dad,' she said, pushing her chair back from the table and getting to her feet. She crossed to the window and gazed out. 'It doesn't seem to be easing off.' The snow, already several inches deep, was falling steadily.

Peter Jackson folded his newspaper as he rose from his armchair. 'I'm ready whenever you are, love. I only have to slip on my shoes. Jean,' he called down the hall. 'We're leaving now. We want to give ourselves plenty of time to get to the station.'

Jean Jackson came bustling along the corridor from the kitchen with a coffee pot in her hand. 'Do you not have time for another cup, Anne?'

'No, thanks, Mum.'

'I don't like the look of that weather.' Jean peered anxiously through the window. 'Are you sure you can't stay another night?'

Anne put a comforting arm around her mother's shoulders. 'I told you, Mum. I've arranged to play with Mary in a tournament at the bridge club this afternoon. But look on the bright side – at least I came up by train. If I'd brought the car I'd have to drive back to Glasgow now.'

Jean mimed a shiver. 'Perish the thought. I only hope the weather's better next weekend. Just about everyone's coming up for your party.'

'I'll be here for that come hell or high water. It'll take more than a few flakes of snow to stop me celebrating my fortieth.'

'It's a pity your sister won't be here,' Jean said. 'It would have been lovely to have had the whole family together.'

'It's a long way to come from Vancouver for a party, Mum. Apart from that, there's no way she could get time off during the school term.'

'I realise that,' Jean said with a sigh. 'But it's still a shame.'

'She'll be across in July. A good excuse for another party.'

Anne bent down and kissed her mother lightly on the forehead.

'Are you ready, Anne?' Peter coughed as he pulled on his driving gloves.

'I'll be right with you, Dad. I just have to nip upstairs and grab my things.'

Anne took the stairs to her bedroom two at a time. Little had changed in the room since she'd left home more than twenty years ago. The same single bed, the same patterned wallpaper, the same beige carpet, the same ornate crucifix positioned above the bed. On the bedside table, beside the reading lamp, stood the alabaster statue of Saint Anthony of Padua to whom her mother always prayed if she lost something of value.

'I'm off now, Edward,' she announced to her childhood teddy bear, which still had pride of place in the middle of the dressing table. Kicking off her slippers, she sat on the edge of the bed to pull on her knee-length boots.

Anne Gibson was a striking figure of a woman. Although close to six feet tall she chose to wear high-heeled boots to exaggerate her height. She was slimly built with long legs and a narrow waist. Her small mouth seemed out of proportion to her large, pale-blue eyes and long, straight nose. Her brown hair, cropped short, was streaked with blonde highlights.

When she'd zipped up her boots she stood up straight and ran her hands down her sides to smooth the skirt of her leather suit. She crossed to the wardrobe mirror to check her appearance, hitching up her skirt slightly so that it brushed against the tops of her boots. She tucked her blouse firmly into her waistband and slipped on her jacket. Her case was lying open on the bed, already packed. Pushing in her slippers, she closed the lid, then picked up her sapphire ring from the bedside table and slipped it on as she leaned across to kiss Edward on the forehead. 'See you next weekend, old boy. It'll be a big party. Everybody who's anybody is coming. Till then, you're in charge.'

She draped her cashmere coat over her arm and picked up her suitcase and her handbag. With a final glance round the room to make sure she'd hadn't forgotten anything, she hurried downstairs.

Peter Jackson had opened the garage doors and was already sitting behind the wheel of his Jaguar, the engine ticking over.

'Bye, Mum. Thanks for a lovely weekend. See you next Saturday', Anne said, giving Jean a cuddle.

'I do hope you're going to be all right.' Jean said, making the sign of the cross as she took a step back. 'I'll say a prayer for you.'

'Don't fret, Mum. I'll be fine.'

'Don't forget to phone me as soon as you get home.'

'I'm going straight from the railway station to the bridge club, so I won't be home much before seven. But I will call you later this evening – I promise.'

Picking her steps carefully across the snow-covered path, Anne opened the car boot and dropped in her coat and her case before climbing into the passenger seat and clipping on her seat belt.

'What do you think, Dad?'

'No problem. I've got the chains on and I saw the snowplough pass by an hour ago. We'll be fine as soon as we get to the main road.' Peter Jackson slowly navigated the hundred yards of driveway that connected his cottage to the main road, the wheel-grip secure as the chains bit into the crisp snow. As he'd anticipated, the main thoroughfare was relatively clear.

'You were very quiet this weekend,' Peter said as he waited for a slow-moving van to pass by before turning into the road. 'Is everything all right?' Anne didn't respond. 'Is Michael still seeing her?' he asked quietly.

Anne turned in her seat to look at him. 'I think so.'

'I don't know how you put up with it, Anne. I really don't. If your mother had any idea what he's been up to, she wouldn't allow him across the threshold.'

'You musn't tell her. You promised.'

'Of course I won't tell her.' The traffic lights up ahead turned to red and Peter applied the brakes gently. 'Why don't you just walk out on him and be done with it?'

'I don't know what to do, Dad. I really don't.' Anne bit her lip. 'The problem is – I still love him.'

'I don't know how you can, after what he's put you through.'

'Last year, when I first suspected he was seeing someone, I decided not to confront him because that could have forced him to choose between her and me – and I wasn't at all sure I'd like the result. I hoped that, if I let the affair run its course, it would come to a natural end and then I might be able to convince him that we needed to see a marriage counsellor.'

'Is it not too late for that, Anne? After all, it's not as if it's the first time he's wandered off the straight and narrow. There was that girl from the squash club you told me about.'

'That was just a weekend fling.'

'For goodness sake, Anne, don't start defending him! For all you know, there may well have been others.'

'I realise that, Dad.' Anne let out a sigh. 'But before I give up on him, I have to do everything I can to try to save our marriage. For better or for worse, and all that.'

Peter snorted. 'It's been nothing but 'worse' for quite some time, as far as I can make out. Do you have any idea who she is?'

'I've got a pretty good idea. I didn't say anything to you before, but I suspected it might be someone from his work so I dropped in unannounced at the office Christmas party. There wasn't much doubt about it. He followed one of his juniors around all night like a lovesick puppy.'

There was an awkward silence for the remainder of the journey

'You're going to be very early for your train,' Peter said as he drew up outside the station. 'I'll wait with you.'

'You'll do nothing of the sort.' Anne spoke firmly as she unclipped her seat belt. 'This weather could turn a lot nastier very quickly. You head straight back home.'

'Are you sure?'

'Of course. Anyway, I could murder another cup of coffee. And I've got my book to read,' she added, tapping her handbag. 'Thanks for the lift.' She leaned across to kiss him on the cheek. 'See you next Saturday.'

Peter hesitated. 'Will *he* –' Peter spat out the word, 'be coming with you?'

Anne took her father's hand and squeezed it gently. 'Despite everything, *he* wouldn't miss my fortieth birthday party.'

'I think you should come up by train.'

'You know Michael. He'd rather drive through a Himalayan blizzard than take a train. Anyway, I'll need the car to carry back all my presents, won't I?' She tickled him playfully under the chin.

'You behave yourself.' He smiled at her. 'And don't forget to phone your mother when you get back to Glasgow.'

Getting out of the car, Anne hurried round to the boot to lift out her coat and her suitcase. The air felt bitterly cold in contrast to the warmth of the car. She slipped her coat over her shoulders and stood waving until the Jaguar had disappeared from sight. The station clock showed five past ten – half an hour to kill. The snow was still falling steadily and the chill wind was piercing her coat. She picked up her case and marched briskly into the buffet where she ordered a black coffee and a tuna sandwich to eat on the train. Sitting down at the table nearest to the radiator, she took her book from her bag and flicked through it until she found her place.

FOUR

The Volvo's wiper blades were having difficulty coping with the driving sleet that was angling down, whipped horizontal by the northerly wind. Despite having the heater at full blast, Michael couldn't find the control to direct the hot air onto the windscreen and his breath was freezing on contact with the glass. His temper was frayed as he crawled along, rubbing vigorously at the windscreen with the heel of his glove in an attempt to improve the visibility.

When he tried to merge with the slow-moving traffic on the Clydeside Expressway, he hit a patch of black ice and lost control. The car skidded sideways. He over-corrected the steering and instinctively slammed his foot on the brake pedal. The wheels locked and he slithered, almost in slow motion, into the back of an Audi in the inside lane. There was a jarring crunch as the two vehicles came together.

The Audi driver, a stocky, over-weight teenager, eased his car forward a few feet before applying the handbrake. Scrambling out, he lumbered round to the back of his vehicle to inspect the damage.

Michael pressed the button to lower his window. 'I'm sorry,' he called out. 'My wheels locked. I couldn't stop.'

'This is ma faither's car, mister,' he bleated. 'If it's damaged I'm callin' the polis.'

The youth was visibly shivering as he bent low and rubbed away the dirt on his rear wing to examine the paintwork. When he stood up straight his straggly hair was matted to the sides of his face. He cupped both hands to his mouth and shouted through the sleet. 'You came aff worst, Jimmy. You've broken your sidelight. I'm no' even scratched.' A broad grin broke out on his face. 'That's yer Vorsprung Durch Technik for you, pal.'

Without waiting for Michael's response, he raised his right arm in a Nazi salute and goose-stepped his way back to his car door.

Michael was fuming as he followed in the Audi's tracks, threading his way past several abandoned vehicles lining the route. By the time he got to his office, it was almost ten-thirty. The journey from Dalgleish Tower, normally fifteen minutes, had taken the best part of an hour. He'd missed his ten o'clock briefing and was in danger of being late for his meeting with DCI Anderson.

When he reached his office block, he drove down the steep ramp to the underground car park and swung towards his reserved parking bay, then slammed his foot on the brake. There, in his bay, stood his Mercedes. 'You're a complete pillock, Paul!' He hammered his fist into the steering column. Glancing round the small car park he saw all the other bays were taken. The nearest parking was the multi-storey, half a mile away, and he'd brought neither a coat nor an umbrella.

By the time he'd sprinted back to the office, Michael was out of breath and soaked to the skin. His hair was sodden with sleet.

'Good morning… Mr Gibson…' Sheila stammered as the drenched figure swept past her into the office.

'Come in here, Sheila.' Instinctively grabbing her note-pad and pen, Sheila followed him into the office. 'Don't even ask,' he seethed. He wrenched off his steamed-up spectacles and rubbed at them furiously with his handkerchief. 'Is DCI Anderson still here?'

'He left about ten minutes ago. He had to be back in Pitt Street at eleven o'clock to deliver a lecture to a graduate trainee seminar. Paul spoke to him to see if he could help, but Anderson insisted he had to talk to you. I told him I'd be in touch as soon as I knew when you'd be available.'

'Do you know what he wanted?' Michael asked, stripping off his jacket.

'He told Paul he wanted to discuss a plea bargain for the Madill case. Do you want me to try to get him on the phone?'

Michael let out a sigh. 'I know him. He'll want a face-to-face meeting. Call his secretary and find out if we can find a slot sometime today. I'll go over to Pitt Street if that's more convenient for him. Then try to find a towel and something for me to wear while I dry off my suit on the radiator. After you've done that, ask Whyte and Davies to brief me on the Madill case and when I'm through with them, tell my bloody son to get his backside in here.'

'Yes, Mr Gibson.'

Ten minutes later there was a knock on the office door and Sheila entered laden with a bath towel, a Paisley-pattern dressing gown, a pair of slippers, a clean white shirt, a pair of black socks, a hair dryer and a steaming cup of coffee. She placed all the items on Michael's desk.

'Inspector Anderson can see you at eleven forty-five,' she said, referring to her notebook.' I've ordered a cab for eleven-thirty to take you across to Pitt Street. A taxi will pick you up from there at twelve-fifteen to get you back here in time for your meeting with Madill and Whyte at twelve-thirty. Mr Whyte and Mr Davies are waiting outside – I'll send them in as soon as you've changed out of your wet clothes. Paul is on standby to see you when you're through with them. Is there anything else?'

Michael managed a weak smile. 'That seems to be everything. Thanks. Tell me, Sheila,' he added, nodding towards the pile of clothes on the desk. 'Is there some poor bugger out there wandering around in his bare feet with no shirt on?'

Sheila blushed. 'Of course not, Mr Gibson.' Half-smiling, she turned to leave. 'Buzz through when you're ready to see Mr Whyte and Mr Davies.'

When her intercom sounded, Sheila whispered to Frank Whyte. 'I'd better warn you. He's in dressing gown and slippers this morning. Whatever you do, don't laugh.'

Peter Davies led the way into Michael's office. He was the senior lawyer in the firm having been the first person hired by Michael's father when he'd set up the practice twelve years previously. He was a small, dapper man with sparrow-like features and a neatly trimmed moustache. 'You managed to make it in then, Michael?' Davies commented dryly.

'Just about, Peter. One of the lucky ones, I guess. Well, gentlemen,' he continued quickly. 'What's your opinion on the Madill case? What's the chance of us getting an acquittal?'

'Not the remotest,' Davies stated. 'You have read the brief?'

'Actually… I didn't manage to find time at the weekend.' Davies tut-tutted and shook his head disapprovingly as Michael avoided eye contact. 'Well,' he continued grudgingly, 'I suppose Frank had better summarise the situation for you.'

Frank Whyte was the latest trainee to join the practice and he was fired with enthusiasm at being given responsibility for his first case. Taking the chair opposite Michael, he opened his manila folder.

'Madill is prepared to swear his innocence on a stack of bibles but the evidence against him is overwhelming. In essence, the prosecution's case is as follows: Madill is an accountant with A.J. Smythe & Sons, a firm of builders' merchants based in Glasgow with branches in Edinburgh, Perth and Inverness. An audit of the firm's books last month revealed that twenty thousand pounds had disappeared from the accounts over the past two years, and during that period a corresponding series of deposits were made into Madill's offshore bank account in the Isle of Man.'

'Madill swears blind that he knows nothing about these deposits,' Davies interjected. 'He claims someone is trying to frame him. It just doesn't hold water. He admits that he asked for monthly statements from his bank, but claims he never looked at them. He insists he didn't know the twenty thousand was in his account. The Sheriff's never going to buy that.'

'I have to go across to Pitt Street now to see Inspector Anderson,' Michael said. 'He wants to talk to me about the case.' Michael turned to Whyte. 'I'll be back here for our meeting with Madill at twelve-thirty and we'll take it from there.'

Paul Gibson was waiting apprehensively outside Michael's office. Aged twenty-one, he was as tall as his father though much slimmer. He had his mother's straight nose and blue eyes, a pale, almost anaemic, complexion and slightly concave cheeks. His shoulder-length, black hair was pulled back from his face and tied at the nape of his neck. He looked uncomfortable in a blue lounge suit, the jacket hanging loosely from his narrow, sloping shoulders. As he waited beside Sheila's desk, he ran his fingers round the inside of his shirt collar.

'I heard him ranting and raving from the other side of the office. Do you know what's biting him?'

'Not really, Paul. All I know is that he arrived half an hour ago like a bear with a sore head, soaked to the skin.'

As Davies and Whyte were filing out, the buzzer on Sheila's desk sounded. She nodded to Paul. 'You can go in now.'

Forcing a smile in Sheila's direction, Paul walked into the office. Despite his nervousness, he couldn't suppress a grin at the sight of his father sitting behind his desk, wearing a dressing gown. 'A bit *Noel Coward*, Dad, don't you think?'

'Cut the wisecracks, Paul. I'm not in the mood. What the hell were you playing at? I let you borrow my car yesterday on the clear understanding that you'd bring it back before eight o'clock this morning, then when I go down to the garage I find my Merc's not there and your clapped-out van's sitting in its place. And to make matters a hundred times worse, I arrive at the office in your mother's car only to find you've taken my parking bay and I end up getting soaked running half-way across Glasgow from the multi-storey.'

'Hardly my fault.' Taking the Mercedes' keys from his jacket pocket, Paul placed them on the desk. 'I thought I was doing you a favour by bringing your car here. I didn't bring it back it last night because I didn't want to take the keys up to the flat and barge in on you while you were having it off with your bimbo. I assumed she'd drive you to the office this morning, so I thought you'd appreciate having the Merc here to get home tonight.'

Michael dug his fingernails into the palms of his hands, so deep that his knuckles turned white. 'Don't ever refer to Philippa as my bimbo,' he said in little more than a whisper.

'Why not? That's what everyone else in the office calls her,' Paul retorted defiantly. 'At least, that's one of the nicer expressions. I've also heard 'slut', 'gold-digger' and 'shag-bag' – take your pick.'

'Stop that right now, Paul.'

'How do you think I feel out there? It's fucking embarrassing. Don't you realise everyone is sniggering behind your back? And what about Mum? You really don't give a shit about her, do you?' Michael glared, tight-lipped, across the desk. 'For Christ's sake, Dad, can't you see what a fool you're making of yourself? It's pathetic – infatuated by a sexy little bit of skirt half your age.'

Michael pulled himself to his feet. 'That's enough.' His voice was shaking. 'I do my best for you, Paul. I give you a good job – a job you're barely capable of holding down. I pay you a bloody good salary, which gets blown on that stupid rock group and God only knows what else. And this is the thanks I get? Well I've had it right up to here with you. I don't want to see you again. Not in the office – not in the flat.'

All vestige of colour drained from Paul's face and his eyes sank deep into their sockets. He turned and walked slowly towards the door, stopping with his hand on the handle. He spun round. 'What's so special about Philippa Scott?' His voice was trembling with emotion. 'Is she a better shag than Carole?'

Stomping from the office, Paul strode past Sheila's desk without as much as a sideways glance.

Michael felt his knees go weak. He grabbed at the edge of his desk for support as he eased himself slowly down onto the chair, his heartbeat racing. He forced himself to breathe in and out deeply, desperately trying to slow down his heart rate. During the past twelve years, Paul had never made any reference to Carole – to that disastrous episode. Michael had succeeded in blocking the incident out of his consciousness, but every horrific detail now came flooding back.

Michael was still sitting in a state of shock when Sheila buzzed through to tell him his taxi had arrived to take him to Pitt Street. He forced himself to his feet and changed back into his clothes. His trousers were crumpled and his shoes were still soggy, but his jacket had dried out reasonably. Throughout the cab journey, his head was reeling. He had to confront Anne tonight – tell her he was going to leave her. He'd promised Pippa that. So it wouldn't be long before Paul found out. Would that be the trigger for him to tell his mother about what had happened with Carole?

FIVE

DCI Charlie Anderson enjoyed delivering the 'Experienced Officer' module to the graduate trainee seminar. He always stuck to the same format – practical advice on criminal detection techniques, interspersed with war stories about his experiences.

Before the start of his talk he'd removed his jacket and rolled up his shirt sleeves, revealing muscular, hairy forearms and thick wrists. As he prowled up and down in front of the class his shirt buttons strained to contain his paunch.

Glancing up at the clock on the lecture theatre wall, Charlie saw there were eight minutes to go. Good timekeeping epitomised an organised mind – an essential prerequisite for detective work. As always, he would set an example by ensuring his lecture finished right on time. He strode across to the flip-chart board, picked up a marker pen and dashed off some hieroglyphic squiggles, then turned towards the twenty expectant faces. 'Does anyone know what that says?' A girl's hand shot up at the back of the room. 'Yes?' he asked.

'It says *The Key Question*, sir,' she responded confidently.

'Excellent! Excellent!' Charlie enthused. 'So you can read shorthand?'

'No, sir.' A suppressed giggle ran round the class. Charlie looked puzzled. 'Sergeant O'Sullivan gave us a talk earlier this morning,' she explained. 'He told us that sooner or later you'd write something on the board in shorthand – and that it was sure to be *The Key Question*.'

The class dissolved in laughter. It took a moment to sink in, then Charlie's deep, belly laugh reverberated around the room. 'So Tony O'Sullivan has actually taken something in, has he? It's a relief to know my efforts over the years haven't been entirely in vain. But seriously,' he asked, 'do any of you know shorthand?' He scanned the blank expressions, shaking his head in disappointment. 'It really is a shame. It's a dying art – but it's invaluable in this line of work.'

Charlie produced his notebook from his hip pocket and waved it aloft between thumb and forefinger. 'This is what it's all about. Don't let anyone try to tell you the notebook's redundant – that recording equipment has made it obsolete. This is where I jot down every word of every interview, in shorthand. Every question I ask, every answer I get.' He paced up and down in front of the class. 'Of course, you can record interviews and then have everything transcribed – each of you has to decide on your own preferred method of working. But there's a huge psychological advantage in using a notebook. As soon as you produce any kind of recording equipment, you introduce a barrier. The person you're interviewing goes on the defensive, he clams up, he measures every word. But if you pull out a notebook, he behaves naturally – he prattles on – and that's when you find things out.

'However, no matter what approach you choose to adopt, some things are fundamental. Good detective work has nothing to do with inspiration, genius or luck. It has everything to do with hard graft, analysing data and assessing probabilities. You have to have a rapport with minutiae – sifting facts, ploughing through seemingly boring details.

'And each and every time – ' Charlie jabbed a crooked index finger at the shorthand on the flip chart. 'There's a *Key Question*, the answer to which will unravel the case. Whether you're trying to track down a murderer, or nick a kid who's pinched a tenner from a shop till, the principle's the same. You ask all the questions you can think of, even though at the time you might not be quite sure why you're asking them, then you structure the data chronologically and sift through what you've got. Brainstorming is a useful technique at this stage – getting a group together to bounce ideas around. You make a series of assumptions and test the facts against each of them in turn, looking for a logical glitch, a non-sequitur. All the time you're searching for *The Key Question*. Somewhere, there will be an anomaly – an inconsistency – there always is. And when you find that the whole case opens up like Pandora's box and everything falls into place.

'My all-time favourite quote is by Gary Player. Once, when he'd won a few golf tournaments in a row, a reporter asked him to what he attributed his lucky streak. Player's reply was: 'You know, it's a funny thing, but the more I practise, the luckier I get'. That sums up detective work in a nutshell. Hard work, graft, determination. That's what gets results.'

Charlie gathered up his notes. 'That's it for today. I hope you got something useful out of this morning's session – and I'd like to wish all of you success in your new careers.'

As the wall clock flicked over to eleven-thirty, Charlie rolled down his shirt sleeves and pulled on his jacket.

Michael Gibson had recovered his composure by the time he arrived at Pitt Street, a few minutes early for his appointment. The officer at the reception desk recognised him.

'You can go straight on up, Mr Gibson. DCI Anderson's expecting you.'

Detective Chief Inspector Charlie Anderson was one of the longest serving members of the Glasgow CID. Well over six feet tall with correspondingly broad shoulders, he gave the appearance of being shorter on account of his pronounced stoop, the legacy of severe arthritis exacerbated by years of sitting hunched over an office desk.

Charlie peered over the top of his half-moon reading glasses when he heard the knock on his door. 'Come in!' His command echoed round the office. When he saw who it was, his features broke into a welcoming smile. Pulling off his spectacles, he rose from behind his desk and enveloped Michael's hand in his huge fist, pumping it up and down. 'Sit yourself down, Michael, and take the weight off your feet.'

Deep crows' feet splayed from the corners of Charlie's eyes and tunnelled under the wisps of white hair at his temples before emerging as deep-rutted wrinkles furrowing round the back of his bald head. By way of contrast he had thick, bushy eyebrows that merged on the bridge of his nose.

Over the years, Michael's father and Charlie had developed a strong, mutual respect. On many occasions they had been adversaries during criminal trials, but each held the other's ability and integrity in high regard. Michael had often been counselled by his father to heed any advice Charlie Anderson had to offer.

Charlie's desk reflected his organised mind. His fountain pen and matching propelling pencil, wide-barrelled and ridged for ease of grip, lay side-by-side, parallel to the top of his ink-blotter. His pending correspondence was arranged in order of priority in the in-basket on the left-hand side of his desk, the memos that had been dealt with stacked neatly in the out tray.

'Your secretary told me you ran into a bit of trouble with the weather this morning,' Charlie said.

'Sorry about that.'

'Couldn't be helped. By the way, how is your father these days?'

Michael shook his head. 'The news isn't great. His dementia is getting a lot worse and his memory plays tricks on him. One minute he's chatting away normally, asking about the family and the business, then all of a sudden he goes off at a tangent. The last time I saw him he seemed to think I was his brother, Vince, who died last year, and he started reminiscing about their schooldays. Nothing coherent – just disjointed thoughts.

'I'm going to visit him this afternoon.' Michael glanced out the window. 'That is – if the weather doesn't deteriorate too much. I don't know how I'm going to find him.'

'I'm really sorry to hear that. I always had a soft spot for old George.'

'I know you did. Thanks for asking after him. What about you? Can't be much longer now till you retire?'

'Another fifteen months – and I'm counting the days, believe you me. Between us girls, I can't keep up with the technology any more. Would you listen to me rabbiting on about 'technology'? I can't even get the hang of bloody emails.' He tapped his knuckles against the computer screen on his desk. 'I switch this damned thing on every morning and that's the one and only time I touch it.' Charlie splayed out his arthritic hands on his desk. 'They don't make keyboards for my kind of fingers. My secretary prints out all my emails, I hand-write the replies and she sends out the responses.'

Michael smiled. 'Not necessarily the most efficient way of working.'

'Let me tell you something. They might call it productivity – I call it encouraging sloppy thinking. Look at that lot.' He waved his hand in disgust at his bulging in-basket. 'I can guarantee that eighty percent of that correspondence will be emails. In my day, if you wanted to send someone a memo, you had to structure your thoughts and hand-write it or dictate it to your secretary, who typed it up. You then had to check it and sign it – and you didn't go to all that trouble unless it was for something important. These days everybody and his wife fires off emails at the drop of a hat without even thinking through what they're trying to achieve – and I'm expected to answer every damned one of them, no matter how trivial. It makes my blood boil. I tell you, the sooner I pack it in the better.'

'The word on the street was you were leaving last year.'

'Last June, actually,' Charlie said, rocking back in his chair. 'My early retirement package had been signed off and I was half-way to my allotment when the Assistant Chief Constable talked me into hanging on for another couple of years.'

'What did Kay have to say about that?'

'Not impressed. She's retired now, so she has time to plan things for us to do together, but this job causes more wasted meals and more missed concerts than you could ever imagine. It was bad enough when I had to opt out of the pantomime on Christmas Eve to sort out a hostage situation at the City Chambers, but last week was the final straw. Kay had invited a few of our friends round for a surprise dinner party for my birthday. It was a surprise all right. I didn't get out of here until well after midnight. You can imagine how that went down.'

'I can make a pretty good guess. How's your daughter, by the way? Is she still teaching?'

'Yes, but in Brussels of all places.'

'What brought that about?'

'Her best friend, Linda, moved to Brussels a couple of years ago. She wanted to make a clean break after a messy divorce so she upped sticks with her three young kids and got a teaching job in the International School. However, as luck would have it, she broke her hip in a skiing accident last month, which means she'll be confined to bed for some considerable time. As she has no one out there to look after her kids, the solution she and Sue came up with was that Sue would take leave of absence until the summer and she and Jamie – he's just turned seven, by the way – have gone over to Brussels to help Linda out. Sue's got a part-time teaching job in the International School and she's settled in well, but of course that means Kay has even more time on her hands as she doesn't have her daughter and grandson to fuss over.' Charlie sighed and glanced at his watch. 'Now then, Michael, you didn't drag yourself half way across the city in a snow storm to listen to an ageing copper wittering on. What can I do for you?'

'The Madill case.'

'Of course. Madill.' Charlie referred to his papers. 'You know how much I hate to see taxpayers' money and police time going to waste. I mean, this one's such an open and shut case I can't believe you're going to try for an acquittal. If we throw the book at him, which we will, the Sheriff's sure to find him guilty and he'll get at least two years.'

'Is there an alternative?'

'You're not your father's son if you don't know there's always an alternative. Here's the deal. You get Madill to change his plea to guilty, with full restitution of the stolen money, and I'll make sure the procurator fiscal only asks for twelve months. With good behaviour he'll be out in six. That eejit's no danger to society. Six months inside will be more than enough to teach him a lesson he won't forget. That way the state saves the cost of keeping him in jail for an extra six months, we save the expense of a trial and I don't have to have two of my officers tied up in the Sheriff court all day tomorrow. What do you say?'

'I'll talk to Madill. But I have to tell you, he swears he's innocent.'

'Of course he does.' Charlie grinned broadly. 'But I also know you can have a very persuasive tongue in your head – when it's in your client's best interest, of course.'

'I'll call you this afternoon and let you know our position,' Michael said, getting to his feet.

'Thanks.' Charlie hesitated. 'One more thing before you go. You do know Jack McFarlane was released this morning?'

SIX

Michael sank back down onto his chair. 'I knew he was due to get out today. I often wake up in the middle of the night in a cold sweat, thinking about what he threatened.' Michael shuddered at the memory of the scene in the courtroom. McFarlane, a crazed look in his eyes, screaming at the top of his voice when the judge passed sentence: '*When I get out I'm going to fucking-well kill you, Gibson! You – and your wife – and your kid!*'.

'That happened a long time ago, Michael. It's possible he's forgotten all about the incident. I'm told he was disruptive during his first two years in Peterhead, but he calmed down a lot after that. I've seen his file. He kept himself to himself and stayed out of trouble. He even earned three years' remission for good behaviour. Just so you know, I got a call from the National Crime Agency a while back to let me know they'll be keeping tabs on him when he gets out.'

'What's their interest in him?'

'He got duffed up a few times while he was in Peterhead by Terry McNee and his cronies, apparently because they think he knows where the proceeds from the Bothwell Street job are hidden. The NCA have got Larry Robertson's card marked for that one, and they're pretty sure he was also involved in a multi-million pound jewellery store heist in London last year, as well as a bank robbery in Birmingham. As you know, the loot from the Bothwell street job was never found and if McFarlane knows where it's stashed, it's only a matter of time until he comes here looking for it. I'll be staying close to the NCA on this one, so at least I'll be able to tip you the wink if and when he comes anywhere near Glasgow.'

'Thanks for that, Charlie. I don't know if you know, but Anne and I moved house a few months back. Paul had decided to move into a flat – you know what it's like when you're twenty-one – independence is everything. After he left home, the house in Bearsden was too big for just the two of us and as neither of us was very keen on gardening, we decided to go for an apartment in Dalgleish Tower.'

'Nice one!' Charlie exclaimed, aware of the sort of money that entailed.

'I must admit, when we decided on Dalgleish Tower, the security aspect was a major consideration.'

'I hear the place is like Fort Knox.'

Michael smiled. 'Not quite. But the building does have a caretaker who lives on the premises, as well as reinforced steel doors and security access codes. I feel pretty safe there – a lot safer than I did in Bearsden.

'Is that the time?' Michael said, glancing at his watch and quickly getting to his feet. 'I'd better be on my way. I've got a meeting with Madill at twelve-thirty to discuss tomorrow's trial. I'll get in touch with you this afternoon and let you know how we're going to plead.'

Harry Kennedy edged his way along the towpath, testing each footstep carefully before committing his full weight, while at the same time trying to avoid the deep snow cascading over the top of his Wellingtons. The wind, whipping off the river, was stinging his eyes and ridges of frost were forming on his thick moustache and his eyebrows. Through the falling snow, he could make out the jib of a crane swaying back and forth high above his head – like the shadowy beak of a giant flamingo searching the leaden skies for food. Harry gripped the guard rail tightly to make sure he didn't stray off the invisible path. Ten feet below, to his left, the icy waters of the Clyde were lapping against the bank.

When he reached the pub, Harry kicked his Wellingtons against a low wall to dislodge the wet snow before pushing the door open. Blinking his eyes to adjust to the dim light, he realised he was the only customer.

'Well, if it isn't Harry Kennedy,' the barman called out, folding his Sporting Life and getting to his feet.

Harry tugged off his raincoat as he dripped his way across to the bar. Though small of stature, he weighed over thirteen stones and had the build of a rugby prop forward; legs and arms like tree trunks, broad, square shoulders and a barrel chest. His head seemed to connect directly to his body with no discernible sign of an intervening neck. His complexion was ruddy and a permanent, impish grin lit up his features.

'It's been so long since I've seen you,' the barman said, 'I was beginning to think you'd gone on the wagon.'

'Don't sound so surprised, Tommy. I'll have you know that I once went for seven years without touchin' a single drop.'

'When was that?'

'Och, it was a while back. Then I said to myself: 'What the hell! Everybody else is enjoyin' my seventh birthday party – why shouldn't I?"

Tommy chortled. 'Same old Harry. What are you having?'

'A pie an' a pint o' heavy, please.' Clambering onto a high bar stool, Harry draped his sodden coat over the adjacent stool and pulled out a tissue to dab the melting ice from his eyebrows and his moustache. He glanced round the bar. 'It's been quite a while since I've been in here, right enough. It was such a long drag from the school. But my new job's just along the road, so you'll be seein' a lot more o' me from now on.'

'Delighted to hear it.' Tommy wiped his hands on a bar towel before opening the glass display cabinet and sliding a mutton pie onto a plate, which he popped into the microwave. Crossing to the hand pump, he started to pull a pint of heavy. 'New job, eh? So you're not still working at the school?'

'I retired from the janitorin' last month. But I fell on my feet all right. I saw a job advertised for a Facilities Manager for yon new block o' flats doon the road. You ken the one I mean? It's called Dalgleish Tower. Fifteen floors o' plate glass – beside the river.'

'I've seen it. Hey, that was lucky – getting another job as quick as that.'

'You're not wrong there. I must tell you about the interview, but. It was a bloody scream.' Harry's eyes sparkled as he recalled his story. 'About a week after I'd sent in my application I got a letter tellin' me to go to the Viewpark Estate Agency in Hope Street for an interview wi' a Mr Chalmers. So I gets myself all dolled up an' I dauners doon to Hope Street. Chalmers turns oot to be wan of thae English chanty-wrastlers, frae Chichester, he telt me, wi' a la-de-da accent you could cut wi' a knife. You ken the kind I mean? Kelvinside, only worse.'

'I know the type well.'

'Anyway, Chalmers starts aff: Do you know why we decided to call the building Dalgleish Tower, Mr Kennedy? I comes back, quick as a flash. You'll have named it after Kenny, I suppose. Then I added. You do realise, Mr Chalmers, that Kenny played for Celtic, so callin' it Dalgleish Tower will alienate the Rangers' fans. Did you notice that nice wee touch there, Tommy? – *alienate*. I'd decided to slip a few big words into the conversation so Chalmers wouldny think he was dealin' wi' some wee, ignorant Glesca keelie. An' they're the majority of your potential customers, I says. Good stuff, eh? – *majority* an' *potential* – in the same sentence. Really floggin' the auld vocabulary for all it was worth, I was. Might it no' be better to call it Mo Johnston Tower?, says me wi' a straight face, seein' as Mo played for both Celtic and Rangers? I said that to him. I did. Honest. He just sat there lookin' flummoxed. He hadn't a bloody clue what I was witterin' on aboot. No' that I'm in any way bothered myself, I added. I'm a Thistle man through and through.'

Tommy smiled as he set Harry's pint down in front of him.

Grinning broadly, Harry took a sip before continuing. 'So Chalmers clears his throat an' says, dead posh like: Actually, Mr Kennedy, we named the building after the fourth Earl of Dalgleish. It was on the tip o' my tongue to say: Oh, aye? Whit team did he play for? But I couldny have done that withoot burstin' oot laughin'. After that, I thought I'd better screw the nut. I mean, I did want the job, efter all. So I just nodded an' said: Oh, the fourth Earl of Dalgleish, is it? That'll be a' right then. That shouldny upset anybody.

'Chalmers went on to ask me a few questions about what kind o' work I'd been doin' at the school, then he offered me the job – just like that. He said he liked my acerbic wit. I'm sure he did that on purpose, the sarky bugger. He kent fine weel I'd have to go an' look that one up.'

'You've made my day, Harry.' Tommy laughed. 'So tell me. How's the job workin' out?'

'Och, it's a doddle. You have to be gey fond o' your own company, mind. You could easily spend all day in Dalgleish Tower an' no' see another livin' soul. The money's no' bad, but the best thing aboot it is that a wee flat comes wi' the job – furnished, an' all. It's toty – a livin' room, one bedroom, a poky kitchen an' a bathroom. It would be helluva cramped for a couple but wi' me bein' on my own, it's just the job. I had to gie up my house at the school when I packed in the janitorin' an' I thought I would need to find somewhere to rent. Then this job turns up out the blue. Magic, eh?'

'And you're a Facilities Manager?' Tommy enthused. 'That sounds dead flash.'

'Ach, it's just a poncy name for a caretaker.' Harry swallowed a mouthful of beer. 'But it's a dead flash building all right. My flat's on the ground floor, along with a gym, almost as big as the one at the school. Security's the big sellin' point though. At least it will be if they ever manage to sell any. They're askin' a bloody fortune for them – it's no' surprisin' there's hardly any selt. The higher up you are the dearer it gets. The flats near the top have stoatin' views but they're lookin' for the best part of hauf a million quid for them.

'Everythin's the latest technology. All the flats have intercoms, double-glazin', central heatin' an' air-conditionin' – even mine. Can you imagine it? Air-conditionin' – in Glesca! Never thought I'd see the day. Though apparently in summer, wi' the buildin' bein' solid glass, we're gauny need it.'

The ping of the microwave interrupted Harry's flow. 'That's your pie ready. If you want a shuftie at the form, by the way, the Sporting Life's over there.' Tommy nodded towards the newspaper lying on the bar.

Harry mimed a shiver. 'Don't mention the gee-gees to me.'

'I thought you were a bit of a punter?'

'I was. That's the problem. I got myself into a lot o' trouble a few months back. Puntin' on tick, like. You aye think the next bet'll get you oot o' trouble. Well I got myself in way ower my heid. I ran up nearly a thousan' quid wi' Larry Robertson, the bookie doon in Dumbarton Road. I couldny settle up money like that so I got a visit from one of Robertson's heavies an' an invitation to drop in an' see the man himsel'. I was shittin' myself, I don't mind tellin' you. I thought I'd be lucky to get oot o' there wi' my kneecaps intact. But, thank Christ, Robertson's no' into violence for the sake of it. I had to agree to pay him off over twelve months, with ten per-cent interest a month on top. It leaves me skint but I still consider myself lucky. I know a bloke in Govan who got his knuckles smashed in for owin' a bookie fifty quid. I've learned my lesson, Tommy. Nae mair puntin' for me.'

Tommy used a bar towel to take the steaming mutton pie from the microwave. Placing a knife on the plate, he pushed it across the bar. 'Mind now, Harry. That pie's bilin'.'

Harry produced a ten-pound note from his trouser pocket and placed it on the bar. He sliced the pie in half and waited until most of the hot liquid grease had spilled out onto the plate before picking it up and biting into it, quickly taking a swig of beer to cool his mouth.

'What exactly does a Facilities Manager do?' Tommy asked as he handed across the change.

'All kinds o' stuff. For instance, this mornin' I spent two hours clearin' the snow from the paths an' the drive leadin' doon to the garage. And if it keeps chuckin' it down like that,' he added, shaking his head ruefully as he glanced out the window, 'that's what I'll be doin' this afternoon as weel. But like I was sayin', you hardly ever see anybody. They go doon in the lift from their flats to the underground garage an' back up again. Nobody ever seems to get oot at my floor.'

'You were saying there aren't many flats sold?'

'So far, just three. Number 15, the top floor, was snapped up by a bloke called Gibson. He's a flash lawyer. No' short o' the readies.' Harry rubbed his thumb and fingers together meaningfully. 'I don't think his missus works. There's a right plonker, name of McFadyen, in number 13. He must be my age. He lives alone an' he never seems to get any mail. I asked him why he bought number 13 when number 14 was the same price in the brochure, but has a better view. He said thirteen was his lucky number. His heid's full o' mince. He dauners aroun' a' day like a fart in a trance. Then there's a couple called Leslie just moved into number 2. Seem nice enough. I think they're both doctors.'

When he'd finished his pie, Harry downed the rest of his pint in one long swallow, wiping his moustache with the back of his hand.

'Same again?'

'No thanks. I just nipped oot for a quick one. I have to be gettin' back because there's a couple comin' to see one o' the flats at twelve o'clock. Normally Chalmers would do the sales blurb himself, but he had to go to a meeting in Edinburgh, so he's lumbered me wi' showing them round.'

Climbing down from his barstool, Harry pulled on his still-sodden raincoat. 'Catch you later in the week, Tommy.'

SEVEN

Michael Gibson was sitting in his office, flicking through his mail, when Sheila buzzed through to let him know Frank Whyte and Archie Madill were waiting to see him. As they walked in, he indicated the two seats on the opposite side of his desk. Madill, a tubby man in his early fifties, was wearing a blue-checked shirt that clashed violently with his red sports jacket.

As soon as he sat down, Madill blurted out. 'I know why you want to see me. You're going to try to talk me into changing my plea to guilty. Well I'm not having any of it. I'm getting legal aid and you have to defend me.'

Michael glanced across at Whyte, giving him a slow wink on Madill's blind side. Whyte had been well coached by Peter Davies.

'Mr Madill,' Whyte began reassuringly, 'we're not here to talk you into anything. We're here to discuss what's in your best interests and advise you accordingly. If you conclude that you want to plead 'not guilty', I will, of course, represent you in court tomorrow to the best of my ability. However, before you come to that decision I think we should discuss the pros and cons.'

Madill's gaze flitted suspiciously between Whyte and Gibson. 'What do you mean – pros and cons?'

'Let's consider the case from the Sheriff's point of view,' Whyte said. 'The prosecution will produce copies of the monthly bank statements you received over the past two years showing a series of deposits into your Isle of Man bank account, totalling some twenty thousand pounds. Your defence, if I understand it correctly, is that someone else must have paid this money into your account in order to frame you and that you never bothered to look at the bank statements because you thought you only had thirty pounds in the account. Is that correct?'

Madill shrugged. 'That's about the size of it.'

Whyte opened his briefcase and took out a sheaf of papers. 'Let's act it out, Mr Madill. You're in the dock, on oath, and I'm the prosecuting counsel.' Madill looked apprehensive and his left eye started to twitch. 'Mr Madill, do you have an off-shore bank account in the Isle of Man?' Madill nodded quickly. 'Why did you open that account?'

'I thought it might come in handy one day.'

'So, because you 'thought it might come in handy one day', you opened an account with a deposit of thirty pounds. You then specifically asked the bank to send you monthly statements – we have copies of the relevant correspondence – which you then proceeded to throw in the bin without looking at them?'

'Yes.'

'When did you open this account?'

'I'm not sure.'

'Approximately when?'

Madill licked at his lips. 'About three years ago, I think.'

'To be precise it was twenty-five months ago.'

'If you say so.'

'In fact, you opened the account in the same week as the first two thousand pounds was appropriated from A.J. Smythe & Sons. By some strange coincidence, two thousand pounds was credited to your account that very week, paid into an Edinburgh branch. Where were you working that week?'

Madill shifted uncomfortably in his chair. His forehead began to glisten. 'I don't remember.'

'Let me jog your memory. For all of that week you were based at A.J. Smythe's Edinburgh office and you – '

Michael held up his hand to interrupt Whyte's flow. 'We can continue in this vein if you like, Mr Madill, but I think you're getting the idea.'

Madill avoided eye contact. 'What do you want me to do?' he mumbled.

'If you go ahead with this defence – and if you're found guilty,' Michael said, 'the prosecution will press for at least two years' imprisonment, which the Sheriff will almost certainly grant. However, if you were to change your plea to guilty you'd get off with a lighter sentence – perhaps twelve or fifteen months – and you would be eligible for remission for half of your sentence. It's your call.'

Madill kept his head bowed for some time before raising his eyes. 'I'll plead guilty,' he said in a whisper.

'I think that's a very wise decision,' Michael said. 'I'll advise the prosecution accordingly.'

When they left the office, Michael buzzed through to Sheila. 'Could you get Inspector Anderson on the phone for me, please. I need to talk to him.'

When Michael's phone buzzed he picked up.

'Good afternoon, Michael. What do you have for me?'

'Madill's seen sense. He's going to plead guilty.'

'Excellent. I knew that persuasive tongue of yours would work wonders. By the way,' Charlie added, 'if you do decide to visit your father this afternoon, be sure to send him my regards.'

'Of course.'

Michael put down the phone and looked out of the window. Glancing at his watch, he pressed the intercom. 'Sheila, I'm going to go to Crighton Hall. I'll be back in time for my meeting with Peter Davies at four.'

Harry Kennedy was dozing fitfully in his armchair when he was roused by the ring of his doorbell. Rubbing the sleep from his eyes, he prised himself out of his seat and went to answer it.

'Good afternoon,' the tall, gangling figure said. 'I'm Donald Moore.' Moore held out a spindly wrist and offered Harry a weak handshake, fingertips only.

'I'm Harry Kennedy, the Facilities Manager. I'm afraid Mr Chalmers isn't here. He had to go to a meeting in Edinburgh and he asked me to show you round.'

'He explained that to me on the phone. I'm sorry we're late. We had to drive up from Gourock and the weather's been absolutely foul.'

Donald Moore was in his sixties with curly brown hair and a wispy beard. He was wearing thick, black-rimmed spectacles. Harry took an instant dislike to him. He didn't trust people with limp handshakes. Mrs Moore shook Harry's hand, but with a much firmer grip than her husband's. She was a small, stocky lady with a pleasant smile. Harry smiled back.

'No problem. I'm glad you made it,' Harry said. 'Step inside for a minute an' I'll get the key to show you round.' Harry went over to the combination safe on his lounge wall and twirled the dial back and forward three times. With a pronounced click, the safe door swung open. 'It's flat number 10 you're wantin' to see?'

'That's right,' said Mrs Moore. 'From the pictures in the brochure it looks lovely.'

'It certainly is,' Harry enthused. He took the key for flat 10 from its hook and dropped it into his jacket pocket before closing the safe door and spinning the dial. Picking up his information folder, he ushered the Moores out into the vestibule. As they crossed the hall towards the glass door, Harry opened his brochure and started reading from the notes. 'Security is a prime consideration in Dalgleish Tower. In order to gain access to the lift or the staircase, a code must be entered via the control panel situated to the right of the access door.'

Harry ostentatiously stood between the Moores and the panel while he keyed in six digits. 'Nobody gets to know the security code except the residents and me,' he stated. 'It's my job to deliver the mail to the flats every mornin' because even the postie doesn't get telt the code,' he announced proudly. Waving the Moores through ahead of him, he summoned the lift and when it arrived he pressed the button for floor 10. The doors closed smoothly and the lift emitted the faintest of hums as it glided upwards. As they were ascending, Harry again referred to his notes. 'Apart from the ground floor, all the floors of Dalgleish Tower have the same layout, comprising one four-bedroom apartment measuring a hundred and fifty square metres.'

The lift doors slid open and they stepped out onto the plush carpeting in the hallway. There was a single door facing them on which was displayed the number '10' in gold numerals. Harry produced the key from his pocket and handed it to Donald Moore. Moore examined the six-centimetre cylindrical bolt, which bore no resemblance to any key he'd ever seen.

'The keys in Dalgleish Tower are state-of-the-art,' Harry read out. 'I'm not exactly sure what that means,' he confided as he took back the key. 'Each key is individually tooled,' he read, 'and cannot be copied by conventional key-cutting equipment.'

Slipping the key into the lock, he rotated it three times anti-clockwise. He read again from his notes. 'As the front door is unlocked you will notice that six bolts have been activated, four horizontal and two vertical, and you will also observe that the door is made of reinforced steel, seven centimetres thick. As you step inside you will notice the solid-oak parquet flooring that runs throughout the apartment. The walls of the apartment are all decorated in white French *tissu*, a fabric wall-covering that is both elegant and hard-wearing.

'The corridor facing you runs east-west, the length of the apartment. The first door on the left leads to the master bedroom which, like all the bedrooms, has a capacious fitted wardrobe, an en suite bathroom and a balcony commanding a magnificent view. The first door on the right leads to the lounge which is forty-two square metres in size and – ' Harry broke off with an embarrassed look on his face. 'This is the first time I've shown anyone round an' there's an awfy lot o' this posy bumf to wade through.' He held up the six pages of notes in his hand. 'I can read it all out if you like, but if I'm borin' the arse off you…?'

'You're doing fine, Mr Kennedy,' Mrs Moore said reassuringly. 'Tell you what. How about if we leave the sales blurb for now and Mr Moore and I have a look round the apartment on our own? If we've got any questions we'll let you know.'

'That's fine by me,' Harry agreed enthusiastically. 'I'll wait for you. Take as long as you like.'

Harry remained in the hall until the Moores had moved on from the master bedroom, then he wandered into the room and gazed out of the window. The sleet had turned to rain and he could make out the shapes of the snow-covered buildings on the far side of the river. He was still admiring the view a few minutes later when he heard a discreet cough behind him.

'Okay, Mr Kennedy,' said Mrs Moore, 'I think we've seen everything we want.'

'Have you got any questions?'

'I think we have all the information we need in the brochure.'

'What did you think of it?' Harry asked as they rode down in the lift.

'Wonderful.' Mrs Moore looked at her husband. 'We'll probably be taking it, won't we, Donald?'

'Provided they'll negotiate on the price, Nancy,' he said sternly. 'Do you know what they'd be prepared to accept, Mr Kennedy?'

'I've no idea. You'd need to discuss that with the agent, Mr Chalmers. I can give you his number.'

'That's okay. I've got it. I'll get in touch with him tomorrow.'

Mud and slush splattered the Mercedes' windscreen as Michael Gibson overtook a line of slow-moving lorries on the M80 south of Stirling. He switched his windscreen wipers to maximum speed to try to clear his vision.

Suddenly, a pair of piercing, pale-blue eyes appeared on the other side of the windscreen – staring straight at him. He swerved instinctively, drifting dangerously close to the rumbling wheels of a container lorry in the inside lane. The eyes were there for only an instant – swept away in the next flash of the wiper blades. A sustained blast on a horn hammered on Michael's eardrums and headlights reflecting in his wing mirror dazzled him. He put his foot to the floor and accelerated away, weaving erratically in the fast lane as he shook his head to try to clear the pulsing pain. Why did he keep seeing those eyes? What was happening to him? Was he losing control? Or what scared him most – was he was going the same way as his father?

He saw the sign for his exit looming up ahead. As soon as he'd swung off the motorway he pulled over at the side of the slip road. Unclipping his seatbelt he stretched for the jar of paracetamol in the glove compartment and spilled several tablets into the palm of his hand – he didn't count how many. Beads of perspiration were running from his temples as he rammed the pills into his mouth. The taste was foul and he had no water. He grimaced as he crunched into the dry pills, trying to generate enough saliva to swallow. Having forced down what he could, he wound down his window and spat the remainder of the pills into the bank of snow by the side of the road.

Leaving the car window open, he made his way slowly in the direction of Carron Bridge. The minor roads hadn't been ploughed or salted and it took him fifteen minutes to negotiate the two miles to Crighton Hall.

'Good afternoon, Mr Gibson. We weren't sure if you'd make it today.' The receptionist's smile seemed forced.

Michael nodded curtly. 'How is my father?'

She didn't answer the question. 'Dr Bell would like a word with you. If you'd care to take a seat I'll let him know you're here.'

Michael didn't sit down. He stood by the window staring out at the falling snow until the receptionist called across to let him know Dr Bell was available.

Michael's footsteps rang out on the marble floor as he strode down the oak-panelled hallway of what had once been a stately home towards the office at the far end. Gavin Bell gestured towards a seat as he opened the folder on his desk. Michael noticed his right eye was bruised and swollen.

'I'm afraid it's not good news.' Michael frowned. 'Your father's Alzheimer's has reached an advanced stage and, together with his schizophrenia, this appears to be triggering unpredictable, irrational behaviour patterns. Yesterday was a case in point. Your father seemed to have got it into his head that we were trying to poison him. In the restaurant last night he grabbed one of the staff by the throat and tried to strangle her. We had to restrain him forcibly.

'I spent the best part of an hour trying to reason with him, but to no avail. He would remain calm for a few minutes, but then the violence would suddenly flare up again.' Bell touched the painful-looking swelling below his right eye. 'Finally, I had to sedate him.'

'How is he today?'

'He seems to be a bit more relaxed.'

'Can I see him?'

'Of course. But do understand that your father's condition has deteriorated significantly in the past couple of weeks, Mr Gibson. You're going to have to reconcile yourself to the fact that in the near future it's possible he won't recognise you.'

Michael walked up the wide staircase to the first floor and knocked gently on his father's door bedroom before entering. George was sitting up in bed, his back propped against two pillows. He was staring out of the window. His skeletal head turned round slowly when he heard someone come in.

'Who is it? What do you want?'

'It's me, Dad.'

'Is that you, Michael?'

'Yes, Dad.' Michael sat down on the upright chair beside the bed. 'How are you getting on?' he asked.

George's rheumy eyes opened wide. 'It's good to see you, son, though, God know, I can hardly see anything these days because of the damned cataracts.'

'Before I forget, Charlie Anderson asked me to pass on his regards.'

'Charlie Anderson? Is that old codger still on the go?'

'He'll be retiring soon.'

'Do you know if Vince is coming today?'

Michael hesitated. 'Vince is dead, Dad. He died last year. You went to his funeral. Don't you remember?'

'Vince is dead?' George rubbed at his eyes with the heels of both hands, then leaned across the bed to whisper in Michael's ear. 'Whatever you do, don't eat anything, son. They're trying to poison us.'

'I don't think so,' Michael said reassuringly. 'Why would anyone want to do that?'

'He wants my room.'

'Who wants your room?'

'Tommy Mooney. He's got the room next door, but mine's bigger. I overheard him telling one of the carers that he wants my room as soon as I pop off.'

'You might have been mistaken, Dad.'

'My eyes might be going, son, but here's nothing wrong with my hearing. I heard him all right.'

'Even if he did say something like that, there's no reason to think anyone would try to poison you.'

George sat bolt upright and tapped the side of his nose knowingly. 'You don't know the half of what goes on around here, son.'

'No one's going to poison you, Dad.' Michael took hold of his father's hand and started to massage his thin, liver-spotted fingers. 'I'll make sure of that.'

George relaxed and let his head sink slowly back onto the pillows.

'You're very good to me, son. I don't know what I'd do without you. Nobody else comes to see me. No one else gives a toss about what happens to me – apart from Vince, of course. He often comes to see me.' George's breathing was shallow. 'He's coming this afternoon.'

George closed his eyes and fell silent while Michael continued to massage his fingers gently. He stayed there, holding George's hand, until he heard the sound of gentle snoring.

Michael walked slowly from the building to the car park and got into his car. He didn't start the engine, staring instead at the Christmas card scene of the granite mansion encrusted in snow and gazing up at his father's bedroom window on the first floor. The lights were on and the lace curtains were drawn. He felt emotionally and physically drained. Closing his eyes, his chin sank onto his chest.

EIGHT

Michael woke with a start, disoriented and shivering. It took him a few seconds to realise where he was. He peered through the gloom at his watch. Twenty past three – he'd been asleep for half an hour. He pulled off his spectacles and rubbed his eyes before replacing his glasses and glancing up towards his father's bedroom window. The lights were out. Fumbling for his mobile phone, he called his office.

'Sheila, tell Peter Davies I'm running late. I'm just about to leave Crighton Hall. I'll be back in the office as soon as I can.'

Firing the ignition, Michael spun the car round in a tight skid in the empty car park and accelerated away down the long, poplar-lined avenue. As he watched the building recede in his rear-view mirror he wondered if his father would recognise him the next time he came to visit.

Roadworks on the Stirling Road slowed down the traffic and it was after half past four by the time Michael pulled up in the parking bay beneath his office. He loped up the stairs, panting for breath by the time he got to the top.

'Is Davies still here?' he asked Sheila.

'He waited for you until half past, Mr Gibson, but he had to leave for an outside appointment. He won't be back in the office today.'

'Damn! I suppose I'll have to smooth his ruffled feathers in the morning. In which case,' he said with a sigh, 'there's not much point in me hanging around here. I'm off home.'

'You haven't forgotten that you have both your car and your wife's car here? What do you want to do about that?'

'Bloody hell! I had forgotten – completely.' Michael paused to consider. 'Would you do me a favour, Sheila, and drive one of the cars over to my flat? I'll drop you back at the office.'

'Of course.'

Sheila got behind the wheel of the Mercedes and drove Michael to the multi-storey car park. The city centre streets had been gritted and most of the snow had cleared away. Traffic was flowing normally.

'I'll wait for you at the car park exit,' she said as he got out. 'Then I'll follow you.'

Michael drove the Volvo slowly, continually checking in his rear-view mirror to make sure Sheila was still behind him. When they reached Dalgleish Tower he operated the remote control to open the doors to the underground garage and signalled to Sheila to drive down first, following her down the steep ramp as the doors clanged shut behind them.

When they got out of the cars, Sheila handed over the Mercedes' key. 'Do you want to take the Volvo or the Merc to drive me back to the office?'

Michael hesitated. 'Do you have time to come up for a quick drink?'

'I never drink during the day.'

'How about making today an exception? I've got a big decision to make and I'm badly in need of some sensible advice.'

Sheila blushed, flattered by the compliment. 'It would have to be a very quick one. I asked Sandra to hold the fort and I told her I'd be back within half an hour.'

Michel flicked open the control panel and tapped in the security code. The lift was waiting. When they arrived at the fifteenth floor he unlocked his front door. 'Let me take your coat.' Slipping her coat from her shoulders, Sheila handed it across. 'The lounge is the first door on the right.' Michael indicated the corridor straight ahead. 'Go on in. I'll join you in a minute. I need to use the bathroom.'

Sheila was standing by the window, gazing spellbound at the view, when Michael came into the lounge.

'Impressive?'

'Incredible, Mr Gibson.'

'I think we might dispense with the *Mr Gibson*. It's Michael.'

Sheila reddened visibly. 'All right. But only when we're away from work. In the office it has to be *Mr Gibson*.'

'That's a deal. What'll you have to drink?'

'Vodka and tonic please, *Michael*. You know, I don't think I could ever get used to calling you by your first name. In ten years of working for your father I never once referred to him as *George*.'

'I'm not my father – at least, I hope I'm not. Ice and lemon?'

'Please. And a very small vodka, with lots of tonic.'

Michael went to the kitchen to fill an ice bucket and carried it to the bar at the far end of the lounge where he fixed Sheila's drink. Opening a fresh bottle of malt whisky, he poured a generous measure into a crystal tumbler and dropped in two ice cubes. He carried the drinks across to the sofa where Sheila was seated and sat down beside her. 'Cheers.' he said, handing her her glass.

Sheila held up her drink and chinked it against his. 'So what's this big decision all about?'

Fixing his gaze on his whisky, Michael swilled the ice cubes round several times before gulping down half the contents in one swallow. 'I'm going to leave Anne,' he said quietly.

Sheila put her glass down on a coaster on the coffee table. There was an uncomfortable silence. 'Are you sure this is something you want to discuss with me, Mr Gibson?'

'*Michael*.'

'*Michael*,' she repeated softly. 'How did Anne take the news?'

'I haven't told her yet. That's why I wanted to get home early today. She'll be here around six-thirty. I'm going to tell her then.'

Sheila hesitated. 'I'm not sure what you expect me to say. Do you want me to try to talk you out of this? Or do you want me to encourage you, or sympathise with you, or what – ?'

'I really don't know what I want,' Michael said, dragging his fingers through his hair. 'I just need to talk to someone. I'm not sure if I'm doing the right thing.' He drained his whisky and held his hand out for Sheila's glass. 'Same again?'

Sheila shook her head as she picked up her glass and covered it with her hand. 'I'm fine.' Crossing to the bar, Michael poured himself another stiff drink. 'If I may be so bold as to ask – why are you going to do this?'

'There's someone else.' Michael took a sip of whisky. 'I suppose you know who she is?'

'I'd have to be blind not to. I think everyone in the office is aware that you are – how can I put it – 'in a relationship' with Philippa Scott. And if anyone had the slightest doubt, the office party last Christmas convinced them. You hardly spoke to anyone else all evening.'

'As obvious as that, eh?' he said ruefully. 'In which case it's probably just as well it's all going to be out in the open. Philippa and I will be moving in together.'

'You have thought this through? This isn't just a seven day wonder?'

'I'm sure. At least – I think I am,' he said, throwing back another slug of whisky. 'Anyway, it's too late to go back now. I've promised Philippa that I'll tell Anne tonight. Tell me honestly, Sheila, what do you think of Philippa?'

Sheila got to her feet and walked towards the window. 'That's a most unfair question. What I think of Philippa Scott is neither here nor there. It has no relevance whatsoever to your decision.'

'I'm sorry. As usual, you're right. It was just something Paul said this morning. He implied that everyone in the office thinks Philippa's a gold-digger. She's not like that. Really, she isn't.'

Sheila turned round to face him. 'It's not me you have to convince, Michael.' She walked towards the coffee table and put down her untouched drink. 'I really must be getting back to the office. Sandra's on her own. And you're not driving me,' she added. 'Not after what you've had to drink. I'll get a taxi.'

'Are you sure? I'm okay to drive.'

'Quite sure.'

'There's a taxi rank outside the building. There are normally plenty of cabs around at this time of day, but I'll come down with you to make sure. If there isn't a taxi waiting, I'll get the caretaker to call one for you. And thanks for the advice,' he added.

'I haven't given you any advice, but I will give you some now. If you're dead set on going through with this, then ease off on the whisky. You'll need to be sober when you break the news to Anne. You don't need me to tell you how she's going to react.'

Michael screwed up his face. 'I'll get your coat.'

Having summoned the lift, they descended in silence to the ground floor. When they went outside there were several cabs waiting in line.

'Thanks for the lift,' Michael said.

'Good luck.' Sheila proffered her hand. As Michael clasped her hand firmly, she leaned forward and pulled him towards her to whisper in his ear. 'For God's sake, Michael, don't waste yourself on Philippa Scott.'

Without waiting for his reaction she broke his grip and ran towards the taxi at the head of the queue. She didn't look back as it sped off.

NINE

Anne Gibson was in a foul mood as she hailed a passing cab outside the St Andrew's Bridge Club. She hated losing and her partner had misplayed a straightforward contract at the last table which had cost them the tournament.

She alighted in front of Dalgleish Tower, stepping carefully from the taxi in order to avoid a large puddle of slush. As the driver got out to open the boot, she belted her coat tightly to protect herself from the chill wind that was whipping round the corner of the building.

'How much is it?' she asked.

'Four pound fifty,' he said, lifting out her suitcase.

She took a five-pound note from her wallet and handed it across. 'That's okay.'

'Thanks. Would you like me to carry your case up the stairs?'

'No thanks, I can manage.'

'Mind how you go. It's starting to freeze and those steps look gey slippy.'

As the taxi sped off into the darkness, Anne negotiated the steps in front of the building gingerly and when she got to the internal door she slammed her suitcase down in frustration. She had trouble recalling the access code at the best of times, but after she'd been away for a few days she could never remember it. She wrenched her diary from her handbag and flicked it open at the back page. 'YK1193,' she muttered to herself, dropping her diary back into her bag. 'YK1193,' she repeated under her breath as she tapped at the control panel.

When she reached the fifteenth floor she opened the apartment door and saw a shaft of light flooding from the lounge into the hallway. She stopped and listened. The noise of the door being opened had roused Brutus and he emerged from the kitchen, bending his back and stretching out his sinewy rear legs. Looking down the hall, he recognised his mistress and padded briskly towards her, tail erect, miaowing loudly.

'Michael, are you there?' Anne called out anxiously.

'Yes!' the familiar voice from the lounge replied.

Anne gave a relieved sigh as she bent to stroke Brutus who was weaving in and out between her legs and rubbing himself up against her. 'Have you missed me, my beautiful big boy?' she whispered, running her fingers through his thick black fur. She took off her coat and draped it on the hallstand. 'You gave me the fright of my life,' she called out. 'You're never home at this time on a Monday. Is everything all right?'

There was no response. Leaving her suitcase in the hall, she walked into the lounge and saw Michael slumped on the settee, a tumbler clenched tightly in his fist, a half-empty whisky bottle on the coffee table beside him.

'For goodness sake, Michael! Is it not a bit early in the day for that?'

'Sit down, Anne,' Michael slurred as he struggled to sit up straight. 'I need to talk to you.'

Anne walked slowly across the room and sat bolt upright on the edge of the chair facing him as Brutus sprang onto her knee and curled up on her lap, purring contentedly. 'Hurry up, then. What is it? I want to take a shower.' Anne sat impassively, gently scratching at Brutus' forehead with her long fingernails. When Michael glanced up, Brutus's yellow eyes seemed to be fixed on him – unblinking, threatening.

'I've thought about this very carefully,' he began in a hoarse whisper. 'Things aren't right between us. Haven't been for some time. So I've decided… I've decided… I'm leaving you.' He lifted the whisky tumbler to his mouth and swallowed the contents.

Anne stopped stroking Brutus and gripped the sides of her chair with both hands. She sat for a moment in silence. 'You can't do that, Michael.' Her voice was quavering. 'We need to talk about this. We have to find a way to – '

'You heard what I said, Anne,' he interrupted, deflecting his eyes from her gaze. 'I'm leaving you.'

'Don't say things like that,' Anne pleaded. 'We can find a way... – we *will* find a way to get through this.'

'It's too late for that.'

'This isn't you talking, Michael. It's the whisky. Have a shower and go to bed. We'll talk about it in the morning.'

'There's nothing to talk about, Anne,' he slurred. 'It's over between us. That's how it has to be.'

Anne stared at him. 'That's not how it has to be, Michael! No matter what's happened, we can work things out. We just need to talk about it – to be honest with each other.'

'It's too late for that, Anne. There's someone else.'

'Someone else? Not the waif from the office, surely?'

'There's no point in discussing this, Anne. I'm leaving. As a matter of fact, I'm leaving tonight.'

Anne placed Brutus gently down on the floor and got to her feet. 'Listen to me, Michael – and listen very carefully.' Her eyes hardened. 'Do you think I don't know what's being going on behind my back? This girl's been around for how long? About a year? At least that's how long I've been smelling Jo Malone perfume on my pillowcase every time I come back from Aberdeen.'

'I'm in love with Philippa, Anne – and she's in love with me.'

'You're deluding yourself, Michael. Can't you see that? She's just infatuated by the idea that 'the boss' fancies her. She'll soon tire of hanging around with a flabby drunk and she'll want the company of people her own age – guys who can last the pace in the nightclubs.'

'There's no point in any of this, Anne. I've made up my mind.' Anne glowered at him in silence. 'You won't have any financial worries,' he added. 'I'll see you're taken care of.'

'You'll see I'm taken care of?' Anne spat out the words. 'You self-centred, patronising bastard! I'm warning you, Michael. If you try to walk out of here tonight, you're through – and I mean through. I'll take you for everything you've got – the flat, the business, your savings, your pension – the lot!' She walked over to the window and stood with her back to him. 'And by the way,' she added, turning round slowly, 'I don't think I mentioned that I had a long heart-to-heart with Saoirse MacBride a few years ago.'

'Who?'

'Don't tell me you don't remember Saoirse? You played squash with her at the club a few times – about seven years ago. Surely you can't have forgotten her? Long black hair, legs up to her armpits, big, green, come-to-bed eyes? You spent a dirty weekend with her in London when you were supposed to be attending a legal conference.'

'How do you – ?' Michael broke off.

'How do I know about Saoirse? Because, after you ditched her, the poor girl came to see me. She wanted to apologise to me. She was distraught and sick with remorse. She'd been caught up in the moment and hadn't thought through the implications of an affair with a married man. She'd imagined your relationship was going to blossom into something beautiful. She told me you'd even offered to give her a job in the firm when she graduated. I assume that was before you got inside her pants. She never dreamt for one minute she'd be unceremoniously dumped after one dirty weekend. She broke down in tears when she told me about it. Her hormones were all over the place. Of course, that's the kind of rotten hand life deals you when you're fifteen.' Anne paused to let her words sink in.

'What are you talking about?' Michael dragged his fingers through his hair. 'She was eighteen.'

'She might have *told* you she was eighteen. And that would certainly have been believable, I'll give you that. But the fact is she was fifteen. What do they call that? Statutory rape, isn't it? How's that going to look on your CV?'

'You're... you're making this up.'

'Oh, I'm not making it up, Michael. I've been saving it up. And what do you expect your latest little sex bomb will do while you're serving time in Barlinnie? Sit at home, knitting socks, till you get out? Maybe she'll come to visit you and bring you some of her home-made apple pie?'

'Why are you doing this, Anne?'

'Why am I doing this? For Christ's sake! If you thought for one minute that I'd sit back and watch you throw away twenty years of marriage so you could set up a cosy little love nest with your latest girlfriend, you must've been mad. You have a decision to make, Michael. Either you stay here – or you live with the consequences of everyone finding out about your underage sex affair. It's your call.'

Anne turned on her heel and strode out of the room. Michael shook his head to try to clear his befuddled brain. He sat, nursing another drink, struggling to think straight. Picking up the phone, he blinked as he tried to focus on the handset to tap in Philippa's number. She answered on the first ring. 'Pippa, it's me,' he croaked.

'Have you told her?' There was both anxiety and excitement in her voice.

'Yes.'

'Fantastic! Come on round. The champagne's on ice.'

'I can't. There's been a bit of a – a bit of a setback.'

'What kind of setback?'

'Anne's turned nasty.'

'What do you mean by 'nasty'?'

'It's to do with money,' he lied.

'Give her whatever she wants. We'll be fine.'

'It's not as straightforward as that. That won't satisfy her. Look, I can't go into details right now. She's liable to come back into the room at any minute.' He pursed his lips. 'She's threatening to talk to the tax authorities. It's no trivial matter. If she does I'll be in big trouble – and so will the firm. It could mean a jail sentence and the end of my career.'

'I don't buy any of this, Michael. What kind of cock-and-bull story are you trying to feed me?'

'I can't talk now, Pippa. I'll call you back later.'

'If this is true, what are you going to do about it?'

'I don't know. It took me completely by surprise. I need time to think. Maybe I can persuade her to change her mind.' There was silence at the other end of the line. 'Are you still there, Pippa?'

'I don't know, Michael. I don't think so.'

He heard the click as Philippa disconnected.

TEN

Tuesday 15 February

Michael Gibson was wakened by slanting shafts of winter sunshine streaming through the lounge window. He got up stiffly from the settee, his head thumping, his mouth parched. He'd slept all night, fully dressed, with his left leg twisted underneath him. As he hobbled down the hall he checked his watch and saw it was almost ten o'clock. He stopped outside the closed bedroom door and massaged his thigh to try to bring some circulation back to his numb leg as he listened for a moment before knocking gently. There was no response. Easing the door ajar, he confirmed the room was empty. The bed was made. When he went to the kitchen he saw an empty cereal bowl lying in the sink. He ran the tap and filled a tumbler with cold water which he downed in one long swallow, then he re-filled the glass and took it to the bedroom where he gulped down a couple of paracetamol tablets. Stripping off, he stood under the hot shower, still massaging his numb leg.

When he'd finished showering, he slipped on his towelling dressing gown and shaved as quickly as he could. His hand was trembling and he twice nicked his chin painfully, sticking small pieces of toilet paper to his face to stem the flow of blood.

It was half past ten by the time he took the lift to the underground garage. Anne's car was gone. He got into his Mercedes and pressed the remote control to open the garage doors and as he drove up the ramp he saw that most of the previous day's snow had melted in the morning sun. The roads were quiet as he made his way across town.

When he arrived at the office, Sheila was seated at her desk with her back to him, typing at her keyboard. 'Good morning, Sheila.'

'Good morning, Mr Gibson.' She replied without turning from her screen.

'Would you come into the office, please?'

Michael slumped onto the chair behind his desk. 'What have I managed to miss this time?'

'There was a staff meeting scheduled for nine o'clock. I cancelled it when you didn't show up. There's nothing else in the diary for this morning. You're supposed to be playing squash with Tom Crosbie at twelve.'

'Cancel it. It would kill me. Anyway, I didn't bring my gear. Is Pippa... Is Miss Scott in this morning?'

'I saw her earlier.'

'Tell her I need to see her straight away.' For the first time he could recall, he noticed Sheila hesitate.

'Very good,' she said stiffly.

A few minutes later Philippa marched in. 'Well?'

Michael scrambled to his feet. 'Pippa, you've got to give me time. It's more complicated than I thought. Anne can cause me a great deal of trouble. I will find a solution, but I need time.'

'For the past year, Michael, there's been one excuse or – as you would put it – one 'reason' after another why you couldn't walk out of your marriage It's such a corny routine. I really don't know what you expect of me, but I'm not prepared to settle for an occasional afternoon shag and a weekend in your flat once a month. So if, for whatever reason, you're not prepared to leave Anne, I think it would be better all round if we call it a day. If and when you sort things out with Anne, perhaps we can think about getting back together. And by the way, that's a very small 'perhaps'.'

'No Pippa, please! I can't stop seeing you! But Anne's threatening me. She knows she can have me locked up and she will if she's crossed.'

'This is getting cornier by the minute. What is she threatening you with?'

'It's to do with tax evasion. Twelve years ago, when my father and I were trying to get the business off the ground, we went through a sticky patch and we filed some highly dubious tax returns in order to keep the business afloat.'

'Is that all? This firm employs some of the best legal brains in the country. Even if your wife does get vindictive, surely it's not beyond our collective wit to mount an effective defence to a twelve year old charge of tax evasion?'

'Effective defence or not – the scandal would ruin the firm. I can't let it get to that.'

Philippa shook her head in frustration. 'This conversation is getting us nowhere. I want a straight answer to a straight question, Michael. Are you, or are you not, going to leave Anne?'

'I... I can't... not right now.'

'So you expect me to settle for being your occasional weekend screw? Is that how it works?'

'It's not like that at all. That's not fair.'

'Not fair? For Christ's sake, look who's talking about being fair! For the past year you've strung me along with promises that we'd be moving in together, and this is all it amounts to?'

'I'll get it sorted, Pippa... I really will.'

'It's too late for that, Michael. I don't want to hear another one of you damned lies.' Philippa's voice was trembling with emotion. 'I'm handing in my resignation, as of right now. I've already turned down several good job offers, out of loyalty to you. Loyalty that was clearly totally misplaced. God, what a miserable little shit you turned out to be. All I can say is – good riddance to you – and to your poxy job.'

The office door rattled in its frame as Philippa slammed it behind her.

ELEVEN

Tuesday 1 March

Paul Gibson was sweating profusely as he struggled to lift a large amplifier onto the tailgate of his van. When a car pulled up behind him and tooted, he recognised the Volvo's horn. 'Hi, Mum!' he called out without turning round.

'That looks very heavy,' Anne said as she was getting out of her car. 'Can't you get somebody to help you with it?'

Paul leaned against the amplifier with his shoulder and pushed until it came to rest against the side of the van. 'I lumbered Gordon with ironing the shirts instead. I'd rather load the van any day,' he said with a grin. 'You're welcome to come up, but I'm afraid I won't have time to offer you a coffee. We're doing a gig in Edinburgh tonight and we should've set off fifteen minutes ago.'

'I'll just come up for a minute and say hello to Gordon. I wasn't planning to stay. I was passing on my way home from the bridge club and I thought I'd drop by to see how you were doing. You're looking pale. Have you lost weight?'

'Give me a break. Not so long ago you were nagging me to ease off on the booze.'

'Are you eating properly?'

'Mum!' Paul closed the rear doors of the van and locked them.

'How's the flat working out?' Anne asked as they walked towards the red-sandstone, tenement building.

'It's fine. A bit cramped, but at least the rent's reasonable.'

'And the band?'

'I don't think The Proclaimers are quaking in their boots yet, but we're doing all right. We've got a booking in Edinburgh tonight, one next Tuesday in Dundee and one the following week in Perth. If tonight's gig goes well there's a possibility that it could become a regular booking for the summer.'

'I'm pleased for you.'

'Dad booting me out of the office was the best thing that could have happened. Gordon and I have been able to rehearse every day for the past couple of weeks and it's starting to pay off,' he said as they started climbing the stone staircase. 'And I don't have to wear suits and ties any more. The only thing I miss is the money.'

As they approached the top of the staircase, Anne pressed an envelope into his hand.

'I wasn't hinting. You don't need to do this.'

'I know I don't *need* to do it. I want to do it. I'm sure you'll find a use for it.' She closed his fist around the envelope.

'You're great,' he said, giving her a hug.

'Gordon!' Paul called out as he opened the door. 'My mother's here.'

'Hi, Mrs Gibson.' The voice came floating out from the bedroom. 'I'll be with you in a minute.'

When Gordon emerged he was carrying two black silk shirts on hangers. 'I'm glad Paul warned me you were here, otherwise you might've heard some unparliamentary language. I hate ironing at the best of times – and with these,' he said, holding up the hangers, 'I'm terrified I'll put the iron straight through them.'

Gordon Parker was a bright, energetic character, slimly built with shoulder-length hair tied back in a ponytail. He and Paul had been in the same class since primary school and for as long as either of them could remember they'd planned to form a group together, finally realising their ambition a few months previously when they'd teamed up with Tommy and Dave, friends of Gordon from university, to form the 'Citizens Band'.

'Any news of a day job?' Anne asked.

Gordon laughed raucously as he shook his head. 'Nothing much doing, Mrs Gibson. There's not a lot of demand for failed electronic engineers these days.'

'It really is a shame,' Anne said in a mildly reproachful tone. 'You could've passed your finals without any problem if you'd spent a bit more time studying and a bit less in snooker halls and discos.'

'I believe my mother might have mentioned that,' Gordon said, winking at Paul. 'But all's well that ends well. When we're playing in front of a packed house at Hampden Park you'll be delighted I didn't waste my talent designing an even faster microchip.'

'You're incorrigible. How's Maureen, by the way?'

'Oh, she's fine. Still wasting her time nursing, I'm afraid. We can't all be touched with genius.'

'Send her my regards. She's a really nice girl. Much too nice for you.'

'So her mother keeps telling me.'

'I hate to interrupt the banter,' Paul interjected, 'but we're running very late. We really should be hitting the road.'

'Of course, I didn't mean to hold you back,' Anne said. 'Get on your way – and don't drive too fast. By the way, that van looks none too safe to me.'

'It passed its M.O.T with flying colours, so will you please stop worrying.'

'I'll be with you in a minute, Paul,' Gordon said. 'I just need a quick pee.'

Paul waited until Gordon disappeared into the bathroom. 'I didn't want to say anything in front of Gordon, but are things any better between you and Dad?'

'We've hardly exchanged a civil word since he broached the subject of leaving me. I refuse to even discuss it with him. He's been sleeping in one of the guest bedrooms for the past couple of weeks and, as far as I'm concerned, he can stay there.'

'I don't know why you put up with all the hassle. You'd be a lot better off without him.'

'I know it's probably unrealistic,' Anne said with a sigh, 'but part of me is still hoping he'll come to his senses and we'll be able to patch things up.'

'You wouldn't take him back, surely?'

'There were good times, Paul. There were some very good times.'

'You should divorce him and be done with it,' Paul snapped. 'Anyway, you can't stop him divorcing you, even if you refuse to cooperate.'

'Somehow, I don't think he'll go down that route,' Anne said with a wry smile.

'Why not?'

'I'll tell you about it later. We don't have time to go into it right now.'

Paul hesitated. 'There's something I need to talk to you about, Mum. Something very important.'

'What is it?'

'Not now. Can I come to see you tomorrow?'

'Who's being mysterious now?' Anne said. 'Come round for a coffee tomorrow afternoon. Make it between three and four o'clock when your father is sure to be at work.'

It was four o'clock in the morning when Paul Gibson and Gordon Parker pulled up outside Paul's flat. Flicking off the van's lights, Paul cut the engine.

'We've had the stony silence routine all the way back from Edinburgh,' Gordon said. 'Can we let it drop now?'

'Why the hell did you do it?' Paul fumed. 'I thought we had an agreement? Nothing before a gig.'

'For Christ's sake! It was no big deal. Just a couple of tabs.'

'It was more than enough to fuck up our chances of ever getting another booking there. Your voice was flat, your timing was off and you forgot the words at least three times. What's the point in us busting a gut rehearsing if you're going to get stoned and ruin everything?'

Gordon pulled a packet of cigarettes from his jacket pocket and lit up, inhaling deeply. 'I've already said I'm sorry,' he mumbled. 'I was uptight. I needed something to relax me before we went on stage.'

Paul's temper calmed as quickly as it had flared up. 'What were you uptight about?'

'If you really want to know, I'm all screwed up about Maureen. We're nuts about each other and we want to move in together, but unless the band takes off in a big way I'm never going to be able to afford to do that. And to add to everything, I've had it right up to here with Maureen's mother. I was round at their place last week and I got the full treatment from the crabbit old bitch. I've never met anyone like her. She puts my own mother in the shade – and that takes a bit of doing. The cantankerous old cow can churn out clichés to a band playing. Gordon mimicked a high-pitched squeak: 'When are you going to get a proper job?' 'When are you and Maureen going to get married?' 'When are going to have the deposit saved up for a flat?' Jesus Christ! Fat chance I've got of ever saving up a deposit. If she knew I still owed you a thousand quid towards the van she'd go ballistic.'

'Talking of which – '

'Oh, fuck! I know I promised you a couple of hundred this month. I will pay you back, Paul – as soon as I can.'

'I'm not exactly flush, you know,' Paul snapped. 'I need the money.'

'I'm sorry. I just – '

'That's okay,' Paul interjected. 'It really is okay.' His voice softened. 'I didn't mean to go on about it.' He punched Gordon gently on the shoulder. 'No point in you going home at this time of night. Why don't you come up and crash out on the settee?'

Gordon sucked hard on his cigarette. 'Are you sure you don't mind?'

'Come on, you daft bampot.' Paul pulled his leather jacket from behind the driver's seat and jumped down. The clouds were high in the sky and a ground frost was forming. He slipped on his jacket and zipped it up.

'What about the gear?' Gordon asked as he clambered down. 'Shouldn't we take it upstairs?'

'I can't be arsed. We'll take our chances and leave it in the van overnight. Just make sure the doors are locked.'

'Suits me. I'm buggered.' They trudged side by side up to the fourth floor landing. As they went into the apartment, Gordon put his arm around Paul's shoulder. 'Would I be dicing with death if I suggested a smoke before we turn in?'

Paul smiled. 'You know the rules. After the gig, anything goes. What've you got?'

'I picked up some hash in Edinburgh.'

'Roll us a couple of joints while I organise the music.'

Paul browsed through the playlists on his laptop while Gordon was working on the joints.

Gordon chuckled when he heard the opening strains of 'Suzanne'. 'Why do you always put on Leonard Cohen when you're going to have a smoke?' he asked, lighting both joints and handing one across.

Paul closed his eyes and lay back in the armchair. He took a long, slow drag, sucking in the smoke and holding it in his lungs for as long as he could before releasing it slowly through his teeth. 'I really don't know. I think maybe it's because when I close my eyes and listen to his voice, I realise you might not be the worst singer in the world.'

Paul ducked as a cushion came flying across the room.

TWELVE

Wednesday 2 March

Anne Gibson sat on the settee in her lounge, totally stunned. Having told Paul about Michael's fling with Saoirse, she'd asked him what he wanted to talk to her about. It had taken a supreme effort on her part to hold it together while he recounted what had happened with Carole, but somehow she'd managed it.

When he'd finished, she'd started to weep, silently at first, then louder and louder as a succession of anguished sobs racked her entire body. Then the tears came in floods. Tears of realisation at the enormity of what had happened mingled with tears of utter frustration – emotions colliding as her world imploded. Everything had fallen into place.

She now understood what had caused the dramatic changes in Paul's personality. She realised why Michael had refused to allow her to get psychiatric help for Paul – and she knew the reason for Michael's breakdown. At the time, she'd thought it had been brought on by work-related stress.

It was all too horrible to contemplate. It should never have been allowed to come to this. If only he'd been honest with her at the time – they could have tackled it together.

Then anger took over. Seething, virulent, all-consuming anger. Michael must have realised the consequences of what he'd done. They were staring him in the face, each and every day for the rest of his life, but still he did nothing.

THIRTEEN

Thursday 3 March

Harry Kennedy had spent most of the afternoon tidying up the gardens in front of Dalgleish Tower and he was settling down to a welcome cup of tea when his doorbell rang. Whistling tunelessly, he pulled himself to his feet and opened his door. 'Och, it's yourself, Mrs Gibson. Come on in. I was expectin' it to be the Moores.'

'Who are they, Harry?'

'The couple who're buyin' number 10. They had a look round the flat a couple of weeks back and they phoned the estate agent this mornin' to confirm they're takin' it. They're comin' round today to take a few measurements. So, what can I do for you, Mrs Gibson?'

'Harry, you've got spare keys for all the flats, haven't you?'

'Yes.'

'Would you do me a favour and lend me your key for my flat? I left my coat at the bridge club and my house keys are in the pocket. My husband won't be home for another couple of hours and I don't want to drag all the way back to Sauchiehall Street in the rush hour as I'll be going there tomorrow anyway.'

Harry's brow furrowed. 'I'd really like to help out, but there's a wee problem.' Anne looked perplexed. 'I've got strict instructions never to let any of those keys out o' my sight. It's written into my contract.'

'Surely you can make an exception just this once? I've got a splitting headache and I couldn't face the prospect of driving back across town. And there's no point in me phoning Paul to ask him to bring his key across,' Anne added. 'He's gone across to Edinburgh.'

'Tell you what,' Harry said, brightening up considerably. 'What I could do is come upstairs with you and open your front door for you. Then Mr Gibson can lock up in the mornin' and you can collect your key from the bridge club.'

'Brilliant, Harry. I knew you'd think of something.' Resuming his tuneless whistling, Harry crossed to his wall safe and started twisting the dial. 'One more favour, Harry. Would you be an absolute angel and get me a glass of water?' Anne took a bottle of pills from her handbag. 'I've had a migraine all afternoon and I'll die if I don't take a Disprin straight away.'

'No bother at all. Nothin' in my contract that says I canny give people a glass of water.' He started whistling again as he bustled to the kitchen.

When Harry returned with the water, Anne was zipping up her handbag. She dropped two soluble tablets into the glass Harry handed her and swilled them round until they dissolved. Grimacing, she swallowed the contents in one gulp. 'Thanks, Harry. You're a lifesaver,' she said, handing him back the glass.

'All part of the service.' Harry took the key for flat 15 from its hook and closed the wall safe, spinning the dial. Locking his front door, he followed Anne across the hall.

'You do the code, Harry,' she said when they came to the internal door. 'I can never remember the damned thing.'

Harry grinned as he tapped at the control panel. 'And I can never forget it. I was allowed to choose the code, so I picked the first six digits of my National Insurance number.'

'So it's all your fault? Why couldn't you have picked something simple for us all to remember? Like 'HARRY', for example?'

'That would have been too easy. You canny be too careful about intruders these days, Mrs Gibson.'

FOURTEEN

Tuesday 8 March

Jack McFarlane's days followed a regular pattern. Rising late, he walked for miles every afternoon, no matter the weather, usually on Hampstead Heath. The early evenings were spent playing darts in a pub not far from Larry Robertson's flat and then he either ate in one of the nearby ethnic restaurants or bought something to take back to the flat, always making sure he was home by eleven o'clock.

This evening he stayed longer in the pub than usual before picking up an Indian take-away and making his way up the hill. He sensed he was being followed all the time, but made no attempt to slip his tail.

When he'd polished off his chicken Madras, he helped himself to a generous glass of malt whisky from the supply he'd found in the kitchen cupboard, then kicked off his shoes and stretched out on the bed to read the newspaper. Dozing, he was jerked awake by the strident ring of the telephone. He rubbed at his eyes and checked his watch, but made no move to answer the phone. After six rings, the caller hung up. McFarlane lay on the bed with his hands cupped behind his head, waiting. Five minutes later the phone rang out again. This time three rings, followed by silence. He sat up and grinned. Six rings, followed by three rings – exactly five minutes apart – between eleven and eleven-thirty. Larry Robertson's signal that he could now go up to Glasgow. No telephone connection – no voice communication on a line that was almost sure to be tapped. He waited a further five minutes before dialling Robertson's number, disconnecting after the fourth ring. The answering code: 'message received and understood'.

Having studied the railway timetables, McFarlane knew there was a train to Glasgow at eight o'clock on Wednesday mornings. He drained his whisky and packed his few possessions into his holdall. Setting his alarm for six o'clock, he stripped off and climbed between the sheets.

The insistent techno beat was pounding in Philippa Scott's ears. She felt completely uninhibited as she moved gracefully and sensually, swaying towards him when he rocked back on his heels, her breasts brushing lightly against his silk shirt, the contours of their bodies moulding together as they moved in time to the driving music.

Arching back her head, she ran the fingers of both hands through her long, loose, auburn hair, glistening with perspiration, while the strobe lights criss-crossing the crowded disco played multi-coloured patterns across their gyrating bodies.

Philippa luxuriated in the heady effects of the champagne and the pulsating rhythm. When the tempo slowed, she clasped both hands behind her neck and moved even closer to him, thrusting her hips forward and grinding into his body. Wrapping her arms around his neck, she slid off the band holding his pony tail in place and ran her fingers through his hair. She closed her eyes and felt her moist, warm sweat trickling down between her breasts. She wanted this night to last forever.

Wednesday 9 March

Jack McFarlane slept fitfully and was already wide awake when the alarm sounded at six o'clock. On the first ring his hand snaked out to silence the bell. Without switching on the light, he dressed quickly. There was sufficient moonlight filtering through the lounge window to allow him to glance round the room to make sure he hadn't forgotten anything. He swung his holdall over his shoulder and slid open the kitchen window at the rear of the building, which gave access to the fire escape leading to the courtyard five floors below. Clambering through, he tugged the window closed behind him and descended quickly to ground level.

McFarlane's every move was followed by the night binoculars trained on him from the attic apartment on the far side of the courtyard. His observer snapped open his mobile phone and connected with the driver of a black Citroën. 'Subject is on the move. He'll be in your line of sight within a minute.'

McFarlane strode down the narrow passageway between the two blocks of flats towards the main road. When he marched past the Citroën, the passenger waited a few moments before slipping out and falling into a matching stride pattern, some twenty yards behind him.

Charlie Anderson had had a boring day. Unless there was a panic on, Wednesday was his day for catching up with his backlog of paperwork and on this particular Wednesday there seemed to be twice as much as usual to wade through. As he slotted the last memo into his out-tray, he glanced up at his wall clock and saw it was after eight o'clock. 'Is that the time?' he mumbled, screwing the top onto his fountain pen and clipping it into his inside jacket pocket. He got to his feet and massaged his aching spine with both hands, then crossed to his filing cabinet and flicked through the top drawer until he came to a bulging manila folder labelled 'Crown versus McArthur'. Pulling it out, he stuffed it into his briefcase. He took off his reading glasses and slipped them into their case, rubbing at his tired eyes as he picked up the phone to call home.

'It's me, love. I'm about to leave the office.'

Charlie pulled on his coat and picked up his briefcase. He was leaning across to switch off his desk lamp when his intercom buzzed.

'Damn!' He flicked the switch across. 'What is it?' he barked.

'There's a Mr Gibson at the front desk, sir. He says he has to see you urgently. I told him you were off duty and asked if someone else could help, but he insists he has to see you. He seems pretty distraught.'

'Send him up.' Charlie let out a weary sigh as he peeled off his coat and hung it back on the peg on the back of the door. He heard footsteps hurrying along the corridor. Michael Gibson stumbled into the office without knocking, pale-faced and visibly shaken. He lurched towards Charlie's desk, almost falling.

'Michael, what on earth's the matter?' Charlie grabbed him by the arm and guided him onto a chair.

'It's Anne.'

'Anne? What about Anne?'

'She's… she's… killed herself.'

FIFTEEN

'What!'

Michael slumped forward and tugged at his tie knot. 'When I got home from work I found her lying there – on the bed,' he gasped. 'There was an empty pill jar by her side. She'd taken an overdose.'

'Are you sure she's dead?'

'I checked. She wasn't breathing.'

'Did you call an ambulance?'

'I tried to. There was something wrong with my mobile – I couldn't get a signal, so I tried to use the phone in the bedroom, but it wasn't working. I couldn't think what else to do, so I drove straight over here.'

Anderson banged on his intercom. 'This is an emergency. Send an ambulance to Dalgleish Tower on Clydeside – suspected overdose – possible suicide. Which floor, Michael?'

'Fifteen. It's the only flat on that floor.'

'Fifteenth floor,' Charlie shouted into the intercom. 'Tell the ambulance crew I'll meet them there with the keys. Get me a squad car out front straight away.' Charlie turned to Michael. 'You don't have to come. You can wait here. Just give me the key to your flat.'

'I'm coming with you.'

'Are you sure?' Michael nodded as he rose unsteadily to his feet.

As soon as they'd scrambled into the back seat, the squad car raced off, siren blaring, catching up with the ambulance a few hundred yards from Dalgleish Tower. Both vehicles screeched to a halt outside the building and two paramedics, carrying a stretcher and an oxygen mask, raced up the steps with Michael and Charlie in close pursuit.

'There's a code,' Michael panted, pushing his way to the front and tapping feverishly at the control panel. As the lift was climbing, Michael fumbled in his jacket pocket for his key. His hands were trembling as he unlocked the front door.

'Which room?' Charlie demanded. 'Quick.'

'First door on the left,' Michael said, leading the way.

Charlie put a restraining hand on his shoulder. 'Leave it to these guys, Michael. They know what they're doing.' Charlie nodded to the paramedics, who hurried towards the bedroom.

Michael slumped to his knees at Charlie's feet. 'Why? Why would she do it?' Burying his head in his hands he started to sob uncontrollably.

One of the paramedics appeared in the bedroom doorway. He caught Charlie's eye and shook his head slowly from side to side.

'Too late?' Charlie mouthed. The medic continued to shake his head, signalling to him to come across. Charlie stopped in the bedroom doorway. The room was empty, the bed was made and there was no sign of any disturbance. He glanced over his shoulder to where Michael was kneeling in the hall, sobbing heavily. 'Check out the other rooms – quickly,' he whispered.

'Nothing, Inspector,' the paramedic reported back a few moments later. 'There's no one in the apartment. Just a frightened cat in the kitchen.'

'Michael,' Charlie said, helping him to his feet, 'come over here.' He led him towards the bedroom. 'There's something very strange. There's no sign of Anne.'

Michael stared open-mouthed, pointing at the bed in amazement. 'But – half an hour ago – Anne was lying there. Oh my God! What's happening?'

'Calm down. I think you could use a drink.'

Charlie turned to the paramedics. 'Sorry about the false alarm, boys. I'll stay with him and try to get to the bottom of this. Do me a favour. When you go downstairs ask Phil, he's my driver, to wait for me? Tell him I don't know how long I'll be.'

'No problem, Inspector.'

Charlie took Michael by the arm to lead him to the lounge and sat him down on the settee. He crossed to the bar and poured two stiff whiskies. Taking the chair opposite, he handed Michael a tumbler. 'In your own time, tell me what happened here this evening.'

Charlie produced his notebook and his propelling pencil as Michael sipped at his drink. 'I got home just before eight o'clock. I'd been playing squash and I'd had a couple of pints and a sandwich with Tom Crosbie after the game. I wasn't expecting Anne to be home. Wednesday's one of her bridge nights and she usually leaves the house around seven.

'The first strange thing was when I got out of the lift. The apartment door was wide open. Brutus – that's Anne's cat – was out on the landing screeching his head off. From the hall, I could see the bedroom door was ajar and there was a light on. I shouted out Anne's name – several times – but there was no reply. I thought there must be a burglar in the flat so I picked up a walking stick from the stand in the hall and tiptoed towards the bedroom.

'When I got to the door – I saw her. She… she was just lying there – face up – on the bed. I dropped the walking stick. There was an empty pill bottle on the bed beside her and a half-full pitcher of water on the bedside table. Oh yes, and an empty glass lying on the bed. She was ghostly white and her eyes were closed.

'I went to the dressing table and grabbed a mirror to hold in front of her lips. Nothing. She wasn't breathing. I tried to call an ambulance, but my mobile wasn't getting a signal and the phone in the bedroom was dead – not even a dialling tone. I didn't know what to do. I took the lift down to the garage and drove across to Pitt Street as fast as I could.'

Michael downed the rest of his whisky in one. 'Do you want another one?' he asked, getting to his feet. Charlie shook his head.

Michael replenished his drink with a shaking hand and came back to the settee. 'This is crazy, Charlie. What's going on?'

'I've no idea. Let's take things slowly. Assuming you didn't imagine something, or – '

'I didn't imagine anything. I saw her. She was lying there.'

'Take it easy. Michael. As I was saying, assuming you didn't imagine anything.' He repeated the phrase slowly but forcibly. 'Then we need to try to establish what happened here tonight. There must be a logical explanation, so let's consider the options. You say Anne normally plays bridge on Wednesday evenings?'

'Yes.'

'In which case we'll start by phoning her bridge club and check if she went there.'

'I told you. She's dead.'

'That may or may not be the case, Michael. Perhaps Anne had fainted, or was in some kind of a coma when you found her? If you want me to help you, you have to let me do things my way. That means checking the facts and eliminating possibilities.'

'Sorry, I didn't mean to fly off the handle.'

'Do you have the bridge club number?'

'It'll be in that book beside the phone. It's the St Andrew's Club.'

Charlie found the number and dialled. 'I'm trying to get in touch with Anne Gibson. Do you know if she's been to the club tonight?'

'I haven't seen her,' the female voice replied, 'but let me check.' Charlie sat back in his chair and loosened his tie knot while he waited. 'No, she hasn't been here at all today.'

'Thanks.' Charlie replaced the receiver. 'She didn't go to her club. By the way, the phone seems to be working all right. Was this the one you tried to use earlier?'

'No – it was the one on the bedside table.'

Charlie went to the bedroom, returning a few moments later. 'That one seems to be working fine too. Perhaps you panicked and didn't hear the dialling tone?'

'I'm telling you – the line was dead.'

'What was the problem with your mobile?'

'I don't know. I couldn't get a connection.'

'Has that happened here before?' Michael shook his head. 'Try it now.'

Michael took his phone from his pocket and studied it. 'It seems okay now. It's getting a strong signal.'

'If Anne didn't go to her bridge club, where else might she have gone?'

Michael paused to consider. 'Perhaps to visit Paul? I had a run-in with him at the office a while back and I haven't seen him since, but I'm sure Anne goes round to his flat quite often.'

'Does she have any brothers or sisters?'

'One older sister.'

'Might she have gone to see her?'

'Not unless she caught a flight to Vancouver.'

Charlie tapped his pen on his teeth. 'How long has she been out there?'

'Since nineteen ninety-nine. I remember the date because she'd had some relationship problems and she wanted to start a new life for the new millennium.'

'How about Anne's friends closer to home?'

'There are several girlfriends she meets up with regularly.'

'Try calling around,' Charlie handed across the phone and the telephone book. 'Check if anyone's seen Anne today.'

Michael dialled a number, with no response. 'Paul's mobile's switched off,' he said, 'and there isn't a landline in his flat. I'll try Mary.' Mary McDonald's phone rang out unanswered. He made several other calls. Of those who answered, no one had seen Anne.

'Would you have said Anne was the suicidal type?' Charlie asked.

'Not even remotely. I couldn't imagine the idea entering her head.'

'Was she under any particular stress that you know of?'

Michael hesitated. 'Our marriage has been pretty rocky recently – not that it has been great for some time. I told Anne a couple of weeks ago – maybe it was three – that I wanted to end it. She went ballistic. No way she would even consider it.

'Since then we've been living in the same flat but we've hardly exchanged a civil word. But suicide?' Michael shook his head. 'I can't get my head round that.'

'Let's go back to the facts. You said the door to the flat was open when you got out of the lift. That's very strange in itself. Someone planning to commit suicide wouldn't normally leave the front door wide open.'

'What are you driving at?'

Charlie took a sip of whisky. 'Let's consider all the possibilities.' Charlie put his glass down on the coffee table and started counting off on his fingers. 'One. Anne fell ill and passed out on the bed, then recovered after you had left the apartment.'

'What about the pill jar and the glass of water?'

'Two. Anne took some pills because she was feeling unwell, possibly too many, and passed out. Three, she deliberately tried to take an overdose, but came round after you'd left.' Charlie picked up his whisky glass and took a sip before continuing. 'And four – I'm afraid I can't think of any delicate way to put this. If it wasn't illness, an accidental overdose or an attempted suicide, that only leaves murder.'

'What?' Michael rasped. 'That's not possible.'

Charlie's mobile started to ring. Tugging his phone from his jacket pocket, he quickly switched it off. 'You told me you saw Anne's body lying on the bed. If she was ill, or had attempted suicide, I concede it's just about feasible that she could've come round after you left the apartment and somehow managed to stagger out. However, it's stretching the bounds of credibility to believe that, on her way out, she tidied away the pill bottle, the water jug and the glass, to say nothing of smoothing down the bed and repairing the phone. There must've been someone else involved. Someone who fixed it to look like suicide, and then removed Anne's body. Could there have been someone else in the flat while you were here?"

'I... I don't know.'

'Did you go into any of the other rooms, apart from the bedroom?'

Michael shook his head in confusion. 'No... No, I don't think so. Just the bedroom.'

'So someone could've been hiding in the apartment while you were here?'

'Well... yes... I suppose so. But this is crazy. Why would anyone murder Anne and then try to make it look like suicide? And why would they then remove her body and tidy up the flat?'

'These are all good questions. I have no answers.' Charlie reflected for a moment. 'There is something else you ought to know, though I doubt if it has any connection with what happened here tonight. The London boys phoned me today to let me know Jack McFarlane caught a train to Glasgow this morning.'

Michael turned ashen and the veins on his neck bulged. He clenched his whisky tumbler in a trembling fist.

'Don't get too uptight about that.' Charlie did his best to sound reassuring. 'There's no way McFarlane could be involved in Anne's disappearance. My men have been tailing him from the moment he stepped off the London train.'

Charlie finished his drink and stood up. 'There's nothing more we can achieve here tonight. I'll go back to the office and file a 'missing persons' report and we'll take it from there. I'll send someone round to Paul's place to check when he last saw his mother. What's his address?'

'Saltoun Street – number thirty-one.' Charlie made a note. 'Do you have a recent photo of Anne I could borrow?'

Michael went to the bedroom and returned with a small silver frame. 'This was taken in Paris last summer. Is it okay?'

Charlie studied it. 'It's fine,' he said, slipping the photo from the frame and tucking it into his jacket pocket. 'I realise this is difficult for you, Michael, but try not to get paranoid about McFarlane. We'll be keeping close tabs on him. I'll call you tomorrow and let you know what progress we've – Damn!' Charlie interrupted himself.

'What's wrong?'

'I've just remembered,' he said punching his fist into the palm of his hand. 'I'm stuck in the High Court all day tomorrow. Don't worry, though. I'll set things in motion tonight and I'll make sure you're contacted as soon as there's any news. In the meantime I suggest you try to get some sleep.'

'Thanks, Charlie.'

'And I also suggest you don't have too many of these before you turn in.' Charlie waved his empty whisky tumbler in the air before placing it on the coffee table.

Charlie pulled open the rear door and got into the waiting squad car.

'Where to, sir?'

'Drop me off back at Pitt Street, Phil.'

As the car pulled away from Dalgleish Tower, Charlie switched on his phone and saw he had a voice message from DS O'Sullivan. Having listened to it, he cursed under his breath.

As soon as he got to his office, Charlie summoned O'Sullivan.

Charlie leapt to his feet when O'Sullivan walked through the door. 'How the hell did you manage to lose him? The London boys managed to keep tabs on McFarlane for three weeks without any problem – and you lose him in Glasgow in less than a fucking hour!'

Tony O'Sullivan stood to attention at the other side of the desk, his eyes riveted to the floor. He was in his early thirties though he could have been taken for a lot younger. Solidly built with short, crinkly red hair, he was blushing furiously, which only served to intensify his normal high colouring and highlight the mass of freckles covering his cheeks and forehead.

'I wasn't expecting him to try to give me the slip so soon, sir,' he mumbled. 'The word from London was that he hadn't once tried to lose his tail during his time there.'

'Tell me what happened.' Charlie slumped back down in his chair. 'Sit down, Tony,' he said in a much calmer tone, waving towards the chair opposite. 'I didn't mean to bite your head off. I've had a pig of a day.'

O'Sullivan took out his notebook and flicked it open. 'I was waiting for McFarlane at Central Station this afternoon. The London train arrived fifteen minutes late. There was no problem picking him out. He strode across the station concourse like he owned the place – dead gallus. As the NCA guys had told us, he was wearing a black anorak, jeans and trainers and carrying a tartan holdall. His head was completely shaved.

'He bought a newspaper and a packet of fags at a kiosk, then went into the station buffet and ordered a coffee. He sat there for about twenty minutes, flicking through the paper, before strolling out into Gordon Street and wandering around aimlessly, stopping occasionally to look in shop windows.

'I stayed about twenty yards behind him all the time. He didn't seem to be going anywhere in particular. Up Hope Street, all the way along Sauchiehall Street to Kelvingrove Park, then he wandered back along Argyle Street as far as the Heilanman's Umbrella. Just meandering around the city as if he was soaking up the atmosphere – or getting acquainted with the place again. I don't know if he suspected he was being tailed. He never once glanced round.'

'He knew all right.' Charlie growled. 'What next?'

'He went into The Horse Shoe in Drury Street and stayed there until the back of six,' O'Sullivan said, referring to his notebook. 'When he came out of the pub he cut across to Buchanan Street and turned into Princes Square shopping centre, but when I followed him inside, he'd vanished. He must've sprinted away as soon as he was out of my line of sight. I ran up the escalator looking for him, but he'd scarpered.'

'He picked the ideal place to lose you,' Charlie mused. 'Princes Square's a rabbit warren – and it's always hoaching. Okay. No use crying over spilt milk. Let's get on with the job of finding him. I want every man we can spare on this one. Check out his old haunts and pay a visit to his former cronies. I don't care who gets dragged out of their bed in the middle of the night. If anyone wants to complain refer them to me.

'The main reason I want him found – and fast,' Charlie explained, 'is that something bizarre happened tonight in Dalgleish Tower, down on Clydeside. Anne Gibson, the lawyer's wife, has gone missing. It's possible she tried to commit suicide, though I suspect she's been abducted or she might even have been murdered. I've got a feeling in my guts that McFarlane's involved.'

'Why is that?'

'Gibson was McFarlane's defence lawyer when he got sent down and, to put it mildly, he didn't do a very good job. McFarlane threatened to get his revenge on the Gibson family when he got out.'

'You think he might have murdered Gibson's wife?'

'I don't know what to think. McFarlane's been a violent bastard all his life – and nursing a grudge for twelve years in Peterhead isn't likely to have mellowed him much. Take this.' Charlie produced the photo from his jacket pocket. 'This is Anne Gibson. I realise she's only been missing for a few hours but unless her husband has flipped his lid completely, something's happened to her. Get the 'missing persons' routine rolling; photo in the morning papers, publicity on television, the works.

'I'm out of action all day tomorrow,' Charlie continued. 'I'm stuck in the High Court as the main prosecution witness in the McArthur trial and God only knows when I'll get called. Tell Colin Renton to drop whatever he's doing and help you with this. Tell him to go round and talk to Paul Gibson first thing in the morning – he's the son. He has a flat at 31 Saltoun Street. I want to know if he saw his mother today.'

'You do realise Colin's working 24/7 for Inspector Crawford on the Castlemilk rape enquiry, sir?'

Charlie waved his hand dismissively. 'Crawford's spinning wheels on that one. He hasn't got a single worthwhile lead and he's got Renton working all the hours God sends just to keep Niggle off his back. I told you. I want you and Renton working full time on this. You brief Colin, I'll square it with Crawford.'

'Very good, sir.'

'I suggest you get things organised here then head off home and grab a few hours' kip. Call me at home tomorrow night if you've got anything to report. If I don't hear from you, we'll meet here first thing on Friday morning.'

When Charlie arrived home he found Kay sitting in the lounge, flicking through a travel brochure.

'What got ruined this time, love?' he asked.

'Shepherd's pie. I left yours in the oven in case you were hungry. Would you like some?'

Charlie shook his head. 'Much as I love your shepherd's pie, I couldn't face anything tonight.'

Kay stood up and gave him a peck on the cheek. 'In which case, I'll turn the oven off.'

'Sorry about that.' He let out a long sigh. 'I really was on my way out of the office when I phoned.'

'God knows, I'm used to it.'

'I think I'll call it a day,' Charlie said, yawning. 'I'm buggered.'

'What was the panic?' Kay asked as she followed him up the narrow staircase.

'You remember Michael Gibson, George's son?'

'Yes.'

'His wife has mysteriously disappeared. Michael came to see me in a blind panic, just after I'd phoned to say I was on my way home. He told me he'd come home from work this evening and found his wife's body in their bedroom. He was convinced she'd committed suicide, but when we went back to the apartment there was nothing there. No body – no sign of a suicide. But we haven't been able to trace her. It's bizarre.'

Charlie stripped off and pulled on his pyjamas before going to the bathroom to brush his teeth. By the time he returned to the bedroom Kay was drifting off to sleep. Climbing into bed, he set his alarm, then switched off the bedside lamp. He closed his eyes but, despite his tiredness, sleep wouldn't come. He turned onto his back and stared at the ceiling, the events of the evening churning through his brain. The more he thought about it, the more convinced he was that it couldn't have been suicide. Either Anne Gibson had been abducted, perhaps murdered, or Michael Gibson was hallucinating – and he wouldn't like to bet on which.

SIXTEEN

Friday 11 March

Thursday had been a totally frustrating day for Charlie. Seven hours kicking his heels in the High Court, only for McArthur to change his plea to guilty just before he was due to be called as a witness.

Charlie arrived at the office early on Friday morning, anxious for news. As he was taking off his coat there was a sharp rap on the door and DC Colin Renton walked in. Charlie had known Renton for years, both having started out together in the Paisley constabulary.

'What did you manage to come up with yesterday, Colin?' Charlie asked.

'Precious little, sir.' Renton's frown exaggerated his craggy features. 'We've put out four 'missing-person' appeals on television during the past twenty-four hours and we ran the story in the national and local papers, but no one's come forward with any information. We've established that the last person known to have seen Anne Gibson before she disappeared was Mary McDonald. She's one of the leading lights in Mrs G's amateur dramatics society. Mrs Gibson dropped in to see her on Wednesday afternoon to discuss the costume designs for their next production.' Tony O'Sullivan walked into the office and waved to Renton to carry on. 'Mrs Gibson left the McDonalds' place in Kirkintilloch around six o'clock,' Renton continued, 'about two hours before Michael Gibson claims he found his wife's body. According to her friend, Mrs G was full of the joys – laughing and joking – no indication of any undue worry or stress.'

'Did you get anywhere?' Charlie asked, turning to O'Sullivan.

'I went up to Aberdeen yesterday to speak to the Jacksons, Anne Gibson's parents. The local constabulary had already broken the news of their daughter's disappearance to them. Mrs Jackson was in bed, heavily sedated, so I didn't get to talk to her. Apparently she's got a heart condition and she took the news very badly.

'Mr Jackson couldn't cast any light on the subject. He last saw his daughter a couple of weeks ago when she went up there for her fortieth birthday party – without her husband. Mr Jackson told me that Michael wanted to leave Anne so he could move in with his new girlfriend.'

'That ties in,' Charlie said. 'Gibson told me his marriage was on the rocks and he was trying to get a separation, so the fact that there's a girlfriend in the frame is no big surprise. Ask around. It shouldn't be too difficult to find out who she is.'

'We know already,' Renton chipped in. 'I went round to Paul Gibson's place yesterday to tell him about his mother's disappearance. He was very upset. He told me his father's involved with a girl called Philippa Scott who used to work in Gibson's law practice. She's now with Colesell and Sharp, a firm of solicitors in Bath Street. Tony and I are going across there this morning to talk to her.'

'Did you get anything worthwhile out of Paul?'

'Not really. The last time he saw his mother was a couple of days ago when he dropped into Dalgleish Tower for a coffee. As far as he's aware she had no particular worries or problems, apart from being uptight about her husband wanting to leave her. He hasn't seen his father since they had a barney in the office and he stormed out – about three weeks ago. Seems he was given the bullet by his own dad.' Renton grinned briefly.

'Have you mentioned to anyone that we suspect Anne Gibson might be dead?'

O'Sullivan and Renton looked at each other, raising their eyebrows and shaking their heads. 'No, sir,' said O'Sullivan. 'All we've said is that she's missing.'

'It's only a matter of time until the story breaks,' Charlie said. 'If there's no news of her whereabouts by this evening, I'm going to launch a full-blown murder enquiry. So, if you think it appropriate, drop the information that she may be dead into the conversation with Gibson's girlfriend. It might be interesting to see how she reacts.'

Charlie checked his watch. 'I'm going to have to leave you boys to it. I've got a meeting with Niggle. He wants to be briefed on the case.'

'Why is he taking an interest?'

'He knows the family. He used to play golf with Gibson's father.'

'One thing before you go, sir,' Renton said hesitantly. 'Have you spoken to DI Crawford about pulling me off the Castlemilk rape enquiry? He almost had a canary when I told him I was working full-time for you.'

'Shit! It slipped my mind. Sorry about that. Don't worry, Colin. I'll square it with Crawford as soon as I've briefed Niggle.'

O'Sullivan and Renton were shown into the reception room of Colesell and Sharp. They sat side by side on the low sofa, flicking through the well-thumbed pages of old magazines, until Philippa Scott joined them. The moment she walked through the door they both scrambled to their feet. Philippa was wearing a cream-coloured suede mini-skirt and matching silk blouse. Her auburn hair was swept back from her face and plaited halfway down her back.

'Sorry to disturb you at work, Miss Scott,' O'Sullivan said, adjusting his tie knot.

'That's okay, officers. Do sit down.' Philippa took the upright chair facing them. Crossing her legs, she clasped her knee in both hands. 'How can I help you?'

'Do you know that Anne Gibson is missing?' O'Sullivan said, taking out his notebook.

Philippa nodded. 'I read about that in the papers.'

O'Sullivan coughed embarrassedly. 'We have reason to believe that you and Mr Gibson have… have a relationship and that – '

'Had,' interrupted Philippa, in a matter-of-fact tone. 'Mr Gibson and I *had* a 'relationship', as you call it. That's no secret. But it's all over now. Has been for some time.'

'When did you last see him?'

'I don't know. Must be the best part of a month.'

'Have you been in contact with him at all during that time?'

'Why would I?'

'I'm not asking why you would,' O'Sullivan said. 'I'm asking if you have been.'

Philippa's complexion reddened visibly. 'The answer is no.'

'Have you seen Mrs Gibson recently?'

'Mrs Gibson? Hardly! My relationship with Michael may be over, but Anne Gibson and I aren't exactly bosom buddies.'

'When did you last see her?'

'God, I don't know. I don't think I've set eyes on her since last December when she dropped in at the office Christmas party.'

'I believe Mr Gibson was planning to leave his wife so he could be with you?'

Philippa shook her head firmly. 'That may have been the case a few weeks ago, but as I've already told you, Michael and I have split up.'

'Can I ask why?' O'Sullivan said.

Philippa shrugged. 'These things happen.'

'Can you think of any reason why Mrs Gibson might choose to disappear?'

'Not at all.' Philippa screwed up her face. 'Why are you asking me all these questions? I hardly know the woman. I've only met her a couple of times in my life and we've never exchanged anything other than casual chit chat.'

O'Sullivan closed his notebook. 'The news hasn't broken yet, but we suspect Anne Gibson may be dead – possibly murdered.'

The colour drained from Philippa's cheeks. 'Murdered?' She stood up and walked towards the window. 'Who on earth… would want to murder her?'

'Can you tell us where you were on Wednesday evening?' Renton asked.

'Wednesday? I can't remember.'

'That was the night before last,' he prompted.

'I was at home, I think. Yes, I was at home watching television.'

'Can anyone vouch for that?' Renton persisted.

'A friend was supposed to be coming round for dinner, but she had to call off at the last minute.'

'So that's a 'no'?'

Philippa spun round, her face flushed. 'I don't believe I'm hearing this. Are you checking to see if I've got an alibi? Are you suggesting that – ?'

'We're not suggesting anything,' O'Sullivan interjected, getting to his feet. 'All we're trying to do is get to the bottom of Mrs Gibson's disappearance.'

'Whatever.' Philippa turned back and stared out of the window.

O'Sullivan exchanged a glance with Renton. 'I think that's all for now,' he said. Ripping a blank page from his notebook, he handed it across. 'If you wouldn't mind jotting down your address and your phone number, in case we have any further questions.'

Taking the pen she was offered, Philippa scribbled quickly on the paper. She thrust it at O'Sullivan and strode from the room.

O'Sullivan turned to Renton and raised an eyebrow. 'What do you make of that?'

'Probably the longest legs I've ever seen. Right up to her oxters.'

'Seriously.'

'Seriously – a friend supposed to be coming round for dinner on Wednesday – then calling off at the last minute? That's a bit too pat for my liking. And she looked distinctly uncomfortable when you asked her if she'd had any contact with Gibson since they broke up. I suspect our Miss Scott might know more than she's letting on.'

O'Sullivan examined the slip of paper in his hand. 'How about that for a coincidence? She lives just round the corner from me. Which means, I suppose, I'll get stuck with the onerous task of going round to her place to continue the interview.' He grinned as he tucked Philippa's address into his notebook.

Charlie Anderson felt distinctly uncomfortable as he sat opposite Superintendent Nigel Hamilton, known throughout the force as 'Niggle' for self-evident reasons. As far as Charlie was concerned, Niggle never contributed anything positive to a situation, his only interest being to make sure his backside was covered. Hamilton's slow, pedantic, sing-song delivery only added to Charlie's irritation with the man.

'What's the latest on the Gibson situation?' Hamilton demanded, rocking back in his chair.

'Nothing definitive to report at this stage. Looks like we might have a murder on our hands, though there's no sign of a body.'

'You need to get to grips with this, Anderson. If the press get a sniff of a scandal concerning the Gibson family, they'll have a field day.'

'I realise that. I've assigned O'Sullivan and Renton to the investigation full time.'

'O'Sullivan? Is that a good call? Wasn't he the one who lost McFarlane?'

'McFarlane gave him the slip. It could've happened to anyone.'

'But it happened to him.' Hamilton sucked hard on his teeth. 'The NCA offered to maintain surveillance on McFarlane while he was in Glasgow, but I told them we would handle it. Made me a bloody laughing stock, that did. And as for Renton, I had Crawford in here yesterday to review his progress, or rather lack of it, on the Castlemilk rape enquiry. He told me you'd messed him about by pulling Renton off the case without so much as a by your leave.'

'I'm sorry about that. I meant to clear it with Crawford, but I was tied up in the High Court all day yesterday and it slipped my mind.'

'Slipped your mind?' Hamilton shook his head. 'Too many things slipping people's minds around here for my liking.'

Charlie bit into his lower lip as he rose to his feet. 'Will that be all?' Without waiting for Hamilton's response, he turned on his heel and strode out of the office.

SEVENTEEN

Monday 14 March

'Anne's been missing for five days, Charlie. Surely there's something you can do?' Michael Gibson was slumped on a chair in Charlie's office. His skin was grey, his eyes red and sunken from lack of sleep. His trousers and jacket were crumpled and his hair dishevelled. He was unshaven and his breath stank of whisky.

'I don't know what to say to you, Michael. We've interviewed all Anne's relatives and friends and we've spoken to her sister in Vancouver, but we've drawn a complete blank. We've established that she left Mary McDonald's place in Kirkintilloch at six o'clock last Wednesday, but no one saw her between then and when you say you found her two hours later. And no one's seen hide nor hair of her since. We've run her photograph in the national and local newspapers and also on television for the past four days. We've combed every square inch within a mile of your apartment block and we're pursuing all possible lines of enquiry.'

Michael got to his feet and started pacing up and down. 'What about McFarlane? Do you still have no idea where he is?'

Charlie shook his head grimly. 'I've alerted the NCA and asked them to let us know if and when he's sighted again in London. They haven't come up with anything. However, I don't think that – '

Charlie's flow was interrupted by his phone ringing. He snatched up the receiver.

'It's O'Sullivan, sir. We've just received a tip off that McFarlane's been seen drinking in a pub in Partick. Do you want him pulled in or should we put a tail on him?'

'Pull him in. Straight away. Looks like we've got a break,' Charlie said, replacing the receiver. 'McFarlane's been spotted in a pub in Partick. My men are on their way to bring him in. I suggest you go home now, Michael. If you don't mind me saying so, you look dreadful. Go easy on the hard stuff. I'll call you later and let you know if we get anything out of McFarlane.'

When Charlie was informed that O'Sullivan was back, he made his way down the stairs, along the corridor and into the interview room. Jack McFarlane was sitting on the opposite side of the desk from O'Sullivan, with Renton standing by the door. As soon as Charlie walked in, McFarlane scrambled to his feet.

'I want my lawyer, Anderson. This is harassment. I've done nothin'. You've got no right to pull me in.'

Charlie waved him back onto his seat. 'Spare me the melodrama, McFarlane. Where were you last Wednesday night between six and eight o'clock?'

'I'm sayin' nothin' until my lawyer's present.'

'Cut the crap. I asked you a question. Where were you last Wednesday between six and eight?'

'Go an' fuck yourself.'

Anderson stared long and hard at McFarlane, then turned to O'Sullivan. 'Let him phone his lawyer. We'll continue the interview when he gets here. Who is your lawyer, by the way?' Charlie made sure he had full eye contact. 'Not still Michael Gibson, by any chance?'

McFarlane looked blank for a moment, then burst out laughing. 'You're sick, Anderson. My lawyer's Frank Morrison. You'll have his number.'

Half an hour later Anderson and O'Sullivan returned to the interview room where McFarlane and Morrison were sitting on the same side of the desk, huddled in conversation.

'Now look here, Inspector,' Morrison said. 'I really must protest in the most vehement of terms. This is victimisation. I've no idea on what pretext you're holding my client but I must insist that you either produce a charge or release him.'

Charlie knew Morrison well – and disliked him intensely. In his mid-fifties – a smooth dresser and a smooth talker – he seemed to be on the payroll of every major perpetrator of organised crime in the city.

Anderson and O'Sullivan took the chairs on the opposite side of the desk. 'There is no charge,' said Charlie. "Your client' – he spat out the words – 'is only here to assist us with our enquiries.'

'What enquiries? As far as I'm aware you've not asked him to assist you with any enquiries.'

'I asked him to account for his movements last Wednesday evening between six and eight o'clock. He refused point blank to answer the question until his lawyer was present.'

Glancing sideways at McFarlane, Morrison gave a slight inclination of the head.

'Mr McFarlane is prepared to answer your questions,' Morrison stated.

'Where were you between six and eight on Wednesday?'

'At my mate's place.'

'What 'mate'?'

'Archie McWilliam.'

'Where does he live?'

'Paisley. He has a flat at the top o' the High Street.'

Charlie changed tack. 'Why did you give Sergeant O'Sullivan the slip when you arrived in Glasgow?'

'I don't know what you're talkin' about.'

'Don't act it with me. You know fine well that we were tailing you from the minute you got off the London train until you gave O'Sullivan the slip in Princes Square.'

'This is outrageous!' Morrison spluttered as he leaned across the desk. 'Having my client tailed is an infringement of his civil liberties.

As he was totally unaware that he was being followed, obviously he made no attempt to give anyone the slip.'

Charlie held up his hand. 'Back off, Morrison. I'm too long in the tooth for this crap. Cut the posturing and let your 'client' answer the question. The sooner he does, the sooner we'll all get out of here.'

Charlie turned back to McFarlane. 'You admit you went into Princes Square shopping centre last Wednesday at approximately six o'clock?'

'Admit?' Morrison interjected. 'Is it now some sort of a crime to go into Princes Square shopping centre?'

Charlie brought his fist hammering down on the desk. 'For fuck's sake!' he roared, struggling to his feet and fixing Morrison with a glare. 'If this is the level of your contribution to the proceedings, I suggest you keep your fucking mouth shut.' Charlie felt an arthritic spasm shoot up his spine. He tried not to let the pain show in his face as he lowered himself back onto his chair. He turned to McFarlane. 'Answer the question.'

'I 'admit' I went into Princes Square. So what?'

'Why did you go in there if not to give O'Sullivan the slip?'

'I wanted to get somethin' for Archie and his missus. They'd invited me to stay with them for a few days and I didn't want to turn up on the doorstep empty-handed.'

'What did you buy?'

'I got Maisie a leather handbag and I picked up a couple o' bottles of Glenmorangie for Archie.'

'Where did you go after that?'

McFarlane shrugged. 'Nowhere in particular. I just wandered back down to Central Station and caught a train to Paisley, then I walked up the High Street to Archie's place.'

'What time did you get there?'

'Christ, I don't know. Sometime between half-six and seven, I suppose.'

'Did you go out again that evening?'

'We stayed in and had a few beers and a blether. Chatted over auld times. After twelve years inside, there's a lot o' catchin' up to do.'

'I suppose this McWilliam character and his wife will corroborate your story?'

'Of course they will,' interjected Morrison. 'Now do you have any more questions or is my client free to go?'

Charlie glared at Morrison. 'He'll go when I say he can go.' He turned back to McFarlane. 'Have you been back into Glasgow since Wednesday?'

'Not until this afternoon. Archie and me were havin' a quiet pint in my old local when your tame gorillas barged in.'

'Have you seen Anne Gibson since you came back?

'Who the fuck's Anne Gibson?'

'The wife of Michael Gibson, your ex-lawyer. Surely you remember threatening to kill her?'

'What the hell are you tryin' to pin on me now, Anderson?'

'When you were sent down for the Bothwell Street job, you screamed from the dock that as soon as you got out you were going to kill Gibson and his wife and his son. Don't tell me you don't remember that?'

'I never said anything like that. I – '

'Anne Gibson went missing last Wednesday,' Charlie interjected. 'The story's been in all the papers. We've reason to believe she may be dead, possibly murdered. She was last seen alive at six o'clock on Wednesday evening.'

'That's quite enough,' Morrison spluttered. 'This is ridiculous. You're haranguing my client about someone who's gone missing – possibly dead. My client has no connection with this person and he has a watertight alibi for his movements at the time in question. Mr McFarlane has been extremely cooperative and has freely agreed to answer your questions. I now must insist that you either produce a charge or else release him.'

Charlie got to his feet. 'You're free to go. How long are you planning to stay around here?' he asked as McFarlane stood up.

'Haven't given it a lot of thought. Depends what turns up.'

'Will you be staying at McWilliam's place?'

'For the time bein.'

Charlie watched from his office window as McFarlane and Morrison crossed the street to Morrison's parked car. 'I hope you've got it organised properly this time, Tony.'

'I've assigned three men to it on shifts to give us twenty four hour surveillance,' O'Sullivan said. 'They'll stick to him like glue. He won't give us the slip again.'

'He bloody-well better not,' Charlie growled. 'Because if he does, you can have the pleasure of explaining it to Niggle.'

Charlie stopped off at the vending machine to pick up a coffee before making his way along the corridor towards his office, twisting and stretching his spine as he went, trying to ease the nagging pain in the small of his back. He sat down on his chair and pressed his intercom. 'Call Paisley Police Station, Pauline. Try to get hold of Bobby Rooney for me.'

When Charlie's phone sounded, he picked up. 'I've got Sergeant Rooney on the line, sir.'

'Hello, Bobby. How's it going?'

'Fine, Charlie. I thought you'd retired?'

'Not long to go now, I'm delighted to say.'

'What can I do for you?'

'Does the name Archie McWilliam mean anything to you? Wife's called Maisie. Has a flat at the top of the High Street.'

'Sure, I know him well. Small time crook. A few burglaries – a bit of shop-lifting – but nothing I'd have thought merited the attention of the Glasgow CID.'

'We're not interested in him, but he's got Jack McFarlane staying with him. Remember him? Bothwell Street bank robbery – about twelve years back?'

'Of course.'

'McFarlane claims to have been with the McWilliams on Wednesday evening from the back of six onwards. Do me a favour.

Nip round to McWilliam's place and take a statement from him and his missus. They're going to corroborate McFarlane's alibi of course, but give me a call off the record and let me know if you think they're at it. It might all be kosher, I just don't know. Wednesday was the night Anne Gibson went missing and I've got a hunch McFarlane's mixed up in it somehow.'

'Will do.'

'Thanks. That's a pint I owe you.'

Charlie disconnected, then called Michael Gibson.

'What happened?' Gibson's voice was slurred. 'What did you get out of McFarlane?'

'Next to nothing. He's got an alibi for the time Anne disappeared. I don't know how genuine it is, but we're not likely to break it. I looked him straight in the eye when I mentioned your name, but not a flicker. If he's lying, he's a very cool customer. We'd no reason to hold him so I had to let him go.'

'I realise you're doing everything you can, Charlie. Sorry about flying off the handle earlier on. It's all getting to me.'

'I understand. Are you going to go into the office this week?'

'I couldn't face it. I've left Peter Davies in charge until further notice.'

'It might be a good idea if you were to go in. It would help to take your mind off things – and it would keep you away from the bottle,' Charlie added.

'Wise counsel, Charlie, as always. I'll give it a try tomorrow and see how it goes.'

Frank Morrison dropped McFarlane off outside Central Station. 'I haven't seen anybody trying to follow us, Jack,' he said, leaning across to check his rear-view mirror again.

McFarlane got out of the car and looked back along Gordon Street. 'I haven't seen anyone either, but there's someone there all right. I can sense it. Thanks for the lift, Frank.'

McFarlane walked into the station and crossed to a ticket booth where he handed across a twenty pound note. 'Single to Paisley Gilmour Street, Jimmy.' Picking up the ticket and his change, he strolled across the concourse to study the departures board. The next train to Paisley was the six thirty-seven. He checked the station clock – twenty minutes to kill. He wandered into the buffet and ordered a pint of heavy. He stood by the door as he sipped at his beer, his eyes scanning the crowds of commuters scurrying towards the platforms. 'I might not be able to see you, pal,' he mumbled under his breath, 'but I know you're out there.'

It was after half-past seven when McFarlane rang Archie McWilliam's bell.

'I was hoping it would be you, Jack,' Archie said. 'How did it go? Did the bastards give you a hard time?'

'Nothin' I couldn't handle. They didn't manage to pin anythin' on me. Not for want o' tryin', mind. By the way, you'll probably get a visit from the pigs. They'll be wantin' to know where I was last Wednesday from six o'clock on. You and Maisie and me spent the whole evenin' here, bletherin' and drinkin'. Right?'

'Of course we did!' Archie slapped his thigh and laughed uproariously. 'I'd better remind Maisie, but.'

Tuesday 15 March

The following day McFarlane and McWilliam spent most of the afternoon in a bookmaker's in Well Street, neither of them coming out in front.

'I think I'd better pack it in now,' Archie said, looking disconsolate. 'While I've still got enough for a bevvy.'

McFarlane checked his watch. 'High time we were out of here anyway.'

They both cupped their hands to light up cigarettes as they walked to the top of Well Street. The rain had eased, but when they turned into the High Street they had to bend almost double into the chilling wind. They went into the Bruce Arms and McWilliam went up to the bar to order two large whiskieswhich he took across to the table by the door where McFarlane was waiting.

McFarlane tossed back his whisky in one swallow, screwing up his face. 'That hit the spot. I can feel the warmth comin' back to my bones.' He studied the faces of all the customers propping up the bar, then whispered to McWilliam. 'Time we were makin' a move.' McWilliam downed his drink and got to his feet, following McFarlane into the toilets. Having checked to make sure they were alone, they emptied the contents of their pockets – wallets, keys, money, cigarettes – onto the ledge above the wash hand basin before stripping off their anoraks, trousers and shoes. Having exchanged clothes, they dressed quickly, then picked up their possessions before returning to the bar.

McFarlane surveyed the scene. The same uninterested customers. No one had entered or left the pub while they had been in the toilets. He nodded to Archie as he pulled up his anorak hood, tugging on the drawstrings and tying them tightly underneath his chin. 'Do the trainers fit?' he asked.

'They're a bit big, but I'll manage.' They strode from the pub and hurried back up the High Street, the wind behind them threatening to lift them off their feet. At the mouth of McWilliam's close they shook hands and McFarlane went inside while McWilliam continued on up the High Street. McFarlane darted straight through the close to the back of the tenement building and, with the aid of a dustbin, clambered over the high brick wall. Dropping to the ground, he sprinted the fifty yards to the end of the muddy lane, the wind and rain stinging his eyes. When he emerged from the lane he slowed to a halting limp. 'Why could you no' take a size ten instead o' a bloody nine, Archie,' he muttered. When he saw a taxi approaching, he flagged it down.

'Where to, pal?'

'Dalgleish Tower.'

'Where's that?

'It's a new block o' flats near the city centre.'

'Is it yon big glass building down by the river?'

'That's it.'

The driver laughed. 'That's the one the Glasgow cabbies call Kenny's Castle.'

Having spent most of the afternoon on another round of interviews with Anne Gibson's relatives and friends, Charlie Anderson had another twenty pages of shorthand notes to show for his trouble, with not a single worthwhile bit of information coming to light.

He was about to go home when his phone rang. He picked up the receiver.

'Is that you, Charlie? 'Michael Gibson's voice was hoarse.

'Yes.'

'It's... it's happened again.'

EIGHTEEN

Wednesday 16 March

Unable to sleep, his brain wrestling to make sense of the previous evening's events, Charlie got up at five-thirty and set off for Pitt Street, getting to his office not long after six o'clock. If nothing else, he thought, this would give him the uninterrupted time he needed to make some sort of impression on his paperwork.

It was still dark outside and the central heating hadn't kicked in. Without taking off his overcoat, he lifted the heavy pile of correspondence from his drawer and placed it in the middle of his desk. He took his fountain pen and his propelling pencil from his inside jacket pocket and laid them neatly beside the papers.

Taking the biscuit tin containing change from his bottom left-hand drawer, he spilled the contents onto the desk. Having selected the coins he needed for a coffee, he swept the rest of the money back into the tin. On the way to the vending machines he stopped off at Pauline's desk and left a hand-written note asking her to schedule an appointment with Dr Stephen McCartney as soon as possible.

When Charlie next looked up at his wall clock it showed half past seven. He got to his feet to stretch his spine. He was stiff and cold but was pleased with the progress he'd made. He eyed the two piles of paper. He'd managed to move more than half the correspondence to his out-tray.

As he sat down again and took the next item from the pile, he heard the welcome click of the central heating cutting in. He shrugged off his coat and was halfway through reading the memo when a sharp rap on the door interrupted his train of thought.

'Yes?' he spoke tetchily, peering over the top of his spectacles. 'Who is it?'

Tony O'Sullivan pushed open the door. Charlie ripped off his spectacles and flung them down on the desk.

'I gather you picked up my call, sir.'

'Who lost him this time, Tony? I'll have his guts for garters!'

'McGinley was tailing him at the time. But it wasn't his fault. McFarlane and McWilliam worked a switch.'

'For Christ's sake!' Charlie gripped the edge of his desk and pulled himself to his full height. 'What the hell's the matter with McGinley? Didn't he realise they were liable to pull a flanker?'

'It was a filthy night, sir. McFarlane and McWilliam went into a pub in the High Street in Paisley where they must've swapped clothes. They headed back towards McWilliam's flat, then split up. McGinley suspected they were up to something, but he didn't spot the switch. He had to decide who to follow and he got it wrong.'

'Christ, it's not that difficult. You follow the one with the fucking big scar down the side of his face. What could be simpler than that?'

O'Sullivan stood with head bowed and bit his bottom lip. He knew from years of bitter experience that the worst thing he could do right now would be to try to defend McGinley's mistake. Attempting to explain that McFarlane and McWilliam both had their faces covered by anorak hoods would only prolong the tirade.

Charlie ranted on for a while before flopping back down on his chair. Picking up his spectacles, he twirled them round in his fingers. 'Well get this. Just as I was about to leave for home last night, I got a call from Michael Gibson to tell me he'd found his wife's body – again. Only this time it wasn't suicide – she'd been murdered. Tied to the bed in their bedroom and her throat slashed.'

O'Sullivan's eyes widened in disbelief. 'You have got to be kidding.'

'If only. But it was the same old story. I rushed across to his flat, but there was no sign of a body – no evidence of a disturbance of any kind. He must have been hallucinating. Just to be on the safe side, send a forensic team across to Dalgleish Tower this morning. Tell them to crawl over the Gibsons' bedroom. The usual stuff – any sign of violence, any traces of blood on the floor or the bed, etc. It's going to be a complete waste of time, but we need to confirm it. Get someone to talk to the caretaker and the other residents – there aren't that many – in case anyone saw or heard anything suspicious last night.'

'Has Gibson lost it completely?'

Charlie shrugged his shoulders. 'I don't know. Maybe he's playing games with us. Maybe he's murdered his wife and he's trying to throw up a smokescreen.'

'Or maybe she's walked out on him and he's having a breakdown,' O'Sullivan suggested.

'There are too many maybes for my liking.' Charlie folded his spectacles and slid them inside their case. 'And to crown a perfect day yesterday,' he added, 'I had Niggle on my back bending my ear about our lack of progress on Anne Gibson's disappearance. He's going to love this morning's update. A reported suicide without a corpse turns into a reported murder without a corpse – and we lose Jack McFarlane into the bargain – for the second time.'

The office soon warmed up. Charlie immersed himself in his paperwork, time passing quickly as he steadily reduced his in-tray. Just after nine o'clock his intercom buzzed. 'It's Pauline, sir. I've spoken to Dr McCartney's secretary. He's had a cancellation for ten o'clock this morning. Is that too soon for you?'

'The sooner the better. Confirm with McCartney's secretary that I'll take that slot, then call the Marriott and leave a message for Michael Gibson. Tell him I'll pick him up outside the main entrance at quarter to ten.'

By the time Charlie had emptied his in-tray it was half past nine. As he stood up to pull on his coat his intercom buzzed.

'Superintendent Hamilton would like you to go up to his office straight away, sir.' Charlie mumbled under his breath. 'Pardon, sir?'

'I said you just missed me, Pauline. I left the office five minutes ago.'

'Er... yes, sir.' Pauline sounded taken aback. 'Five minutes ago...'

Just before ten o'clock, Charlie and Michael Gibson walked up to the psychiatrist's reception desk, their footsteps making no sound on the red, thick-pile carpet. 'We have an appointment with Dr McCartney,' Charlie said.

The receptionist consulted her desk-diary. 'Detective Inspector Anderson?'

'Yes.'

'If you'd care to take a seat, gentlemen.' She indicated the row of black leather armchairs opposite. 'I'll let Dr McCartney know you're here.'

They had been seated for only a few minutes when the receptionist called across. 'He can see you now.'

Charlie strained to lever his bulky frame from the narrow chair and led the way down the corridor. He knocked discreetly on McCartney's door and entered the oak-panelled office. Stephen McCartney, a tall, casually dressed man in his mid-forties, rose from behind his desk to greet them. He had a muscular build and his face was deeply tanned from his recent skiing holiday.

'How are you keeping, Charlie? It must be at least a year since I last saw you.'

'I'm fine, Stephen. This is Michael Gibson.' McCartney smiled welcomingly as he took Michael's hand in a firm grip. 'Michael's had a traumatic time of it over the past few days,' Charlie explained. 'His wife, Anne, has disappeared without trace and he's had two bizarre experiences. Last Wednesday he imagined she'd committed suicide, then last night he imagined she'd being murdered. I thought it would be useful if he talked to you.' McCartney nodded. 'I'll leave you two to it,' Charlie said, turning to leave.

'Wait a minute,' Michael said hesitantly. 'Would it be possible for you to stay? Would that be all right, doctor? If Charlie were to stay?'

'No problem from my point of view.'

'Could you stay, Charlie? You've been through all this with me. I'd really like you to stick around.'

Charlie looked enquiringly at McCartney. 'Is that a good idea?'

'It might be helpful. If you've already heard Michael's story, it could be useful to know if his recall of the events remains consistent – whether or not his memory's playing tricks on him.'

'If it might be of help, sure, I can stay.' Charlie conjured up a mental image of Niggle sitting behind his desk – pursed lips sucking hard on his teeth – spindly fingers tapping rhythmically on his desk. 'I'm in no rush to get back to the office.' Pulling off his coat, he took the chair against the far wall.

'Lie down and try to relax,' McCartney said. Michael stretched out full-length on the couch. 'I'd like to record our conversation, if that's okay?' Michael nodded. McCartney leaned across and activated his recording device. 'Before we discuss what happened, tell me a bit about your wife; her personality, her interests – anything that comes to mind.'

'Where do I begin? Anne was a couple of years younger than me. Convent educated, conservative, strait-laced in many ways – but she was fiercely determined about things that mattered to her. When things were going her way she was all sweetness and light, but if crossed, she could be a real vixen.'

'How would you describe your marriage?'

'We were together for more than twenty years. We met while we were at Glasgow University where she was studying European History. I was actually dating her sister at the time and it was she who introduced me to Anne. Anne got me involved in the University drama club, which was one of her passions. She was very talented, both in the production side of things and in acting. We started going out together and we soon fell head over heels in love. She was only nineteen at the time. Unfortunately, I got her pregnant. I wanted her to have an abortion, but she wouldn't hear of it – strict Catholic upbringing and all that. So I married her. At the time, it seemed like the right thing to do.'

'So she had the child?'

'Yes.'

'Do you have any other children?'

'No. Just Paul. He's grown-up now. Or I should say, he's twenty-one. I wouldn't say 'grown-up' is a good way to describe him.'

'During the time you've been married, have you had any affairs?'

Michael hesitated. 'That depends on what you call an affair. I had a couple of one night stands a while back, but the only thing I would really describe as an 'affair' would be my relationship with Philippa.'

'Who is Philippa?'

'A girl I've been seeing for the past year.'

'Did your wife know about her?'

'Yes.'

'Did she know about your one night stands?'

'She knew about one of them.'

'And your wife? Did she have any affairs?'

'Not that I know of. She could have, I suppose, though I wouldn't have thought that likely.'

'Despite your infidelity, would you describe your marriage as stable?'

'Up until a few weeks ago, yes. Then I told Anne I was going to leave her. She blew up. She refused point-blank to even discuss the subject. She hardly spoke to me after that. We continued to live in the same apartment, but we led completely separate lives. She preferred to continue with a complete sham of a marriage rather than let me leave her.'

'How did you react to that? Did you feel resentful?'

'I was very angry. I desperately wanted to be with Philippa.'

'Why didn't you just walk out?'

'Anne was... she was threatening me.'

'With what?'

'She had a hold over me.' Michael looked anxiously at the recording machine and then across to where Charlie was seated. 'I'd rather not say anything more about that.'

'Okay, let's move on. Tell me about the suicide incident.'

'Last Wednesday, when I came home from work, I parked my car in the underground garage and took the lift. When I arrived at my floor, the apartment door was wide open. Brutus – that's Anne's cat – was out in the hall, miaowing noisily. I wasn't expecting Anne to be home. Wednesday's one of her bridge nights. I called her name out several times, but there was no response. I could see there was a light on in the main bedroom – the door was ajar. I thought there must be a burglar in the apartment so I picked up a walking stick from the hallstand and crept towards the bedroom.

'Then I saw her – lying face up on the bed. There was an empty tumbler by her side. There was a half-full water pitcher on the bedside table and an empty pill jar on the bed. Her eyes were closed. She was pale, but she looked very peaceful.

'I grabbed a mirror from the dressing table and held it against her lips. It didn't steam up. She wasn't breathing. I tried to call an ambulance, but my mobile wasn't able to pick up a signal and the phone in the bedroom was dead. I was in a state of panic. I went down to the garage and drove as fast as I could to Pitt Street, to police headquarters. I couldn't think what else to do. Charlie came back to the apartment with me but – and this is the incredible thing – when we got there, there was nothing. Anne's body wasn't there.'

'Tell me about the bedroom. Apart from Anne's body lying on the bed, was everything else normal?'

Michael looked perplexed. 'What do you mean by 'normal'?'

'Was everything else as you would have expected to find it? For example, were the curtains open or drawn?'

Michael thought for a moment while he pictured the scene in his mind. 'Drawn, I think. Yes, I'm pretty sure they were drawn.'

'You said your mobile couldn't pick up a signal. Could your battery have been flat?'

'No. It was fine not long after, when Charlie came back with me to the flat.'

'And you said the phone in the bedroom was dead. Was it in its usual place?'

'Yes, on the bedside table, at my side of the bed.'

'Were the phone wires cut?'

'I don't know. I didn't check. When there was no dialling tone, I just dropped the receiver and ran out.'

'Can you remember what Anne was wearing?'

'Yes. A white blouse and a green leather skirt.'

McCartney got to his feet and paced up and down the room. 'The next part will be difficult for you, Michael. I'm going to ask you to tell me what happened last night, when you thought Anne had been murdered. Do you feel up to it?' Michael nodded and closed his eyes. 'Go ahead then, in your own time.'

'It all started just as before.' Michael's tongue flicked over his lips. 'I came home from the office around seven o'clock. When I got out of the lift the apartment door was wide open and the cat was out in the hall, screeching its head off. I felt like I was reliving a bad dream. I called out, but there was no reply. I didn't go to the hall-stand for a stick. There was no need. I knew there wasn't a burglar in the apartment.

'I went to the bedroom door, fully expecting to see Anne lying on the bed. But not like that!' Michael opened his eyes wide and sat bolt upright, beads of sweat forming at his temples.

'Lie back and try to relax. We can take a break, if you like?'

'I don't want a break. I want to keep going.' He lay back down and closed his eyes. 'It was horrible – utterly sickening. Anne was bound to the bedposts, thick white rope round her wrists and ankles. She was gagged with brown sticky tape – the kind removal companies use. She was wearing the same white blouse and green leather skirt, but her throat… her throat was slit wide open. She was staring… staring straight at me – with her cold, blue eyes……- just like McFarlane's.' Michael's breathing was coming in short gasps, his voice laboured. 'Blood was pumping from her body. Her blouse was changing from white to crimson before my very eyes. Dark stains were spreading across her skirt. Blood was seeping through the duvet. I fell to my knees and closed my eyes. The cat was shrieking even louder. I threw up all over the bed. I couldn't help myself.

'When I forced my eyes open, all I could see was my vomit mingling with Anne's blood. I nearly passed out. I staggered to my feet and tugged out my mobile. But again, there was no signal. I wanted to run from the room but I made myself pick up the phone, even though I knew the line would be dead. It was. I dropped the receiver and ran to the lift and when I got to the ground floor I hammered on the caretaker's door.

'Harry let me in and I phoned Charlie. He was there in less than fifteen minutes. Charlie went upstairs and when he came back down he told me he'd found nothing. I didn't believe him. I didn't want to go up again, but Charlie made me. There was nothing,' he gulped. 'Nothing at all.'

McCartney paused before speaking. 'You mentioned that Anne's eyes were like McFarlane's. Who is McFarlane?'

Michael stared across at Charlie, then turned back to McCartney. 'He murdered Anne,' he whispered. 'I knew he would. He comes after me in my dreams – always the same nightmare. His face appears out of nowhere and he's mocking me. His eyes lock onto mine and no matter how much I try I can't deflect my gaze. I can't close my eyes and I can't lift my arms to shield my face.

'His face grows bigger and the purple scar on his cheek becomes more and more vivid. My body starts to shrink and he opens his mouth wide as he approaches me. I'm running backwards as fast as I can but he's closing on me relentlessly. There's no escape. He's licking his lips. He's going to swallow me whole when he gets close enough. I stumble and fall and...' Michael sat up and sank his face in his hands, his whole body quaking.

McCartney waited until Michael had recovered his composure before taking him by the shoulder and guiding him back to the prone position. 'Do you know McFarlane, Michael? Or is he just someone who appears in your nightmare?'

'I know him all right. I defended him in the High Court twelve years ago – I was an advocate at the time. He got sent down for armed robbery, but he's out of jail now and he's after me.'

'Why would he be after you?'

'He blames me. He thinks I let him down.'

'Do you think you let him down? Do you blame yourself?'

Michael swallowed hard. 'Though he protested his innocence, I was sure he was guilty. Nevertheless, I'd taken on his case and it was my responsibility to present his defence in the best possible light. I failed miserably. I wasn't sharp. I missed numerous opportunities to pressurise prosecution witnesses, to challenge circumstantial evidence.

'When it became apparent the case was slipping away, I tried to persuade him to change his plea to guilty in order to get a lighter sentence. He took exception to this advice. He dismissed me as his advocate and proceeded to conduct his own defence. However, he was found guilty by a majority verdict and sentenced to fifteen years.

'As he was being led from the dock he screamed out – I'll never forget his words: *When I get out I'm going to fucking-well kill you, Gibson. You – and your wife – and your kid.*' Tears welled in Michael's eyes. 'I should have represented him much better than I did. I was under a lot of stress at the time – personal problems, family problems. If I'd performed to the best of my ability, there was a possibility he might have got off with a 'not proven' verdict. The episode affected me badly. I had a breakdown and I was off work for several months.'

'Did you seek psychiatric help at the time?'

'Yes.'

'Who did you consult?'

'Dr Trayner.'

'Tell me about your nightmare. How often does it occur?'

'It used to be about once a month. But since the headaches started it seems like every other night.'

'How long have you been suffering from headaches?'

'About six months.'

'Do you know what brings them on?'

'Not specifically.'

'Describe them.'

'Sharp, stabbing pains at the base of the skull and behind my eyes. They're at their worst first thing in the morning. They tend to ease off during the day.'

'Are you taking anything for them?'

'Just paracetamol.'

'How many?'

'I don't know. Quite a lot, I suppose.'

'Have you seen a doctor?'

'No.'

'Why not?'

'I'm… I'm scared… my father… I'm scared I might be going the same way as my father.' Michael's voice was barely audible.

'Do you now accept, logically, that Anne's suicide and murder couldn't have happened as you described?'

'Last Wednesday, I didn't accept that. It was all so real and there could've been a logical explanation for everything that happened, however unlikely. Someone could've removed Anne's body and tidied up the flat before I returned with Charlie. But last night – no.' Michael shook his head. 'It couldn't have happened. It all seemed so real at the time, but no one could possibly have cleaned up the mess I saw in fifteen minutes.'

'Had you been drinking before you came home?'

'I've been hitting the bottle pretty hard recently, but not yesterday afternoon. I'd been to the office and I was stone cold sober when I came home. What's going on, doctor?' Michael pleaded. 'What's wrong with me?'

McCartney leaned across to switch off the recorder. 'I don't know, Michael. This is only a preliminary session. Clearly, there's a lot to be looked at in more detail. Are you going to be in Glasgow for the next few days?'

'Of course. Where would I go?'

'In which case I'd advise you not to go back to your apartment for the time being. Is there anywhere else you could go?'

'I stayed at the Marriott last night.'

'Then check in there for a few more days and come back to see me on Friday. Would ten o'clock be okay?' he asked, consulting his desk diary.

'Yes.' Michael hesitated. 'What about the cat? I'll have to go back to the flat to feed the cat and change its litter.' He sounded strangely distant. 'If Anne comes home, the first thing she'll ask about will be the cat.'

McCartney looked across at Charlie. 'Is there someone who could handle that?'

Charlie thought for a minute. 'The caretaker. I'm sure he wouldn't mind doing it. I'll have a word with him.'

'Good. Take two of these in the evening before you go to bed,' McCartney said, writing out a prescription. 'They'll help you sleep. Cut down on the paracetamol – and I recommend you lay off the booze completely.'

Michael folded the prescription and slipped it into his wallet. 'There's one other thing, doctor. When I went to pack my toilet bag last night – before going to the hotel – my razor – I use a cut-throat – was missing.'

'When did you last see it?'

'Yesterday morning. I shaved with it before I went to work.'

McCartney exchanged a quick glance with Charlie. 'I think you've been through enough for today. We'll talk about the razor on Friday.'

Michael got up from the couch and shook McCartney's hand. 'Thank you. And thanks for staying, Charlie.'

'I'll call you at the Marriott as soon as we have any news,' Charlie said.

When Michael had left, Charlie turned to McCartney. 'What do you make of it, Stephen?'

'It's all pretty weird. The guy is clearly unstable and needs careful handling. What can you tell me about this McFarlane character?'

'He's bad news – dangerous and violent. It runs in the family. I sent his old man down twice for armed robbery. I knew Gibson was uptight about him coming out of prison, but not to the extent of having nightmares about it.'

'Gibson's story – was it the same as the version he gave you?'

'Essentially, yes. A few more details on some points, a few less on others. But that's inevitable when you recount something twice. One thing I did notice. He said that when he thought Anne had committed suicide she 'looked very peaceful'. I don't recall him saying anything like that at the time.'

'That figures. When he got to the bit about entering the bedroom yesterday it was almost as if he wanted to find her body lying peacefully on the bed, just as he'd imagined her the previous week. He'd adjusted to the fact that she was dead and he wanted to confirm in his mind that it was a peaceful suicide.

'However, his subconscious wouldn't let him off so lightly. He had to suffer more. He had to witness a violent murder. Did you notice that, at the start, when he referred to his wife it was in the past tense? 'She *was* a couple of years younger than me', 'she *was* fiercely determined' – as if he knew she was dead. Later on, he left open the possibility of her being alive when he said: 'If Anne comes home, the first thing she'll ask about will be the cat'. His mind seems to be struggling to make the distinction between fantasy and reality.

'However, would I be right in saying that all that's actually been established is that Anne Gibson is missing?'

'That's correct.'

'So, apart from Gibson's story, there isn't a shred of evidence that his wife is dead. Maybe she's run off with another bloke, for God's sake. Perhaps Gibson's ego won't let him face up to that possibility and his subconscious is trying to block the idea out of his mind.

'First, he imagines suicide. But Gibson has a logical mind. If his wife had committed suicide her body would have been discovered by now. As time goes by he has to go a step further and imagine she's been murdered and her body's been hidden.

But why he invents such a violent murder is hard to fathom. I'm surmising, Charlie. It'll take time to unravel what's going on inside his head.'

'What about his wife having a hold over him? He's never mentioned anything about that before.'

McCartney grinned. 'He didn't seem too keen to expand on that in your presence. I'll try to get him to open up on that when we're on our own on Friday.'

'And his mobile phone and his land line mysteriously not working for a while, then working normally again. What's that all about?'

'I've no idea.'

'And what about the missing razor? Presumably he's not imagining that?'

'I don't know. That's something else I'll probe into on Friday.'

'He said he had psychiatric treatment around the time of McFarlane's trial. I wasn't aware of that. From a Dr Trayner – do you know him?'

'It's not him – it's her. And yes, I know her well. We were in the same year at Glasgow University. She has a practice on the south side.' McCartney stroked his chin reflectively. 'Tell me about Gibson's bedroom. Is there any possibility that Anne Gibson could have been murdered as he described and then the killer cleared up the evidence before you got there?'

Charlie shook his head emphatically. 'None whatsoever. The bedroom was as clean as a whistle. As Gibson said himself, nobody could've cleared up the mess he described in fifteen minutes. To be on the safe side I've sent the forensic boys across to crawl all over the place, but I'll bet anything you like they'll draw a blank.'

'Do you know anything about the family background? Is there a history of instability?'

'I know his father, George, very well. He also was a solicitor – spent most of his career working for 'Coppell and Morris'. He did a bit of conveyancing but his speciality was defence briefs in the Sheriff court. That's how I got to know him. A shrewd old bugger was George. He'd mastered the art of plea bargaining before the term had been invented. But as honest as the day is long. When you did a deal with George Gibson, you could be one hundred per cent sure he'd honour his side of the bargain.

'George had always aspired to be an advocate, but he failed the bar exams. When Michael took up law he worked for several years as a solicitor, then trained as an advocate. I was never quite sure if this was Michael fulfilling his personal ambition or George pushing him to achieve what he himself had never managed. In any event Michael turned out to be a competent, rather than a brilliant, advocate – that was, until a wheel came off about twelve years ago.

'A couple of weeks prior to McFarlane's trial, Michael had got very bad press for his handling of the defence brief in a high-profile rape case. When you questioned him this morning he told you he 'wasn't sharp' during McFarlane's trial. That was the understatement of the century. I was in the public gallery throughout the proceedings. He was pathetic. He seemed to be in a constant dwam – lost in another world. Several times the judge had to call his name two or three times before he responded.

'McFarlane's trial put the kybosh on any aspirations Michael might have had of becoming a top-flight advocate – though I hadn't realised until today he'd undergone psychiatric treatment as a result.

'Old George took it very badly. He'd been planning to retire round about that time, but in order to allow Michael to step down from advocacy without losing face he sank his capital into setting up 'Gibson & Gibson'. I know they struggled for quite some time to get the practice off the ground – a solicitor who was overdue for retirement and a failed advocate wasn't the ideal combination to inspire confidence. But, credit to them both, they worked their arses off and they managed to build the firm up to be one of the most successful in the city.'

'Michael's reference to 'going the same way as his father'. What was that all about?'

'George cracked up a couple of years back. It started as eccentric behaviour – he would suddenly burst out laughing in court at the most inappropriate moments. He would ask witnesses bizarre personal questions – totally unrelated to the case in hand. He got argumentative with the Sheriff, once even accusing him of bias when he disagreed with a verdict. Because of his years of distinguished service he was given a fair amount of latitude, but eventually it got out of hand and he was suspended for contempt of court. Michael managed to persuade him to seek medical help. I believe schizophrenia was diagnosed.

'Round about the same time a spate of fires started breaking out in the district. One day, one of my officers caught George red-handed, kindling a fire behind Bearsden railway station. We were going to prosecute but Michael persuaded me to drop the charges. The deal was that Michael would have George committed to Crighton Hall on a voluntary basis.

'As there was little to be gained by dragging a sick old man through the courts and ruining his reputation, I went along with it. What do you think? Could this be at the root of Michael's problem? Could there be something hereditary?'

'Certainly, there could be. But it's the combination of circumstances that's worrying. The guy's enduring repetitive, terrifying nightmares; he seems to have a drink problem; he's living in constant fear that McFarlane is out to kill him; he's suffering from debilitating headaches and he's convinced his wife's been murdered. Add to that his previous breakdown and the possibility of inherited schizophrenia and you've got a walking time-bomb on your hands. There's no way to predict what he might do next.'

When Charlie got back to Pitt Street he found a note on his desk from Pauline, requiring him to report to Superintendent Hamilton as soon as he got back. He trudged up the staircase and tapped lightly on the door, hoping Hamilton might still be at lunch. His hopes were dashed by the summons to enter.

'You wanted to see me?'

'What's going on around here, Anderson?'

'Going on?'

'Who the hell managed to lose McFarlane this time?'

'I don't have the details. I've been with Michael Gibson all morning, visiting a psychiatrist. Gibson imagined he'd found his wife's body again last night – this time with her throat slashed – but once again the corpse had disappeared into thin air.'

'It's not just the air that's thin around here. My patience is wearing *very* thin.'

'Gibson's a sick man. He's unstable and his testimony's unreliable. It'll take time to diagnose his condition.'

'Diagnose his condition?' Hamilton feigned incredulity. 'For Christ's sake, Anderson. Do I have to spell everything out in words of one syllable? We're not running the fucking National Health Service. I don't give a monkey's about the state of Gibson's health. There are two things, and two things only, that interest me right now. Number one is Anne Gibson. She's been missing for a week. If she's alive, I want her found to kill off the speculation that's building up in the press – and if she's been murdered, I want the body found and the culprit brought to book. Am I making myself clear?' Charlie ignored the rhetorical question as he stared out of the window. 'And the other priority is the whereabouts of McFarlane. The NCA are biting my arse on this one. They're on the blower to me every five minutes, wanting to know if he's made a move towards recovering the proceeds of the Bothwell Street job – and all I have to report is that we don't even know where the hell he is!

'It's not good enough. This not the quality of work I expect from my senior officers. I want to make myself very clear. If Anne Gibson's body isn't found within the next twenty-four hours – dead or alive – there will be repercussions.'

Charlie was seething when he stomped back to his office. He'd never been closer to punching a senior officer in his life. He buzzed through to Pauline and asked her to find O'Sullivan and Renton, then sat behind his desk, breathing in and out deeply, trying to compose himself while waiting for them to arrive.

'What do you have?' he asked as they walked in together.

'As expected,' Renton said, 'forensic drew a complete blank at Gibson's place. No trace of vomit or bloodstains. No sign of a forced entry. No evidence of a disturbance of any kind.'

'And McFarlane?'

O'Sullivan shook his head ruefully. 'I'm afraid we've got nothing on him yet. We're watching McWilliam's flat and we've issued McFarlane's description to all the Paisley cabbies in case someone picked him up after he gave us the slip. So far, no one's come forward with anything.'

'Well you should both be aware that Niggle is not at all a happy bunny,' Charlie stated. 'In fact, he thinks we're a complete bunch of wankers and he's threatening to have us for breakfast if we don't get a result on the Gibson case within the next twenty-four hours. Quite frankly, I don't give a bugger what he thinks about me. The guy's a bloody politician, not a copper. All he's bothered about is covering his arse. But, like it or not, he's the boss around here and you're going to have to work with him for the foreseeable future, so pull out all the stops.'

Thursday 17 March

The following morning Charlie again arrived early at Pitt Street. At eight o'clock his phone rang. He picked up the receiver. 'DCI Anderson?'

'Speaking.'

'It's Bobby Rooney, from Paisley, Charlie. You'd better get some of your blokes across here sharpish.'

'What's up?'

'A body's been found in the woods. I think it's the missing woman.'

NINETEEN

'The missing woman? Anne Gibson?' Charlie demanded.

'Yes.'

'Are you sure?'

'As sure as I can be – the body fits her description.'

'Where was she found?'

'In the Gleniffer Braes. There's a small copse of trees near a drinking fountain, just back from the road. The body was found in there. From the description I've been given it looks like it was a particularly brutal murder. My guys are up there now, cordoning off the area.'

'Have you notified forensics?'

'Not yet. I decided to call you first.'

'Leave everything with me, Bobby. I'll handle it from this end. Tell your boys I'll be across as soon as I can get there – should be in about half an hour.' Charlie replaced the receiver and flicked his intercom switch. 'Do you know if Tony O'Sullivan's in yet, Pauline?'

'I saw him at the coffee machine ten minutes ago.'

'Ask him to come to my office straight away.'

'I've just had a call from Bobby Rooney,' Charlie said when O'Sullivan stuck his head round the door. 'It seems that Anne Gibson's body's been found in the Gleniffer Braes on the outskirts of Paisley. You and I are going over there right now. Tell the duty officer to send a forensic team across and organise an ambulance. I'll pick up my car and meet you out front.'

There had been a welcome change in the weather overnight. The rain clouds had vanished and the sun was rising in a clear blue sky as Charlie filtered onto the M8 in the direction of Paisley. A couple of miles down the road he ran into road works and progress was slow while three lanes of traffic funnelled into one. When he switched on the car radio the painfully cheerful voice on Radio Scotland was advising everyone to avoid the westerly direction on the M8 for the rest of the morning.

'Thanks a bunch.' Charlie flicked off the radio. By the time he reached the exit for Paisley the traffic flow had improved, though the commuter traffic was still heavy as he made his way towards the town centre. Turning off the main road, he cut through the side streets.

'You seem to know this part of the world well,' O'Sullivan commented.

'This is my home territory. I was brought up in this neck of the woods.'

It was almost nine o'clock by the time they crossed the Glenburn housing estate and started to climb. The sight of the Gleniffer Braes brought happy memories flooding back to Charlie. It had been a long time since he'd last driven towards these hills. Would the big car park still be there, he wondered? It was near the crest of the hill, a couple of hundred yards beyond the drinking fountain.

In his youth, the car park had been a favourite spot for courting couples. He and his mates had often driven up there with their girlfriends after an evening in the pub or at the dancing. He smiled to himself as he recalled the well-worn chat-up lines: 'Have you ever seen the lights of Paisley from the top of the Gleniffer Braes? They're really quite spectacular'. The girls all knew the score – most of them had been up to the car park dozens of times – but they always acted surprised. 'No. I've heard about them, but I've never actually seen them'. 'Would you like to see them tonight?' 'That sounds like a nice idea'.

When you got there, especially on a Friday or Saturday evening, it was hard to find a place to park – the car park was invariably crammed – although, judging by the number of steamed-up windows, not much viewing of the lights of Paisley was being done. He smiled again as he recalled the first time he'd brought Kay up here. He wondered if the car park was still as popular.

Charlie dropped into first gear to negotiate the steep hill. 'The drinking fountain Bobby Rooney mentioned is on the left-hand side as we go up,' he explained. 'I hope it hasn't changed too much. It was rather special. A battered metal drinking cup attached to the rock face by a steel chain. When the snow on the high hills melted, the spring water would gurgle out from a fissure in the rock. I often stopped there to have a drink when I was out walking. But I suppose the communal drinking cup will have been banned now by some European Community hygiene regulation or other.' Charlie chuckled at the thought. 'There was a plaque on the wall,' he added. 'It had a picture of a bloke on it and there was a poem inscribed round the outside. It was all about 'The Bonnie Wee Well at the Breist of the Brae' and there was something about a lark drinking there in the morning – but I can't remember the rhyme.'

Charlie came upon the fountain before he was expecting it. It seemed to be lower down the hill than he remembered. 'Something's different,' he said. 'I think the road's been straightened. I'm sure it used to pass much closer to the well.' He glanced to his left, but he'd passed too quickly to notice if the drinking cup was still in position.

Charlie continued up the twisting road and turned off when he reached the entrance to the car park. It had been extended to more than twice its previous size. Courting must be alive and well in Paisley, he thought.

This morning, however, there was only one other vehicle parked there – a police patrol car. Charlie got out from behind the wheel and leaned on his car door as he breathed in the cool, sweet air. 'If you close your eyes you could imagine you're a million miles from a city up here,' he said. 'Half the beauty of this place is the silence.'

Closing his eyes, he breathed in again deeply and filled his lungs before exhaling slowly. When he opened his eyes he scanned the hills far beyond the conglomerates of Paisley and Glasgow. 'Magnificent, isn't it?' He pointed towards a snow-capped peak rising in the far distance. 'That's Ben Lomond – and there's the Campsies. But unfortunately, Tony,' he said with a sigh, 'we're not here today to admire the view.'

He looked across towards the clump of trees, two hundred yards away – as Bobby Rooney had described, just behind the drinking fountain. Leading the way, he set off across the hillside and clambered over the low stile as he made his way towards the two grim-faced, young constables. He flashed his warrant card. 'DCI Anderson. Glasgow CID. This is DS O'Sullivan. Bobby Rooney called us out.'

'We were expecting you, sir,' one of the constables said.

'Where's the body?'

'In there.' He indicated a gap in the trees. 'I should warn you before you go in, it's not a pretty sight.'

'It never is, son.' Charlie ducked under the tape that had been stretched between two fir trees and braced himself as he walked towards the gap. He froze, completely stunned. He couldn't believe his eyes. The body, spread-eagled, tied by the wrists and ankles to four saplings. The white rope. The mouth taped with brown sticky tape. The eyes open and staring. The throat slit wide open. The erstwhile white blouse stained crimson. The green leather skirt saturated with blood. Charlie's head started to spin. The clean air smelled foul in his nostrils. He couldn't breathe.

Charlie heard the engines before he saw the vehicles. Glancing across, he saw a police car and an ambulance snaking in convoy up the winding road. He plodded back across the hillside to meet the cars.

Charlie recognised the officer who got out. 'Good morning, Eddie.'

'Morning, Inspector.' Sergeant Eddie McLaughlin opened his car boot and pulled out three cameras which he swung round his neck, then he hauled out a heavy black bag.'

'Can I give you a hand with your gear?'

'No need, thanks. I'm used to it. Where is she?'

'Over there. In that clump of trees.' They walked together towards the copse. 'One important question, Eddie. I need to establish if she was killed here or if her body was brought here after she was murdered.'

'I'll see what I can do.'

Charlie and Tony spoke to the two constables while McLaughlin photographed the corpse and meticulously examined the surrounding area.

'Who found her?' O'Sullivan asked.

'A guy out walking his dog early this morning. I took his statement. His dog ran into the copse and didn't come out when he called. He went in to look for it and found her, then he called '999' from his mobile.'

They were still in discussion when they heard McLaughlin shout across to the ambulance crew. 'Okay, boys, I'm finished. You can take her away.'

'What do you reckon, Eddie?' Charlie asked.

'She's been dead between twenty-four and forty-eight hours. I'll give you a more accurate figure after the autopsy. I've taken soil samples, but it won't be easy to establish with any degree of certainty whether or not she was murdered here. She lost so much blood that you'd normally expect the earth to be impregnated if she'd been killed here, but with the porosity of the soil and the amount of rain we've had in the last forty-eight hours the blood could easily have been washed away.'

'The murder weapon?'

'The cause of death was repeated slashes to the throat – there are at least ten wounds – all delivered with a sharp knife or blade, probably not serrated.'

'Was she sexually assaulted?'

'I'll have to wait for the post-mortem to confirm that but my initial impression is no. Her clothes don't seem to have been interfered with.'

'As soon as you have the photos I'd like copies.'

'Are you going back to your office now?'

'Yes.'

'I'll send prints across. You'll have them within the hour.'

Charlie and Tony followed behind as the stretcher was carried across the hillside and they watched in silence while it was loaded into the ambulance. McLaughlin's car, followed by the ambulance, turned round in the car park and weaved their way down the road. Charlie waited until they were out of sight before signalling to O'Sullivan to get into the car. Neither of them spoke as they drove down the hill. Charlie didn't glance to his right as they sped past the drinking fountain. The silence wasn't broken until they were back on the motorway.

Stephen McCartney's receptionist buzzed through to him. 'Inspector Anderson called fifteen minutes ago, doctor. He asked to speak to you but I explained you couldn't be interrupted during a consultation. He said it was extremely urgent. I told him your agenda was full today but he insisted he had to see you. He wanted to know if he could come across at lunch time?'

'For Charlie Anderson to skip his lunch, it must be important. Tell him to come over at twelve. Oh, and do me a favour, Margaret. Nip round the corner and get me a sandwich.'

'What kind?'

'Cheese and tomato, lots of pickle.'

Stephen McCartney was sitting behind his desk, flicking through The Herald and munching his sandwich, when Charlie walked in.

'Finish your lunch,' Charlie said, taking the chair opposite. 'Good of you to see me at such short notice.'

'What's the panic?' McCartney asked through a mouthful of crumbs.

Charlie took three photographs from his inside jacket pocket and dropped them onto the desk. 'What do you make of these?'

McCartney winced as he studied each photo in turn. 'You sure know how to spoil someone's appetite. Anne Gibson, I assume?' Charlie nodded grimly. 'Where was the body found?'

'In the Gleniffer Braes – on the outskirts of Paisley.'

McCartney raised an eyebrow. 'When?'

'Early this morning.'

'Has Michael been told?'

'Not yet. I wanted to talk to you first.'

'What do you make of it?'

'There's not a shadow of doubt that Gibson saw his wife's dead body. The description he gave us is too accurate for coincidence to even enter the equation. But whether he saw the body in Dalgleish Tower or in the Gleniffer Braes is an open question. And whether or not he murdered her is also up for grabs.'

'Was she sexually assaulted?'

'We won't know for sure until after the post-mortem, but it seems unlikely.'

'Statistically, that increases the probability that Gibson killed her,' McCartney stated. 'In murder cases, where a female victim is found tied to a bed, or to anything else, there's often a sexual motive. When a husband murders in a fit of rage or jealousy, sexual assault is much rarer. I'm not saying this means Gibson killed his wife. Only that the probability is increased.'

'Point taken. But even if you believe Gibson to be capable of doing this, it doesn't stack up. He said he was in his office on Tuesday up until six-thirty. Assuming that checks out, he phoned me from the caretaker's flat in Dalgleish Tower just after seven. It wouldn't have been possible for him to drive to Paisley and back in that time, never mind commit a murder.

'And if he did kill his wife,' Charlie continued, 'why on earth would he implicate himself by giving us such an accurate description of the corpse? And why the cock-and-bull story about Anne committing suicide last Wednesday?'

'I haven't the remotest idea. The time of death – when was that?'

'The initial assessment is that she was killed between twenty-four and forty-eight hours ago, which is consistent with the murder having taken place on Tuesday evening – when Gibson claimed to have found his wife's body.'

'Remind me. When did she first go missing?'

'Just over a week ago.'

'So the murderer kidnapped her and held her somewhere for a week before he killed her?'

'Search me.' Charlie scratched at his bald head. 'This is a right bloody mess, Stephen. Where the hell do we go from here?'

'Have the press got wind of the story yet?'

'Not as far as I know.'

'If you consider Gibson to be a suspect, of course you'll have to pull him in. But I'm not at all sure how he would react if you were to show him these,' McCartney said, sliding the photographs back across the desk. 'They could easily tip him over the edge.'

'I've no intention of doing that.' Charlie picked up the photos and slipped them back into his pocket. 'I'm on my way across to the Marriott now to break the news to him.' Charlie hesitated. 'I was wondering if there was any chance you might be able to tag along?'

'It certainly would be better if we were both there. Do you know if he's in the hotel right now?'

'I took the precaution of having him watched. I checked just before I came here. He went into the lounge bar at eleven o'clock and he's still there.'

McCartney buzzed through to his receptionist. 'When's my next appointment, Margaret?'

'One o'clock. A therapy session with Mr McLeod.'

'Is there anyone else who could see him?'

Margaret perused the diaries. 'Dr Orr's available. She's familiar with Mr McLeod's case. I could ask her to take the session.'

'Do that. Something urgent's cropped up and I have to go out for an hour or so but I'll be back in time for my two o'clock appointment.'

Police Sergeant Norman Hudd turned off the road into the drive leading to the Jacksons' cottage. 'Why do we get all the best jobs, Sharon?'

'This is the second time this month I've had to break the news to parents that their daughter's been killed,' Sharon said. 'It doesn't get any easier.'

Hudd pulled up outside the cottage and they both got out of the patrol car, their footsteps scrunching on the gravel path as they walked up to the front door. Hudd rang the bell, which clanged noisily. Peter Jackson came to the door.

'Sorry to disturb you, sir. I'm Sergeant Hudd and this is Police Constable Hoggard. Could we possibly come in for a minute?'

Jackson looked puzzled. 'What's wrong?'

They both took off their caps as they stepped across the threshold. 'Is Mrs Jackson here, sir? We'd like to speak to her as well.'

'There is something wrong. It's about Anne, isn't it?' he insisted. 'It's something serious.'

'I'm afraid so, sir. Would you please call your wife?'

'Jean!' he shouted. 'It's about Anne.'

Jean Jackson appeared in the hall, wiping flour from her hands on her pinafore. 'What is it, Peter?' She stopped in her tracks when she saw the two uniformed officers. 'Oh my God!' She hurriedly made the sign of the cross. 'What's happened?'

'I think it would be better if you sat down,' Sharon said, crossing to Jean's side and taking her by the arm to guide her onto a chair. 'I'm afraid we've got some bad news, Mrs Jackson,' she said quietly.

Hudd took out his notebook. 'It concerns your daughter, Anne Gibson,' he intoned gravely. 'I'm very sorry to have to inform you that… that your daughter is dead.'

Jean Jackson stared blankly at Hudd for a moment, then started screaming hysterically. 'It's not true! I don't believe it! I won't believe it! No!'

Sharon put her arm around Jean's shoulder to try to console her. Peter Jackson turned to Hudd. 'What happened?' he asked calmly.

'How did Anne die?'

'It looks as if she was murdered, sir.'

'How?'

'I believe it was knife wounds.'

'Where was she killed?'

'Her body was found this morning in some woods near Paisley.'

Peter Jackson stared across at his wife. 'Jean.' She didn't look at him. 'Jean,' he repeated forcibly. 'We'll have to tell them. They'll find out soon enough.'

TWENTY

Charlie Anderson and Stephen McCartney went up to the reception desk in the Marriott where Charlie showed his badge discreetly to the receptionist. 'Police,' he said quietly. 'Who's the duty manager today?'

'Mr Graham.'

'Could I have a word with him?'

'I'll get him for you.'

Charlie looked across the lobby towards the open-plan, sunken lounge that ran the full length of the hotel. Leaving McCartney at reception, he walked down the steps to where Colin Renton was sitting on the settee, flicking through a newspaper. 'Is Gibson still here?' he asked.

Renton nodded as he folded his paper. 'He came down to the bar just after eleven o'clock. He's over there, at the table facing the swimming pool.' Renton indicated where Michael was sitting, reading a paperback. 'He's on his third pint of lager if I'm not mistaken.'

'You can knock off now, Colin,' Charlie said. 'I'll take over.'

Charlie returned to reception as Keith Graham was coming across the lobby.

'How can I help you?'

'We need to talk to one of your guests and I'm afraid we've got bad news to impart to him. I'd like to do it in private rather than in the bar. Is there a room we could use?'

'Of course. The office at the far end of the lounge,' he said, pointing. 'I'll make sure you're not disturbed.'

Michael scrambled to his feet when he saw Anderson and McCartney approaching. 'What's happened?' he demanded.

'Come with us,' Charlie said, leading the way to the office. 'It's bad news, Michael,' he said, closing the office door behind them. He paused. 'I'm afraid Anne is dead.'

Michael leaned on the window ledge for support. 'I knew it,' he said in barely a whisper. 'I knew she was dead.' He stared out of the window. 'Where was her body found?'

'In woods on the outskirts of Paisley,' Charlie said.

'Really?' He shrivelled his brow. 'How did she die?'

McCartney moved across Michael's line of vision. 'Exactly as you described, Michael,' he said.

Michael stared right through McCartney. 'Of course. Of course.' He turned towards Charlie – his eyes still focused in the middle distance. 'You think I killed her.' His tone was matter-of-fact. Charlie didn't respond. 'I had a motive. I wanted to leave Anne and she was digging her heels in. An open and shut case, wouldn't you say? There are a lot of things I have to do.' His voice was trance-like as he continued to stare unblinkingly. 'I'll have to let Paul know, of course. Then I'll have to tell Anne's parents. They live near Aberdeen. They're going to take the news very badly, especially Mrs Jackson.'

Charlie was about to interrupt but McCartney's hand on his sleeve restrained him. 'Let him talk,' he whispered.

'Then there's the people at the bridge club. They're going to have to be told. As well as the amateur dramatic society.' Michael glanced at his watch. 'I don't know how I'm going to find the time to fit all this in. And there's the cat. Who's going to take care of the cat? I don't like cats.' He started towards the door. 'I really must go. I have to tell Paul straight away.'

Charlie glanced towards McCartney, who nodded. 'If you like, we could do that, Michael,' Charlie offered. 'We've already arranged for someone to break the news to Mr and Mrs Jackson – we could tell Paul as well.'

'Could you? That would be kind.' Michael paused and blinked. 'If you gentlemen would excuse me for a minute. I've been drinking lager all morning. I'll burst if I don't go to the bathroom.'

Charlie and McCartney accompanied Michael to the toilets and waited for him outside.

'Where do we go from here, Stephen?' Charlie asked.

'That depends on what action you're planning to take. Are you going to arrest him?'

'I'll certainly have to take him in for questioning. We've got to get to the bottom of where and when he saw his wife's corpse.'

'Don't rush him. Take him in, by all means. In fact, it would be better if he wasn't left on his own right now. But don't pressurise him too much, especially during the next twenty-four hours. Whether or not he did it, he's right on the edge.' McCartney looked at his watch. 'Can you handle things on your own from here, Charlie? I really do need to get back to the office.'

'Sure. Thanks for your help.'

As McCartney was leaving, Michael emerged from the toilets.

'I'd like you come with me to Pitt Street, Michael.'

'Of course, Charlie.' Michael's voice was still dreamlike. 'There are lots of things we need to get organised. Would it be okay if I go up to my room to collect my things?'

'Sure. I'll come with you.'

They crossed the foyer and Charlie held down the button to summon the lift. 'What floor is it?' he asked as the doors opened.

'Number four.'

They went inside the lift and Charlie pressed the button for floor four. As the doors were closing, Michael stepped out into the foyer.

TWENTY-ONE

Charlie stomped into his office and slammed the door behind him. Stripping off his coat, he threw it onto the desk and collapsed in his chair. He flicked the intercom. 'Find Tony O'Sullivan, Pauline. I need to see him straight away.'

'I'm glad you're back, sir,' O'Sullivan said as he breezed into the office. 'There's been a development.'

'Fire away.'

'It's concerning McFarlane. You recall that he gave us the slip in Paisley on Tuesday?'

'How could I ever forget?'

O'Sullivan let the heavy-handed sarcasm wash over him. 'A taxi driver's come forward. He picked up someone answering McFarlane's description in Paisley round about five-thirty – which was just after McGinley lost him. And – wait for it – he asked to be taken to Dalgleish Tower.'

Charlie let out a low whistle. 'Dalgleish Tower? Tuesday evening? The night Anne Gibson was murdered?'

'There's more. I checked with the drivers who service the rank outside Dalgleish Tower. One of them recalls picking up someone answering McFarlane's description outside the building later that same evening, round about eleven o'clock.'

'To go where?'

'He was dropped off in the city centre.'

'Do we know where he is now?'

O'Sullivan shook his head. 'He hasn't been seen since. We're still watching McWilliam's place but he hasn't been back there.'

'I want him found.'

'We've got every man we can spare working on it.'

'Anything else?'

'That's it.'

'I've got a couple of things for you. First, there's the Gibson boy – Paul. He needs to be told that his mother's body's been found. Would you handle that? I realise it's not the nicest job in the world, but someone has to do it.'

'I suppose so… '

'You know where he lives?'

'Yes. Saltoun Street. I dropped Renton off there last week when he went to talk to Paul about his mother's disappearance.'

'I want to break the news to Gibson's girlfriend personally. What did you say her name was?'

'Philippa Scott.'

'Have you got her address?' O'Sullivan reached into his pocket for his notebook and handed across the slip of paper with Philippa's address and phone number. 'What impression did you form of her?' Charlie asked.

'Sophisticated, intelligent, sexy – a right cracker, in fact. As Renton said – the longest pair of legs you're ever likely to see. But there was something about her manner that didn't quite gel. We got the impression she was holding back on something.'

'One more thing,' Charlie said. 'Gibson told me he left his office at six-thirty on Tuesday evening. Get someone to check out what time he arrived in the office that morning – and also find out if he was out of the building at any time during the day. Also, get the word out,' Charlie added casually, 'that we're looking for Gibson. He did a bunk from the Marriott and I want him picked up as soon as possible.'

O'Sullivan looked quizzical. 'Did a bunk? How could that have happened?' he asked incredulously. 'I thought Renton was supposed to be keeping an eye on him?'

'Renton didn't lose him,' Charlie growled. 'I bloody-well did. Gibson told me he wanted to go up to his room to get his things. I went into the lift with him, then the bastard stepped out just as the doors were closing. By the time I fumbled around to find the button to hold the lift doors open, I was halfway to the first floor.'

'Unlucky, sir.' O'Sullivan did his best to suppress a grin. 'Could have happened to anyone.'

'I'm warning you, if one word of this gets out around the office I'll have your stripes.'

'My lips are sealed.'

'Get out of here.'

As O'Sullivan was leaving, Charlie's intercom buzzed. 'Two messages for you, sir,' Pauline said. 'Sergeant McLaughlin from forensics would like to see you urgently. It's regarding Anne Gibson's autopsy. And there was a call from a Sergeant Hudd in Aberdeen. He asked if you would phone him back as soon as possible.'

'What it is to be popular,' Charlie sighed. 'Tell Eddie he can come over now, then try to get Hudd on the phone for me.'

Pauline buzzed back straight away with Hudd on the line.

'A bit of a strange one for you, sir. It's about the Gibson case.'

'Go on.'

'I drew the short straw this morning. I got the job of breaking the news of Anne Gibson's murder to her parents, Mr and Mrs Jackson. As you'd expect, they were distraught when they heard the news. However, it transpires that, during the period Anne Gibson was supposedly missing – that's to say, from Thursday March 10th until Tuesday March 15th – she wasn't missing at all. According to Mr Jackson, she was hiding out at her parents' house near Aberdeen.'

'What?'

'She told her parents she needed to get away from her husband and she didn't want him to know where she was.'

'I don't understand any of this, Sergeant.' Charlie stopped to consider. 'I think I'll need to talk to the Jacksons.'

'That would certainly be best, sir. I didn't know what questions to ask.'

'I'll come up to Aberdeen as soon as I can. I'll try to make it tomorrow. I'll call you back when I've set up the arrangements.'

'Very good, sir. I'll wait to hear from you.'

Charlie's thoughts were interrupted by the buzzer. 'Sergeant McLaughlin is waiting to see you.'

'Send him in.'

'What have you got for me, Eddie?' Charlie asked.

'The post-mortem confirmed what I told you this morning. Anne Gibson was murdered between four p.m. and eight p.m. on Tuesday. The cause of death was twelve slashes to the throat with a sharp blade – it was a pretty frenzied attack.'

'Could the wounds have been made by a cut-throat razor?'

'Possibly. There are severe rope burns on the victim's wrists and ankles which indicate that she struggled violently before she died. However, there was no sexual assault. And robbery wasn't the motive either – her watch wasn't taken and neither were her rings, which must be worth a small fortune. You asked me to establish whether or not the murder took place in the woods.'

'And?'

'As I said earlier, it's not going to be possible to determine that with any degree of certainty. Based on the earth samples I took, I'd say the body was brought to the copse some time after the murder, but that's just an educated guess, not something that would stand up in a court of law.'

'Is that it?'

'A couple more things. There was an inordinate amount of make-up mingled with the blood around her throat – hard to be sure, but it seemed to be some kind of theatrical make-up, mostly red and black. And if you think that's weird, wait till you hear this. The blood samples I analysed – from her throat, her blouse and her skirt. They're all a mixture.'

'What are you talking about, man?'

'They're a mixture of bloods – her own blood and animal blood. It appears to be sheep's blood.'

TWENTY-TWO

Dusk was falling by the time Charlie pulled up outside Philippa Scott's apartment block. A glass door had been installed at the entry to the Victorian tenement building and on the right-hand side of the door there was a row of buzzers alongside a list of names and floor numbers. Peering at the list, Charlie pressed the buzzer beside the name 'Scott'.

There was a long delay before the intercom was activated.

'Is that Miss Scott?' Charlie spoke into the intercom. 'Miss Philippa Scott?'

'Yes. Who are you? What do you want?'

'DCI Anderson – Glasgow CID. I'd like to ask you a few questions.'

'What about?'

'Anne Gibson.'

'I've already spoken to two of your officers.'

'I realise that.'

'Can't this be done later? It's not convenient right now. I'm getting ready to go out. I'm being picked up in half an hour.'

'It's important. I won't keep you any longer than necessary.'

Philippa hesitated. 'Oh, very well. If you must. It's the third floor'

When the door release buzzer sounded, Charlie pushed it open. The building had no lift and he was wheezing by the time he'd climbed the stairs. He took out his warrant card and showed it to Philippa as she opened her apartment door. She was wearing a loose-fitting silk dressing gown and her hair was wrapped in a bath towel.

Charlie stepped into the hallway, closing the door behind him. Philippa led the way to the lounge where she indicated a chair. 'I don't know how I can help you.' She stood by the window, towelling her hair vigorously. 'I've already told your men everything I know.'

'I'm afraid I've got some serious news. Anne Gibson's body has been found.'

Philippa stopped towelling her hair. 'Was she – ?' She broke off.

'Was she – murdered?' Charlie offered. 'Is that what you were about to ask?'

Philippa nodded, wide-eyed.

'Yes.'

'Oh my God!' The towel slid from Philippa's fingers as she clasped both hands to her face. 'How? Where?'

'Her throat was cut. Her body was found this morning in a copse near Paisley.' Charlie paused to let the news sink in. 'You told my officers that you and Michael Gibson split up several weeks ago?'

'That's correct.'

'Have you seen or heard from him since?'

'I haven't had any contact with him. I told your men that.'

'That all sounds very final, considering that only a few weeks ago he was about to leave his wife so he could be with you.'

'That's water under the bridge. It's all over between Michael and me.'

'But with Anne no longer… How can I put this delicately? No longer… standing in the way. Won't that change things?'

'For God's sake! What a horrible thing to say.' Philippa thumped her fist down on the back of the settee. 'How many times do I have to tell you? Michael and I are no longer an item.'

'Are you seeing anyone else?'

Philippa's voice shook with temper. 'I don't see how that's any of your damned business.'

'Anything that might be connected with Anne Gibson's death is my business.'

'I don't have to listen to this. You don't have a warrant. You've no right to barge in here making totally unfounded insinuations. I'd like you to leave, Inspector – this very minute.'

Charlie stood up. 'As you wish.'

Charlie turned up his jacket collar and belted his coat tightly as he huddled in the shadows of the apartment block opposite. He'd been waiting for almost half an hour when a red Ferrari drew up and a young man jumped out, pressed a buzzer, then disappeared into the building. He was tallish and Charlie could see his hair was tied back in a ponytail, but it was too dark to make out his features. Ten minutes later he reappeared with Philippa. Charlie jotted down the car registration number. He remained in the shadows until the Ferrari had roared off.

Friday 18 March

The following morning Charlie walked to the corner shop at the end of his street where he bought The Herald and a packet of strong mints. It was a bright, clear day and he was quite looking forward to the trip to Aberdeen. At least he'd be able to relax on the train for a few hours. He strolled back up his drive and turned his key in the lock. 'I'm back, Kay.'

'I'm in here!' Whistling tunelessly, Charlie wandered down the hall to the kitchen where Kay was unfolding the ironing board, a basket of unironed clothes stacked on the chair beside her. 'Why so cheerful this morning?' she asked.

'Because I've got a relatively quiet day in prospect.'

'I hope I'm not about to spoil it for you.'

'What do you mean?'

'There's some kind of a panic on. Tony O'Sullivan called a couple of minutes ago. He wants you to phone him back straight away.'

Charlie snatched up the phone. 'What's up, Tony?' he demanded

O'Sullivan's voice was terse. 'There's been another murder, sir.'
'What are you talking about, man? Who's been murdered?'
'Paul Gibson.'

TWENTY-THREE

'Paul Gibson! What in the name of God happened?'

'You asked me to break the news to Paul about his mother's murder. I didn't want to do that over the phone, so I went across to his flat a couple of times yesterday afternoon, but he wasn't around. I drive past his place on the way to work so I stopped off this morning on the off-chance and when I went up to his flat, I found the door wide open. The lock had been forced. I found his body in the bedroom, lying on the bed. His throat had been slashed. His hands and feet were bound with white rope and his mouth was gagged with brown sticky tape.' There was a stunned silence at the other end of the line. 'Are you still there, sir?'

Charlie spoke in a hoarse whisper. 'I'm here.'

'Will you still be going up Aberdeen?'

Charlie paused to collect his thoughts. 'I think I have to. I need to talk to the Jacksons and find out what the hell Anne Gibson was up to. You take charge of things here. I'll get back from Aberdeen as quickly as I can. We'll meet up later this afternoon in my office. Tell Renton to be there. We need a council of war.'

Charlie climbed aboard the train and took a seat opposite a teenage girl with a crying infant in her arms. He eyed the baby nervously, wondering if it might cry all the way to Aberdeen.

Charlie balanced his briefcase on his knees and flicked it open, pulling out a folder of papers. He put on his glasses and scanned the first memo, but by the time he got to the end of the first paragraph, he realised he'd taken nothing in. Going back to the top of the page, he started reading again slowly.

The rhythmic motion of the train and the warmth of the carriage were soporific. His eyelids were heavy and he allowed them to droop. His chin came to rest on his chest.

The girl with the infant tapped Charlie on the shoulder. He awoke with a start. 'We're in Aberdeen, mister. If you don't get off now you'll be back in Glasgow before you know it.'

It was half-past eleven when Charlie stepped off the train. He had a stiff back and there was a crick in his neck. He walked as briskly as he could to the end of the platform, twisting and stretching his spine as he went to try to loosen his knotted muscles. At the ticket barrier, he saw a uniformed officer scanning the faces of the passengers pouring off the train.

Charlie waved to him. 'Sergeant Hudd?' He nodded. 'DCI Anderson,' he said, offering his hand. 'I didn't know so many people commuted from Glasgow to Aberdeen. The train was packed.'

'Would you like a coffee before we go to see the Jacksons?'

'If we have time, I could murder one, but I do need to catch the 14.05 back to Glasgow.'

'We should be okay,' Hudd said, checking his watch. 'I told Mr Jackson to expect us around twelve. We've got time to grab a quick coffee in the buffet.'

Charlie appreciated the warmth of the cup as he cradled it in both hands while sipping at his drink.

When he'd finished his coffee, Hudd checked his watch. 'Time we were making a move, sir.'

'What state are the Jacksons in?' Charlie asked as they were walking towards Hudd's car which was parked just outside the station entrance.

'Not good. Mrs Jackson, in particular. She took the news very badly.'

'I'm afraid there's worse to come.'

'Sir?'

'I heard this morning that there's been another murder. The Jacksons' grandson, Paul Gibson, has been murdered.'

'Good grief!'

'What do you think? Should we break the news about Paul to the Jacksons today?'

Hudd looked dubious. 'I think we should take medical advice before doing that. I'm not at all sure Mrs Jackson's heart could stand the shock. She's already in a bad enough state.'

'I agree. We'll say nothing about Paul's death this morning. But I'm afraid that means you'll have to discuss it with the medics and decide how and when to break the news to them about their grandson. I have to get back to Glasgow this afternoon.'

'Very good, sir,' Hudd said with a heavy sigh.

Fifteen minutes later they pulled up outside the Jacksons' cottage. Peter Jackson came to the front door, his face waxen and stubbled as if he had neither slept nor shaved. 'I heard your car coming up the drive,' he said. 'Come on in.'

'Mr Jackson, this is DCI Anderson from Glasgow,' Hudd said by way of introduction.

Jackson shook Charlie's proffered hand. 'Mind your head, Inspector,' he said, eyeing Charlie's height. 'I have to duck to get through the doors in here and I'm only five feet ten.'

Jackson led the way to the lounge, Charlie bowing low as he passed under the lintel. Jean Jackson was sitting on the settee, a black shawl wrapped tightly round her shoulders. She didn't acknowledge their presence. 'Jean hasn't spoken since we got the news about Anne,' Jackson said quietly.

'I'm sorry to intrude at a time like this, but I'm afraid I do need to ask you some questions.'

'I understand. Sit down.'

Charlie took out his notebook. 'When did you last see your daughter?'

'Last Tuesday morning, the fifteenth. I dropped her off at the station in Aberdeen. She told me she was taking the train to Glasgow and she said she'd be coming back the following day.'

'Did she say why she was going to Glasgow?'

'She told me she was going to audition for a part in a production her am-dram group are putting on later this year.'

'How long had she been staying here, prior to her trip to Glasgow?'

'Since the previous Thursday, the tenth.'

'Between the tenth and the fifteenth of March your daughter was reported as missing. There was a nationwide search going on for her. Were you not aware of that?'

'Of course I was. Her picture was on the television and in all the papers.'

'What were you playing at, Mr Jackson? Why were you hiding her?'

Jackson paused. 'You have to understand what was going on. Anne was scared of Michael. Terrified wouldn't be overstating it. She and Michael hadn't been hitting it off for some time. That was patently obvious – he didn't even come up here for her fortieth birthday party.

'The day she supposedly went missing, she arrived here out of the blue. When I asked her what was going on she told me the reason she'd come here was to escape from Michael. He'd been putting her under intense pressure for some time to agree to a separation – and she was having none of it.

'The previous evening he'd come home in a raging temper, blind drunk, and had ranted on about leaving her. When she tried to walk out of the room he attacked her – threw her to the ground and kicked her in the stomach. She showed me the bruises. Her rib cage and the small of her back were a mass of black-and-blue. I wanted her to go to the police, but she wouldn't hear of it.

'You have to understand what she was like, Inspector. Anne was very strong willed and she was used to getting her own way. She could twist her mother – and me, for that matter – round her little finger.

'She said she just needed to get away from Michael for a few days to think things through. She told us to ignore the fuss in the newspapers and on television – she said Michael had orchestrated all that. It would only be for a week or two at most, she said, then everything would be back to normal.'

'Mr Jackson, did you not realise the seriousness of the situation? My men wasted days searching for your daughter – and all the time she was hiding out here.'

'I'm sorry. Truly, I am. Jean and I pleaded with her to at least let the police know she was safe – it was such an awful waste of time and money to have those men searching for her. But she wouldn't hear of it. She could be extremely stubborn.'

Charlie shook his head in exasperation. 'What did she do while she was here?'

'Not very much. She spent most of the time in her room, reading and listening to music. She never went out in case anyone saw her.'

'Did anyone visit her or make contact with her while she was here?'

'She got a letter, a couple of days after she arrived. It had a Glasgow postmark, but I didn't recognise the handwriting on the envelope. I think it must have been bad news because she seemed very upset when she read it.'

'Is the letter still here?' Charlie asked.

Jackson shook his head. 'As soon as she'd read it she crumpled it and threw it onto the fire, then she ran upstairs to her room.'

'Were there any other contacts?'

'She got a phone call on the morning of the fifteenth – the day she went back down to Glasgow. I answered the phone. The caller was a man, but I didn't recognise his voice.'

'So someone knew she was here?'

'Apparently.'

'Was the phone call the reason for her return to Glasgow?'

'Almost certainly – she'd said nothing about going to Glasgow before she received the call. It was strange. Anne didn't say a single word to the caller. I know that for a fact because I was in the room at the time. She took the phone from me, listened for a few seconds, then hung up and announced she was going to Glasgow.'

'Is there anything else you can tell me? Anything at all?'

Jackson shook his head. 'I'll do everything I can to help you catch the animal that murdered my daughter, Inspector, but that's all I know.'

Charlie stood up and put away his notebook. 'Thank you, Mr Jackson. Once again, I'm sorry to have intruded on your grief.'

Jackson led the way to the front door. Waiting until they were in the hall, out of his wife's earshot, he spoke in a hushed voice. 'Do you have any idea who did this, Inspector?'

'There are some leads we're following up, but nothing concrete.'

'It was Michael, wasn't it?'

Charlie looked him straight in the eye. 'I understand you're upset, but why do you say that?'

'Anne told me he threatened to kill her if she refused to give him his freedom. There's insanity in the Gibson family. You mark my words, Inspector. Michael's father went mad and Michael's gone the same way.'

There was a line of taxis waiting in the rank outside Queen Street station. Charlie got into the cab at the head of the queue and arrived back in Pitt Street just before six o'clock to find O'Sullivan and Renton waiting for him in his office, O'Sullivan in an obvious state of agitation.

'There's been an almighty cock-up, sir!' O'Sullivan blurted out as soon as Charlie walked in. 'Paul Gibson's not dead.'

'What?'

'The news has just come through. Apparently it's one of his friends who's been murdered. A bloke called Gordon Parker.'

'What the hell are you on about?'

'I told you this morning that I'd found a body in Paul Gibson's bed. A young guy – early twenties – long hair. I'd never actually met Paul – I just assumed it had to be him. However, this afternoon the forensic boys were in the flat, taking photographs and prints, when Paul breezed in, large as life, wanting to know what was going on. It transpires that he spent last night in Edinburgh. He'd been through there rehearsing with his mates and he'd given a key to his flat to Gordon Parker so Parker could spend the night there with his girlfriend. Apparently Paul often let Parker use the flat when he wasn't coming home because Parker and his bird both live with their parents and they don't get many opportunities to shack up together.'

'You do realise,' Charlie said, shaking his head in disbelief, 'that I was within a whisker of telling the Jacksons that their grandson had been murdered – and that the shock might have killed Mrs Jackson?' O'Sullivan stood grim-faced. 'Do we know when Parker was killed?' Charlie asked.

'Around seven o'clock this morning.'

'And the girlfriend? Where was she?'

'I've spoken to her. Her name's Maureen Donnelly. She's a nurse in the Western. She became hysterical when I broke the news. I didn't manage to get much sense out of her, other than the fact she left the flat around six-thirty because she was going on duty at seven. When she left, Parker was fast asleep.'

Charlie pressed his intercom. 'Pauline, this is urgent, and I mean urgent. Get Sergeant Hudd in Aberdeen on the line. I don't care where he is or what he's doing, it's imperative that I speak to him immediately.'

'We've got another tricky problem on our hands,' said O'Sullivan.

'Tell me about it!'

'Paul Gibson hasn't been told yet about his mother's death yet. He's still in shock after finding out about Parker's murder. I don't know if he's up to handling the news about his mother.'

'Jesus wept! Neither do I.' Charlie buried his face in his hands and rubbed hard at his eyes. 'Where is Paul now?'

'Downstairs. PC Freer's with him. After I took his statement, I suggested he stay here for a while. I reckoned that if Parker's murder was a case of mistaken identity – if the killer's intended victim was really Paul – it might be better if he stayed away from his flat for the time being.'

Charlie grunted his agreement. He open his desk diary to check a number, then picked up the phone and dialled. A female voice answered. 'This is Inspector Anderson. Would it be possible for me to speak to Dr McCartney?'

'He told me a few minutes ago that he was about to go home, but I haven't seen him leave the building yet. If you hold on, I'll check if he's still in his office.' Charlie drummed his fingers impatiently on his desk while he waited. 'You're in luck. He's still here. I'll put you through.'

'Stephen, I'm glad I caught you. There's been a development in the Gibson case and I need your advice. Would it be possible for you to stop off at Pitt Street on your way home?'

'I'll be there in fifteen minutes.'

As soon as Charlie hung up, the phone rang. 'I've got Sergeant Hudd on the line for you,' Pauline said.

'Hudd? This is Anderson. Have you broken the news about Paul Gibson's death to the Jacksons?'

'Not yet, sir. The doctor recommended that – '

'Thank Christ for that!'

'I beg your pardon?'

'There's been a case of mistaken identity, Sergeant. Paul Gibson isn't dead. I'll explain to you later what happened. In the meantime say nothing to the Jacksons about another murder.'

'Thank you, sir. Thank you very much. That's a hell of a relief. That was one job I really was not looking forward to.'

Charlie dropped the receiver onto its cradle and wiped the beads of perspiration from his brow.

'Did we manage to check out Gibson's movements on Tuesday?' he asked.

'I went to his office today,' Renton said. 'I spoke to Peter Davies, one of Gibson's colleagues. He had a meeting with Gibson from – let me see.' Renton flicked through his notebook. 'From 17.37 to 18.24 on Tuesday afternoon. A stickler for accuracy, our Mr Davies. A man after your own heart, sir.' Renton smirked.

'Was Gibson in the office all day?'

'I didn't get a definitive answer to that. His secretary, Sheila Thompson, wasn't there. Her mother's ill and she took the day off to visit her in Falkirk. I spoke to the other secretary, Sandra. She checked Gibson's diary and the meeting with Davies was the only one scheduled for Tuesday afternoon. It seems he spent most of the day ploughing through a backlog of paperwork, but Sandra's desk isn't outside his office so she couldn't vouch for him being there all day. I've got Sheila Thompson's home address and phone number. I've been trying to call her but she's not back yet.'

'Give me her address,' said Charlie. 'I'd like to talk to her myself. One more thing, Colin. Check out who this car belongs to.' Charlie copied the registration number from his notebook onto a slip of paper. 'It's a red Ferrari. The owner is Philippa Scott's latest squeeze.'

'A Ferrari, no less? Miss Scott's not exactly slumming it, then?'

Anderson, O'Sullivan and Renton were still locked in discussion when Stephen McCartney walked into the office. Charlie levered himself to his feet. 'Tony, organise the coffees while I fill Dr McCartney in.'

By the time O'Sullivan returned with four coffees balanced on a tray, Charlie had described the day's events. 'We've now got two murders on our hands,' he said, 'and we've got both Gibson and McFarlane wandering around Glasgow like loose cannons. I need to know what's going on inside Gibson's head. What he's likely to do next. He told us he had psychiatric treatment about twelve years ago. Remind me. What was the doctor's name?'

'Susan Trayner.'

'I'd like to talk to her. Could you set up a meeting?'

McCartney raised an eyebrow. 'You're talking about confidential doctor / patient consultations.'

'I'm talking about trying to nail a ruthless killer who's struck twice and for all we know might strike again.'

McCartney hesitated. 'It would have to be strictly off the record.'

'I know the score.'

'When would you like to see her?'

'As soon as possible – tomorrow lunch time, if she can make it.'

McCartney took his mobile from his jacket pocket and went out to the corridor. 'Susan? It's Stephen McCartney.'

'Stephen! I haven't heard from you in ages. To what do I owe the pleasure?'

'I'm looking for a favour. Someone I know would like to pick your brains over lunch tomorrow. Are you free?'

'If it's 'One Devonshire Gardens', I could be talked into it.'

'I think it's more likely to be a bowl of soup upstairs at the Chip.'

'Oh, he's a copper?'

'Got it in one. DCI Charlie Anderson.'

'How will I recognise him?'

'He's over six feet tall, hunched shoulders, bald as a coot with thick, jet-black eyebrows.'

'No distinguishing features at all, then?'

'I'll ask him to wear a red rose in his lapel, roll his left trouser leg above the knee and carry a copy of the Sun.'

'Don't do that. He'll merge with the crowd.'

Stephen chortled. 'What time would suit you?'

'How about twelve o'clock?'

'That should be fine. I wouldn't normally ask you to do this, Susan, but it's a very serious business. Murder, in fact.'

'Anything I should know in advance?'

'I bumped into a guy called Michael Gibson this week. He told me he consulted you about twelve years ago. Do you remember him?'

'Sure. I saw him several times over a period of years.'

'Check your files on him. All strictly off the record, of course.'

McCartney returned to Charlie's office. 'Dr Trayner will meet you tomorrow at noon, upstairs in the Chip.'

'Thanks for that, Stephen. Now for the next dilemma. How do we handle Paul? He's still in shock following the news of the death of his friend. Should we break it to him that his mother's body's been found? And should we tell him there's a possibility that Parker's murder might have been a case of mistaken identity and there could be a killer out there who's after him?'

'Why do I get all the easy questions?' McCartney picked up his coffee and swilled it round in the plastic cup. 'On balance,' he said, 'I think it would be better to tell him everything. He's going to have to find out sooner or later. It's going to be really tough on him, but drip-feeding the information to him over the next few days won't make it any easier. I'll talk to him, if you like.'

'Thanks.' Charlie smiled wryly. 'I was kind of hoping you might volunteer. Colin, go with Dr McCartney and make sure he gets anything he needs.'

As they left the office, Charlie pressed his intercom. 'Pauline, find out who's doing the forensic report on the Gordon Parker murder and get them on the line.'

Pauline called back within minutes. 'It's Sergeant McLaughlin. I have him for you.'

'Eddie? Anderson here. What do you have on the Parker murder?'

'The slashes to his neck are similar to Anne Gibson's wounds. The white rope used to tie him up is identical, as is the brown tape across his mouth. Not much doubt that it was the same killer and almost certainly the same murder weapon.'

'That's what I thought. Tell me, could this killer have struck before? Have there been any other murders recently that fall into the same pattern?'

'There's been nothing remotely like this in Scotland in the past ten years. I make a point of studying all the pathology reports to try to spot any potential serial killer trends. It's a sort of hobby of mine.'

'I always knew you had a weird streak. You don't, by any chance, support Queen's Park?'

McLaughlin chuckled. 'I'm strictly a rugby man. However, there is one thing you should be aware of concerning Parker's blood sample.'

'Don't tell me it was mixed with sheep's blood, for Christ's sake.'

'Not this time. But it looks like Parker was into hard drugs – probably speedballs.'

'Remind me?'

'A mixture of cocaine and heroin,' McLaughlin said. 'The stimulation of the cocaine suppresses the sedative effects of the heroin and gives the user an immediate, intense rush of euphoria. There were several puncture marks on his left forearm. All quite recent, so he hasn't had the habit long. On the other hand, from the analysis of his blood, he must've injected a hell of a lot last night. The way he was carrying on I wouldn't have given much for his life expectancy, even if he hadn't been murdered.'

'We're uncovering a real can of worms with this one, Eddie. Let me know if you come up with anything else.'

When Stephen McCartney walked into the office, Charlie put down the memo he was reading. 'How did it go with Paul?'

'Not good. It was a traumatic shock, as you can imagine. I've given him a sedative. I've convinced him not to go back to his flat for the time being. I've booked him into Traquair House in Rutherglen. It's a private clinic run by Mike Glen, a colleague of mine. Paul can stay there for as long as he needs to and we'll be able to keep him under observation as there will inevitably be a delayed reaction. I'm going to drive him across to the clinic now and I'll stay with him until he's settled in.'

'What do you reckon, Stephen? What kind of bloke are we looking for? What kind of mind does it take to commit two murders like that?'

'Vindictive, ruthless and highly disturbed. But don't necessarily assume the murderer is male. I wouldn't rule out the possibility of a female killer.' Charlie raised his eyebrows. 'I've no particular reason to suppose the killer is female,' McCartney continued. 'However, knife slashes require no great strength and the victims could just as easily have been tied up by a woman who was threatening them with a gun, for instance. Or perhaps we're looking for more than one person. Perhaps the killer is working in tandem with an accomplice.'

Charlie smiled ruefully. 'I was sort of hoping you might help me to eliminate a few possibilities, not open it up to encompass the entire adult population of the west of Scotland.'

Maisie McWilliam answered the phone. 'It's Jack,' the deep voice said. 'Is Archie there?'

'Hold on. I'll get him for you.'

Archie McWilliam hurried to the phone. 'How's it goin', Jack?'

'Fine. How are things at your end?'

'The cops are still watchin' the building. It wouldn't be safe for you to come back here.'

'I thought as much. I'm callin' from a phone box but I don't want to stay on the line too long in case they're tracin' calls to your phone. Would you do me a favour?'

'Fire away.'

'Could you fling my things into my holdall and bring it up to Glasgow tomorrow?'

'No problem. Where'll we meet?'

'You remember where we used to drink on Saturday nights?'

'You mean – '

'Wheesht! You know where I mean?'

'Of course.'

'I'll see you there tomorrow night at seven – and make sure you're not followed.'

'Don't try to teach your granny to suck what-nots.' Archie laughed. 'See you tomorrow. And don't forget – you're on the bell.'

TWENTY-FOUR

Saturday 19 March

Charlie Anderson twisted and turned in bed, unable to sleep. His brain was churning. He was convinced McFarlane was involved in the murders, but every time he closed his eyes his mind filled with unanswered questions. How was Michael Gibson able to describe his wife's corpse so accurately? What was McFarlane doing at Dalgleish Tower on the night of the murder? Why had Gibson absconded from the Marriott? Why had Anne Gibson hidden out at her parents' cottage? What was Philippa Scott's role in all of this?

He rolled over and fumbled under his pillow for his watch, pressing the button on the side to illuminate the face for the umpteenth time. Almost four o'clock and he hadn't managed to get a wink of sleep. Looking across, he could make out the shadowy outline of Kay lying on her side.

He slipped out from under the duvet, picked up his slippers and dressing gown and tiptoed out of the bedroom. He went down the stairs to the kitchen and put on the kettle. While waiting for the water to boil, he went to the hall and took a notepad and his propelling pencil from his briefcase. The kitchen was bitterly cold. He pulled his dressing gown tightly round his waist, re-tied the cord, then plugged in the electric fan heater and switched it on. Tipping two spoonfuls of instant coffee into a mug, he poured on boiling water and added three heaped teaspoonfuls of sugar, which he stirred in slowly.

'Any chance of a cup?'

Charlie turned round with a start to see Kay standing in the doorway, huddled into her dressing gown. 'What are you doing up?' he asked.

'I could ask you the same question.'

'I couldn't sleep, love, so I thought I might as well try to do something useful. He indicated his notebook. This Gibson case is getting to me. It's a mass of contradictions. I need to write everything down in a structured manner to try to get my head round it.'

'Well you might as well tell be about it. I'll never get back to sleep now.'

'Are you sure?'

'As long as I get a coffee first.'

Charlie made a mug of coffee for Kay, then sat down beside her at the kitchen table, wrapping both hands round his mug to warm them while he organised his thoughts.

'Let's start with the assumption that Michael Gibson isn't insane and he isn't hallucinating. In which case the facts are as follows.' Opening his pad at a clean page, Charlie started making notes as he spoke.

'On the 9th of March Gibson 'finds his wife dead' in Dalgleish Tower – suspected 'suicide'.

On the 10th, Anne Gibson goes into hiding near Aberdeen.

On the 15th, she travels back to Glasgow, telling her parents she'll be returning to Aberdeen the following day.

On that same evening, Gibson 'finds his wife dead' in Dalgleish Tower – murdered.

Also on that day, Jack McFarlane is known to be in the vicinity of Dalgleish Tower around the time of the murder.

On the 17th, Anne Gibson's body is found in the woods near Paisley – and the autopsy reveals sheep's blood on her clothing.

The following day, Gordon Parker is murdered, presumably by the same person. Possible case of mistaken identity for Paul Gibson.'

Charlie put down his pencil and sipped at his coffee while studying the sheet of paper. 'What do you think?' he asked.

'If Anne Gibson turned up safe and well in Aberdeen on the 10th, then it sounds like she faked her suicide on the 9th,' Kay offered.

'I agree. It would've been perfectly feasible for her to play dead when Michael came home and then clear away the pill-jar, tidy up the room and make herself scarce before Gibson and I returned to Dalgleish Tower. Nothing else would explain what Gibson saw and also be compatible with Anne turning up at her parents' house the following day. But I can't for the life of me understand her motive.'

'Why do you think she went back to Glasgow on the 15th?' Kay asked.

'I've no idea. And what happened to her when she got there?' Charlie added. 'Who did she fall foul of? McFarlane? Gibson? Someone else? Gibson says he found his wife's body in Dalgleish Tower. If this is true, this time she wasn't acting. And if he did find her body – who killed her?'

'And what's the sheep's blood all about?' Kay asked. 'Did that get onto her clothing in Dalgleish Tower, or in the woods near Paisley?'

'We don't know.' Charlie shook his head as he turned over to a fresh page in his notepad.

'Let's look at it on the assumption that Michael Gibson *did* murder his wife. It wouldn't have been possible for him to have killed her in the bedroom in Dalgleish Tower and then to have cleaned up such a mess in fifteen minutes without leaving any trace of blood.'

'Perhaps he killed her somewhere else,' Kay suggested, 'then took her body to the Gleniffer Braes?'

'That doesn't stack up with Gibson leaving his office at six-thirty and phoning me from the caretaker's flat in Dalgleish Tower at five past seven.'

'In which case, Jack McFarlane, or someone else, might have killed her and taken her body to the Gleniffer Braes.'

'So how could Michael Gibson describe the corpse so accurately?' Charlie put down his pencil, pushed his chair back and swung both feet up onto the kitchen table. He closed his eyes. 'I'm missing something, Kay. I'm missing something.'

Charlie walked up the crazy-paving path, lined with wilting daffodils, towards the modern apartment block. He pressed the bell push of the ground floor flat. There was no response. When he sounded the bell again, Sheila Thompson came hurrying to the door. Keeping the security chain in place, she eased the door ajar.

'Who is it?' She peered through the gap. 'What do you want?'

'It's Inspector Anderson, Miss Thompson. Sorry to disturb you on a Saturday morning. Could I possibly have a few minutes of your time?'

Sheila closed the door while she unhooked the chain, then opened it wide. 'Sorry about the unwelcoming reception. I didn't recognise you, Inspector. Come on in.'

'No need to apologise. A very sensible precaution. I only wish more people would do that.' Charlie stepped into the hall. 'How's your mother keeping? I heard she wasn't well.'

'Oh, it's nothing serious. A touch of flu, that's all. She's over the worst of it.' Sheila ushered Charlie towards the lounge. 'What can I do for you?'

'Are you aware that Mr Gibson's wife has been found murdered?'

'Yes. It's in the morning paper. It's a terrible business.'

'What you don't know is that there was another murder yesterday. Gordon Parker, Paul Gibson's best friend, was also killed. I'd like you to keep this information to yourself, but we suspect the killer's intended victim may have been Paul.'

'My God!'

'Did you know that Mr Gibson has disappeared?'

Sheila looked incredulous. 'Disappeared? What do you mean?'

'He absconded from the Marriott Hotel on Thursday afternoon and hasn't been seen since.' Sheila shook her head in confusion. 'When did you last see him?' Charlie asked.

'On Tuesday. He came into the office on Tuesday. I remember that clearly because it was the first time I'd seen him since his wife had… had... gone missing.' Sheila's voice tailed off.

'Was he in the office all day?'

Sheila stopped to think. 'Most of the day, apart from an hour or so in the afternoon.'

Alarm bells started ringing inside Charlie's head but his outward demeanour gave no indication of surprise. 'When, exactly, did he go out? Think carefully. It may be important.'

'He arrived around nine o'clock and busied himself with his backlog of paperwork. He didn't go out for lunch – he had a sandwich in the office. About four o'clock he told me he'd had enough and said he was going home. I reminded him that Peter Davies had scheduled a promotion review in his agenda at five-thirty. Mr Gibson didn't want to defer that again – it had already been rescheduled several times – so he went out around four o'clock and returned around five-thirty for his meeting with Mr Davies. He left for home straight after that meeting.'

'Do you know where he went between four and five-thirty?'

'I didn't ask – and he didn't volunteer the information.'

'Did he behave any differently when he returned to the office?'

'Meaning what?'

'Did he seem anxious, flustered, agitated?'

'He was certainly on edge. But he'd been like that all day.'

'Have you seen or heard from him since Tuesday?' Sheila shook her head. 'Thank you. You've been most helpful.'

Sheila closed the front door behind Charlie and slipped the security chain back in place. She stood leaning with her back to the door, her heart pounding. 'You can come out now. He's gone.'

Michael Gibson appeared in the bedroom doorway. He was unshaven and his eyes were red from lack of sleep. 'Why did you tell Anderson that?' he roared, thumping both his fists against the wall. 'Why did you tell him I left the office at four o'clock on Tuesday?'

'Because it's the truth. That's why. Why shouldn't I tell the police the truth? What lies have you been telling them? How can you expect me to cover up for you if you don't tell me what lies you've been telling?'

'I'm sorry. I didn't mean to go off the handle.' He ran his fingers through his tousled hair. 'I need to work out what to do now.' Going into the lounge, he poured himself a stiff drink.

'Whisky's not the answer, Michael.'

'It helps me think.' He took a long swallow, screwing up his face when the neat spirit hit the back of his throat. 'What can I do?' he muttered. 'Now my alibi's blown.'

Sheila looked at him in astonishment. 'What alibi?'

'I told Anderson I was in the office all day on Tuesday and that I didn't leave until six-thirty. That would've meant it was it impossible for me to drive to Paisley and get back to Dalgleish Tower by seven. But now he knows I was out of the office between four and five-thirty, that changes everything.'

'Where did you go? I need to know the truth. Did you drive to Paisley?'

'Good God, no.'

'What did you do?'

'I went to see Pippa.'

'You did what? I thought it was all over between you and her? Why did you go to see her?'

'I needed to talk to her. She'd been avoiding me. She hadn't returned my phone calls or answered any of my texts. I called her office on Tuesday morning, but I couldn't reach her. Her secretary told me she was with a client. I scheduled a meeting with her at four-thirty under a fictitious name, then I got her phone number from her secretary on the pretext that I wanted to leave a confidential message on her answering machine concerning the meeting. I did leave a message – imploring her to meet me at her flat at four-thirty.'

'Michael… You… You do know – ?'

'Know what?'

'That Philippa's involved with someone else.'

'What are you talking about?'

'She's seeing Jonathan Sharp.'

'She can't be! I don't believe you.'

The realisation hit Michael like a blow from a sledgehammer. Was that all their relationship had ever meant to Philippa? The life style? The status of being with 'the boss'?

'Didn't she tell you that – when you went to see her?'

'I didn't see her,' Michael spluttered. 'She didn't turn up. I rang her door bell, but she wasn't there. I waited in the car outside her apartment block for an hour but she didn't show up. Finally I gave up and went back to the office.'

'Why did you lie to the police?'

'I panicked. I didn't want to give them the impression that I was running back to my mistress as soon as my wife had gone missing. I didn't want Anderson to think I'd anything to do with Anne's disappearance.'

'You've got to tell him the truth. He knows now that you lied about the time you left the office. You'll only make things worse if you don't give yourself up.'

'I can't. I've got to find McFarlane. He murdered Anne. And you heard what Anderson just said – he tried to murder Paul. If I don't get to him first, he'll kill me. I know he will.'

'Stop talking like that! You're no match for McFarlane. Even if you did find him, what would you do?'

'I will find him.' Michael's eyes hardened. 'And I'll kill him.'

'This is crazy talk. Stop it at once. Go to the police. They'll give you protection until they find McFarlane.'

'The same way they protected Anne? The same way they protected the poor sod who got killed in place of Paul? And let's suppose, for the sake of argument, that they do catch him. What then? Will they be able to convict him? Even if they do – what'll happen to him? Another stretch in jail; a life sentence for him –

and a lifetime of nightmares for me, living in dread of the day he gets out.

'I've lived with it for the past twelve years – waking up in the middle of the night in a cold sweat wondering where and when he's going to strike. There's no way I'm going to go through all that again. I'm going to finish it once and for all.'

Michael picked up the bottle and poured neat whisky down his throat until he felt his eye sockets burn. 'I've got to go. Thanks for not giving me away to Anderson.' Crossing to the front door, he unhooked the security chain and opened the door a few inches, looking and listening, then slipped outside and pulled the door closed behind him.

Sheila sank down on the settee with her head in her hands.

Charlie climbed to the top of the spiral staircase in 'The Ubiquitous Chip' and looked around the crowded bar. When Susan Trayner half-rose, raising her hand tentatively in recognition, Charlie crossed to her table.

She looked to be in her mid-forties, her straggly, prematurely greying hair piled on top of her head and held in place by a wooden clasp.

'What can I get you?' Charlie asked. His first impression was that her strong features were forbidding, but her hazel eyes were soft and friendly and she had an engaging smile.

'Nothing, thanks. I've got a mineral water,' she said, holding up her glass.

'Would you not like something to eat?'

'No thanks.'

Charlie crossed to the bar to order a coffee. While waiting to be served, he glanced back over his shoulder and studied Susan's profile; skin-tight jeans and a clinging polo-neck sweater which showed off her still youthful figure to advantage.

Charlie carried across his coffee and sat down on the bench seat beside her. 'It's good of you to see me on a Saturday. I'll be as brief as I can. The reason I wanted to talk to you is that I'm hoping you might be able to straighten out a few things in my mind.' Charlie paused while he stirred several spoonfuls of sugar into his coffee. 'We're talking purely hypothetically, you understand.' Susan nodded her assent. 'If I were to take the case of, for example, an advocate who felt he'd let down a client. Do you think that would be enough to induce a nervous breakdown?'

'Probably not in itself, though it could be a contributory factor.'

'What else might it take?'

'Perhaps personal problems – family problems – that sort of thing.'

'Such as?'

Susan hesitated. 'How important is this?' She spoke tersely. 'I'm not in the habit of going into such details.'

'I wouldn't be asking if lives weren't at stake. It is that critical.'

She took a sip of mineral water. 'Very well. As long as it's clearly understood that we're talking in complete confidence.' Charlie nodded. 'Let me paint a scenario for you. Imagine that our hypothetical advocate's wife has gone away for the weekend to a bridge congress and he's arranged an assignation with an old girlfriend, who happens to be his wife's sister.'

'Her sister!'

Susan nodded. 'He gives his nine year-old son extra pocket money to go to the cinema with his pal. However, the boy forgets his money and when he runs back home to get it, he hears a noise coming from his parents' bedroom. He walks in unannounced and finds them together.'

'Actually sees his father screwing his aunt?'

'Maybe he sees something even more traumatic. Something a bit kinky.' Charlie raised an eyebrow. 'The girl, naked, spread-eagled, tied to the bed.'

The coffee spoon fell from Charlie's grasp.

'Nothing aggressive or violent, you understand. She's an old flame from his university days – a more than willing participant, enjoying every minute of it. In fact the bondage game was initially her idea, but he finds it incredibly exciting. The feeling of power and domination turns him on enormously. When the son bursts into the bedroom he sees his father lying naked on the bed, fondling his aunt's breasts. The boy stands frozen, wide-eyed in the doorway, his gaze locked onto his father's erect penis, already encased in a condom.

'The boy screams: 'Stop it, Daddy! Stop it! Don't hurt Aunt Carole!' He rushes off to his room and locks himself inside. It takes the father the best part of two hours to coax him out. He tries to explain to the child that he hadn't been hurting Carole – that they'd only been playing a game.

'But it's when he tries to make the boy promise never to mention this game to his mother that he realises he's lost his son. A wedge has been driven between them. The child used to hero worship his father, but his respect for him crumbles and disintegrates. The sparkle of unquestioning trust dies in the boy's eyes as he sits, tight-lipped, steadfastly refusing to make the promise.

'His aunt becomes hysterical. She pleads with him to promise not to say anything to his mother. She even gets down on her knees and begs him. The boy starts wailing. Eventually, he makes the promise, then runs out of the house in floods of tears.

'Over the next few days, the child doesn't say a word to his father. The father tries to bribe his way back into his son's affections by buying him the expensive baseball bat he'd been hankering after for months, but when he takes it to him the boy won't even acknowledge the gift. The father leaves the bat on top of his son's bookcase. Weeks go by and the boy still won't go anywhere near it. He doesn't even unwrap it from its polythene sleeve. Every time the father goes into the child's bedroom, the bat is lying in exactly the same position. The permanent reminder – the rejected thirty pieces of silver – the phallic symbol of an engorged penis wrapped in a sheath.

'The incident has a traumatic effect on the father. His work suffers dramatically – he loses his power of concentration. He spends every waking minute fretting about whether the son will tell his mother about the incident, but his wife never gives any indication of having found out. He's torn in two. He consults a psychiatrist who recommends him to confess everything to his wife in order to have a basis for re-establishing credibility with his son. Objectively, he agrees with the advice, but he can't bring himself to tell her what happened.

'Having previously tried to interest his wife in mild bondage games to enliven their sex life, he knows how much the very idea disgusts her. He shudders to think how she would react if she ever found out he had allowed their son to witness him indulging his fantasies with her sister. In the event, he does nothing – never broaches the subject again – neither with his wife nor his son. Time doesn't heal. In the months that follow the mental anguish builds up. The boy becomes introverted and withdrawn. From being good at sports and a high achiever at school, he loses interest in everything and falls behind his peers. The wife's sister is totally traumatised by what happened – to the extent that she applies for a teaching job in Canada because she can't handle the way her godson looks at her every time he sees her.

'The mother becomes concerned about her son's welfare and she wants to consult a psychiatrist to try to find out what's wrong with him, but the father dismisses the idea, telling her the boy's just going through a normal, adolescent phase – while all the time he's living in constant dread that his son might blurt out what had happened to his mother in a fit of pique over some unrelated, trivial incident.

'That, Inspector, is the kind of pressure that might induce a breakdown.'

Charlie drained his coffee cup. 'Jesus wept!'

TWENTY-FIVE

As soon as Charlie got back to the office he summoned O'Sullivan and Renton. He noticed Sullivan was frowning.

'Let me bring you up to date,' Charlie began. 'This morning I was convinced McFarlane was our man. It was only a matter of smoking him out and gathering the evidence. Now I'm not so sure. It seems that Gibson has been stringing us along with a pack of lies. His secretary told me he was out of his office between four and five-thirty last Tuesday. Ample time to drive to Paisley and back – and commit a murder.

'You had the clue staring you in the face, Colin,' Charlie said, turning to Renton. 'But you missed it. You scoffed at Peter Davies telling you his meeting with Gibson had started at 5.37. Did you not ask him why?' Renton looked puzzled. 'Nobody schedules a meeting to start at 5.37,' Charlie said. 'It had to be scheduled for 5.30, so why did it start at 5.37?'

'Davies might've turned up late?' Renton suggested.

Charlie shook his head. 'Totally out of character for such a precise man.'

'Gibson's previous meeting overran?'

'He didn't have any other meetings that afternoon.'

'Gibson got caught short in the bog?'

Charlie laughed. 'Nice try. Possible, but too much of a coincidence. Never trust coincidences. Facts and probabilities are our only friends. If you'd followed through and asked Davies why the meeting had started late, he'd almost certainly have volunteered the information that Gibson had been out of the office.

But on the other hand,' Charlie said, rubbing his chin. 'If Gibson did murder his wife, what the hell was McFarlane doing taking a taxi to Dalgleish Tower? There are too many loose ends, boys. I don't like it.

'You're not looking happy,' Charlie said, eyeing O'Sullivan's worried expression. 'What's up?'

'I just had a phone call from PC Chadwick in Partick. He told me that Mrs Donnelly – she's the mother of Maureen, Gordon Parker's girlfriend, had been to see him. She was in a right tizz. It seems that Maureen's gone missing.'

'Missing?'

'I went across to the Western yesterday to break the news to her about her boyfriend's murder. I spoke to her just as she was coming off shift. She insisted on knowing how Parker had been killed, so I told her. She was distraught – verging on hysterical. I offered to give her a lift home, but she said she wanted to walk. She only lives half a mile from the hospital. I watched her go off down the road towards her house, but apparently she never arrived.'

Archie McWilliam swung Jack McFarlane's tartan holdall ostentatiously over his shoulder as he loped down Paisley High Street. He was sure he was being followed. Whoever was tracking him would know the holdall belonged to McFarlane and would deduce he was on his way to meet him. That would make it all the more satisfying for him, and frustrating for his tail, when he gave him the slip.

He checked his watch. Twenty-four minutes past five. Bang on schedule. The High Street was crowded with Saturday afternoon shoppers spilling out onto the pavement. McWilliam maintained a steady pace, weaving his way through the throng, knowing his tail would have no problem keeping up with him – and no problem staying hidden. That was fine. This wasn't the time or place to make his move. He turned left before

Paisley Cross and strode down Moss Street towards Gilmour Street station.

When he walked into the station, he saw there were two people queuing at each of the three ticket booths. Ideal. He made a pretence of studying the departures board, although he knew the Paisley to Glasgow timetable like the back of his hand. The next train to Glasgow Central was the five thirty-six, leaving from platform 1.

As the town hall clock started chiming the half-hour, he joined one of the queues, fidgeting at first, then calling out loudly to the woman at the front to hurry up. He glanced towards the station entrance but no one seemed to be paying any attention to him. When he reached the ticket window he pressed his face close to the glass. 'Single to Glasgow Central, pal. As quick as you can.' He pushed the correct money across, grabbed his ticket and ran up the staircase leading to the platforms.

Platform 1 was at the top of another flight of steps at the far end of the concrete corridor. His footsteps rang out as he put on a sprint when he heard the train rumbling to a halt above his head. Several people were hurrying to catch this train; breaking into a trot when they heard the engine apply its brakes. Which one of them was tailing him? When he reached the platform, he ran towards the back of the train while most of the other late passengers scrambled towards the nearest compartments. He pulled a carriage door open wide and clambered on board, then closed the door and wrenched down the window, watching while the guard checked everyone was safely on board. The piercing whistle sounded and the train started to trundle forward.

McWilliam waited until they had gathered some momentum, then he flung open the carriage door and jumped down onto the platform. The guard, leaning out of his window, swore at him and shook an angry fist. McWilliam stood chortling. He gave a flamboyant two-fingered salute to the guard – and to whoever else might be staring back at him in frustration.

Swinging the holdall over his shoulder, he skipped down the steps and out of the station. He jumped into the taxi at the head of the rank. 'Govan Cross Subway, Jimmy,' he announced as he pulled the cab door shut. 'Put your foot down.' He smiled contentedly as the taxi sped off.

McWilliam watched out of the rear window throughout the fifteen minute journey to Govan. Although he saw no sign of being followed, he couldn't be sure he was in the clear. He was confident he'd shaken off whoever had followed him on to the train, but it wasn't beyond the bounds of possibility that someone else had been detailed to monitor the taxi rank.

He got out the cab at Govan Cross and paid his fare. Hurrying to the subway station, he bought a ticket and slipped it through the barrier before trotting down the staircase to the Inner Circle platform. While waiting for a train to arrive, he sat on the bottom step and studied the face of everyone who came down after him. Only half a dozen passengers had appeared by the time the train pulled in. Of these, none looked suspicious and only two were remote possibilities. He boarded the train near the front and stood beside the doors, waiting for the warning beep to sound. As soon as the doors started to close he stepped from the train onto the empty platform. He watched the faces through the windows as the train quickly gathered speed and rushed past him into the tunnel. He thought he detected a look of anger in the eyes of one of the men who'd followed him down to the platform. Perhaps he'd imagined it. No matter, he was confident he was now in the clear. Grinning broadly, he punched the air in triumph as he crossed to the Outer Circle platform. A train arrived almost immediately and he got on board.

McWilliam alighted at Hillhead. When he emerged from the subway station, darkness had already fallen. He bought a copy of the Evening Times from a street vendor. Crossing Byres Road, he turned up Dowanside Road, cut across Caledon Street to Highburgh Road and from there he walked towards The Rock, the pub where he had his rendezvous with McFarlane.

He continued past the pub, almost as far as the Clarence Drive traffic lights, then spun on his heel and froze, looking for any telltale movement; anyone stopping suddenly, turning away, trying to hide in the shadows. There was nothing suspicious. Checking his watch, he saw he was twenty minutes early.

He retraced his steps and went into the lounge bar, where he ordered a pint of heavy and a large whisky, carrying his drinks across to an empty booth. He swallowed the whisky in two gulps and shook the dregs into his beer. He unfolded the Evening Times and turned to the sports results, cursing when he saw that St Mirren had lost. He had almost finished his pint when he saw Jack McFarlane enter the lounge. He stood up and waved.

'Same again, Archie,' Jack shouted across, pointing to the empty glasses on the table in front of him. McWilliam nodded in confirmation, holding up a thumb and forefinger spaced wide apart to indicate he was drinking doubles. McFarlane ordered at the bar and asked a waitress to bring the drinks across. 'First things first, Archie. How did Thistle get on?'

'I didn't check their result. But St Mirren lost two-one at home.'

'See's the paper, then.' McFarlane flicked to the sports pages. 'A one-each draw at Motherwell. No' bad, eh? Is it no' about time you gave up supportin' St Mirren and started to follow a decent team?'

McFarlane dodged the playful punch that came his way, bumping into the waitress in the process and causing one of the pints on her tray to wobble. 'Sorry about that, dear. My fault entirely. Don't worry about the pint that got shoogled. It was his.' McFarlane smiled as he gave the waitress a generous tip.

'Any problem getting here?'

'Not at all. I enjoyed myself. I used the 'steppin' aff the train' routine twice. It was just like the auld days.'

'Thanks for bringin' that, by the way,' McFarlane said, eyeing his holdall.

'How've you been getting' on? Did you find somewhere to kip down?'

'I'm stayin' at Larry Robertson's place. That's why I suggested we meet here. He lives just round the corner in one of them flash, detached houses in Turnberry Road. He's got it done out real nice. As they say, there's no such thing as a poor bookie.'

'Have you been able to get things sorted out?'

'There was a wee hiccup yesterday, which might delay things for a day or two, but I'm still hopin' to get everythin' done in time to head back down to London next week.'

Michael Gibson thumbed through the notes in his wallet while waiting his turn in the slow-moving queue for the cashpoint. He counted a hundred and eighty pounds. He stuffed his wallet back into his inside jacket pocket and turned up his collar, both to protect his neck from the drizzle and to obscure his features from the people lined up behind him. When he eventually got to the head of the queue, he slipped his card into the slot. It seemed to take an age before a message appeared, requesting him to enter his PIN. Why was the machine responding so slowly? His imagination started running riot. Had the police instigated a check on his card? Had his account been blocked? Was a signal being transmitted at this very moment to the police, identifying where he was?

Glancing anxiously over his shoulder, he tapped in his number. The machine paused for what seemed like an eternity, before a dimly-lit message appeared on the screen. He bent forward and squinted at the display. 'PIN invalid', he read. 'Do you wish to cancel or retry?'

He shook his head to try to clear his befuddled brain. He was sure he'd typed in the correct number. Was this a ruse to keep him here while a squad car was speeding across the city to intercept him? The queue behind was muttering impatiently as the drizzle gave way to a squally shower. Peals of thunder rolled in the far distance and large raindrops came plopping down, bouncing high from the wet pavement. He felt the eyes drilling into the back of his skull as he pressed 're-try'. Licking his lips, he carefully re-entered his code. Again it seemed to take an inordinately long time before a message appeared asking how much he wanted to withdraw. He selected three hundred pounds and hopped from one foot to the other while he listened to the slow, mechanical counting of the money. Whipping out his card, he grabbed the notes as soon as they appeared and stumbled off down the street.

Having stopped off at an off licence to buy a half-bottle of whisky, Michael headed for Sauchiehall Street, shaking the rain from his sodden jacket as he entered the Lorne Hotel. He walked the length of the lounge bar, scanning the faces of all the customers. There was no sign of McGurk. Choosing an empty table at the far end of the bar, he ordered a whisky. He picked up the newspaper he found lying on an adjacent chair and held it up in front of his face, sipping at his drink and continually checking his watch. McGurk was late. Had something gone wrong? He put down the paper and caught the waitress's eye. 'Same again, please.'

She brought his drink across on a tray and set a bowl of peanuts down on the table in front of him. He shovelled a handful into his mouth. Realising this was the first thing he'd eaten all day, he wolfed his way through the bowlful, washing them down with whisky. How long should he give McGurk? He was already half an hour late. Five more minutes, he decided. He couldn't risk sitting here any longer; someone might recognise him. He picked up the newspaper again and used it to shield his face.

Every time he heard the lounge door open, he stole a glance over the top of the paper. At last, he saw him. Bernie McGurk was in his late fifties, a small, wiry man with lank, grey hair and an unkempt pepper-and-salt beard. His crumpled, ankle-length black coat had seen better days. His left leg was shorter than his right and his shoe was built up to compensate. Despite that, he walked with a pronounced limp.

McGurk waved in Michael's direction as he shuffled the length of the lounge and sat down opposite him. 'Long time no see, Mr Gibson. Sorry I'm a wee bit late.' His smile revealed his unlovely, yellow teeth.

'What are you drinking?' Michael asked.

'Same as yourself, Mr Gibson,' he replied, nodding towards Michael's glass. Michael called across the waitress and ordered two more whiskies.

'Did you manage to get it for me?' he said in a whisper.

'Of course.' McGurk took a large brown envelope from the voluminous inside pocket of his coat and placed it on the empty chair between them. 'Have you used one of these before?' he asked in a low voice.

Michael shook his head. McGurk checked to make sure the envelope was out of sight of everyone in the bar before easing the pistol out and placing it on the chair.

'It's straightforward. It's a basic semi-automatic pistol. Safety catch off,' he said, easing across the switch. 'Safely catch on.' He flicked the switch back. 'Understood?' Michael nodded. 'There are six rounds in the clip in the butt. You said that would be enough?'

'More than enough.'

'Minimum recoil, so just aim and fire,' McGurk said slipping the pistol back into the envelope.'

'Two hundred and fifty, you said?'

'That's right.'

Michael put the envelope into his jacket pocket and took out a wad of notes which he pushed under the newspaper lying on the table. 'It's all there. You can count it.'

'Wouldn't dream of it. If I can't trust a gentleman like you, who can I trust?' McGurk said, taking the money, which quickly disappeared into his coat pocket. 'What was the other thing you wanted to talk to me about? The thing that was too hush-hush to mention on the phone?'

Michael remained silent while the waitress placed their drinks on the table in front of them. He waited until she was well out of earshot. 'I need some information. Jack McFarlane's in town and I want to know where I can find him.'

'McFarlane?' Bernie let out a low whistle as he picked up his whisky and swilled it round the glass. 'He's bad news. You don't want to be messing with the likes o' him.'

'That's my problem. All I want you to do is find out where he's hanging out.'

'I don't know about that.' McGurk took a sip from his drink and put the glass down on the table. Taking a packet of cigarette papers from his coat pocket, he unfolded his tobacco pouch and started to roll a cigarette. 'If word ever got back to McFarlane that I'd been asking questions about him, my life wouldn't be worth a monkey's.' He stuck the unlit cigarette into his mouth and sucked on it hard.

'I'll pay well. Five hundred. A hundred up front and four hundred when you get me the information.'

'I don't know. I don't like it.'

'Here's a hundred.' Michael slid another wad of notes under the newspaper. 'And there's four hundred more when you let me know where I can find him.'

McGurk picked up his whisky glass and cradled it in both hands before swallowing the contents. He snatched up the money and stuffed it into his pocket. 'I'll do my best, but I can't promise anything.'

'Fine.'

'Where can I contact you?'

'You can't. I'll get in touch with you. How much time do you need?'

McGurk shrugged. 'Not a lot. My contacts either know where he is or they don't. Phone me at eleven o'clock tomorrow morning and I'll let you know what I've got.'

'Thanks. Stay here and have another drink. We don't want to be seen leaving together. I'll call you tomorrow.' Michael crossed to the bar and paid for another whisky for McGurk before walking out of the door into the cool evening air.

The rain had eased off as Michael walked back along Sauchiehall Street towards the Kelvingrove Art Gallery. Cutting into the park, he found a quiet bench beside the river. In the gloom he opened the brown envelope and took out the pistol which he balanced it in the palm of his hand. It felt comfortable. He checked to make sure the safety catch was on, then tucked it carefully into his right-hand jacket pocket.

Picking up some loose pebbles, he started lobbing them in the general direction of the river Kelvin. He couldn't see them land, only the splash told him when they hit the water. He drank from the whisky bottle until he felt drowsy. Tugging off his jacket to use as a blanket, he stretched out on the park bench and soon passed out in a drunken stupor.

Michael slept fitfully, confused images churning in his brain. He was in the master bedroom of his house in Bearsden – he recognised the chintzy decor. Carole was tied to the bed, spread-eagled – naked apart from a red silk scarf blindfolding her eyes and a black velvet choker round her throat. He was lying beside her, also naked, caressing her breasts as she moaned softly in anticipation.

Suddenly the blindfold slipped from her eyes. But the eyes weren't Carole's – they were Anne's. Cold, blue eyes – glazed and staring unblinkingly at him – dead eyes. The furniture and the wallpaper began to swim out of focus and the room transformed itself into the stark black-and-white decor of his bedroom in Dalgleish Tower. The choker round her neck began to unwind all by itself and blood started weeping from an open wound in her throat. A bloodstained, ivory-handled, cut-throat razor appeared from nowhere on the pillow beside her head.

Michael tried to re-tie the choker to stem the flow, but the blood kept seeping through his fingers; at first, a trickle, then it oozed and bubbled, splashing onto his bare arms and chest. He tried to roll away from the crimson flow but it followed him, gushing from her throat and pouring towards him in a deluge.

He scrambled from the bed and ran towards the bedroom door. It was locked. He couldn't wrench it open. Blood was everywhere now, filling the room; ankle-deep and rising inexorably. The body on the bed started to twitch and jerk violently, arms and legs flailing frenziedly against their restraining bonds. He stood by the bedroom door, petrified, tugging with all his might at the unyielding handle.

Suddenly the head detached itself from the writhing corpse and floated up towards the ceiling, torrents of blood spurting in all directions from the severed neck. The head started moving rapidly across the room towards him. Two shafts of blue light sprang from the dead eye-sockets and locked onto him while the features twisted into those of McFarlane. The jagged purple scar appeared, engorged with blood, pulsing like a living organ on the side of his face, growing larger all the time, coming closer and closer, pounding louder and louder…

A strangulated cry died in Michael's throat. Throwing his arms in the air, he rolled over and crashed head first from the park bench onto the gravel path, splitting his forehead on a jagged stone. He lay there, stunned and disoriented, a rhythmic, pounding crescendo hammering at his eardrums. He struggled groggily to his feet. He saw the half-empty whisky bottle lying on the ground and instinctively grabbed it by the neck to use it as a weapon. The footsteps receded. The two joggers disappeared into the distance, totally unaware of his presence.

Michael's forehead was stinging, his mouth parched. Blood from his head wound was trickling into his eye. He limped down to the river's edge and cupped the icy water in both hands, splashing it onto his face and into his mouth.

He scrambled back up the bank, pulled on his jacket and sat down on the bench. Suddenly remembering the pistol, he tugged it from his pocket to check it wasn't damaged. Fortunately, he hadn't fallen on the gun. He unscrewed the top of the whisky bottle and his hands were shaking as he lifted it to his mouth, whisky spilling round his swollen lips as he gulped to swallow. He put the bottle down on the bench and pressed the palm of his hand hard against his forehead to try to stem the flow of blood. He felt nauseous. Reality and nightmare were merging. What was happening to him? Was he going mad? He stared fixedly at his upturned, bloody palm. Was this the hand that had slit Anne's throat?

TWENTY-SIX

Sunday 20 March

It was a spring-like morning and Charlie Anderson had to tug down his sun-visor to keep the low early morning rays out of his eyes as he drove towards Dalgleish Tower. He parked in the shadow of the building and plodded up the steps to ring Harry Kennedy's bell.

'Sorry to disturb you so early on a Sunday morning.'

'No problem, Inspector. Come on in. I'm always up and about by seven. I often have a wee catnap in the afternoon, mind you, but I'm not one for lyin' in bed in the mornin'. What can I do for you?'

'I need your help, Harry. Every time I think I've taken a step forward in the Gibson investigation, five minutes later I find I've gone two steps backwards. When that happens, the only thing to do is go back to square one and start all over again. So, if you'll bear with me, I'd like to ask you a few questions – most of which you've probably answered already.'

'Fire away. Would you like a wee cup of tea or a coffee before we start?'

'Coffee sounds good.'

'Milk and sugar?'

'Black – three sugars.'

Charlie settled into an armchair while Harry busied himself in the kitchen. When Harry returned, he handed across a steaming mug, then took the chair opposite.

Charlie opened his notebook and rolled down the lead in his propelling pencil. 'First question. How difficult would it be for someone to get into this building undetected?'

Harry sat forward on the edge of his seat. 'There are only two ways to get in,' he said, stroking his moustache. 'Anyone can walk through the front entrance, as you just did, but that only gets you as far as my door. To get access to the lift or the staircase, you have to go through the connectin' door and for that you need the security code. There's an intercom for each apartment beside that door, as well as a camera. If you ring an apartment bell, the resident can see who it is and open the door if he wants to let you in.'

'The only other way in is through the garage. You'd need a remote control gadget to open the garage doors, then you'd need the security code to get through to the lift or the stairwell.'

'How many people have door keys and remote controls?'

'Let's start from the bottom,' Harry said, numbering off on his fingers. 'On the second floor, there's the Leslies. They moved in recently. There's just the two of them – husband and wife – both doctors. They've got keys and remote controls. The tenth floor flat has been sold to a Mr and Mrs Moore. They've got one door key for now, but not a remote control. They haven't moved in yet.'

'Know anything about them?'

'Just that they come from Gourock. Apart from that I don't know anything.'

'Okay, go on.'

'On the thirteenth floor, there's McFadyen. He's got a door key but he didn't want a remote control because he hasn't got a car. To tell you the truth, I think he's a bit glaikit, Inspector. He hardly ever comes out of his apartment – once a week to the best of my knowledge, to go the messages. Apart from that, he stays put all the time and he never seems to get any visitors.

'The only other occupied flat is number 15, the Gibsons. Mr Gibson has a key and a remote control, as has – ' Harry lowered his eyes. 'As *had*, Mrs Gibson. Their son, Paul, has a key and a remote control as well. He used to come round a lot – there's no mistakin' his van – it's got 'Citizens Band' in big letters plastered on the side. But recently he only ever came here during the day to see his mother – never when his father was at home.

'Mr Gibson ordered an extra key and a remote control. Very hush-hush, it was. He gave me a good bung to keep quiet about it. For a 'friend', if you get my meanin'.' Harry tapped the side of his nose knowingly. 'The young lady seemed to have the run of the place whenever Mrs Gibson was away for the weekend.'

'If somebody wanted to get a spare key, what would they have to do?'

'There's a form that has to be filled in and countersigned by Mr Chalmers – he's my boss. He manages the estate agency that handles everythin' to do with the building. When Chalmers has signed off the authorisation, I send the form to London where the keys are cut. It takes a couple of weeks.'

'Has anybody else got keys that you know of?'

'I've got a complete set in there.' Harry pointed to his wall-safe. 'And Mr Chalmers has a set in his office. As far as I know, that's it.'

Charlie noted down the information and put away his notebook. 'I'd like to talk to the Leslies and McFadyen in case they heard or saw anything.'

'Your blokes have already taken their statements.'

'I know. But I'd still like to talk to them.'

'Fine. But you'll have to come back later on to see the Leslies. I saw them goin' out just before you arrived. I think they're church-goers. McFadyen's sure to be in, but whether or not he'll open his door to you is a different matter entirely.' Harry chortled as he got to his feet. 'I'll open the access door for you so you can get to the lift.'

Charlie got out of the lift at the thirteenth floor and pressed the doorbell.

'Who's there?' a gruff voice barked through the intercom.

'Police, Mr McFadyen. DCI Anderson, Glasgow CID. I'd like a word with you, if you don't mind.'

There was a pause. 'Show us your badge. Hold it up to the spy hole.' Charlie took out his warrant card and held it against the door. 'Not that close. I canny see it right.' Charlie stepped back a pace and held it up again. 'Are you on your own?' McFadyen demanded.

'Yes.'

There was a further delay before Charlie heard bolts being withdrawn and locks being turned. A small, wiry figure in his sixties appeared in the doorway. He was going thin on top and wore heavy black-framed spectacles. His dressing gown and bedroom slippers looked to be several sizes too big for him.

'What do you want?'

'I'd like to ask you a few questions about your neighbours.'

'I've already had your lot nosin' around asking all kinds of damn fool questions.'

'I won't keep you long.'

McFadyen eyed Charlie up and down. 'You'd better come in,' he said grudgingly. 'Mind and wipe your feet.' Charlie wiped his feet very deliberately on the doormat before stepping across the threshold. McFadyen locked and bolted the door behind them before leading the way to the lounge, which was cluttered with furniture of every conceivable shape and size. It reminded Charlie of Steptoe's junkyard. 'I won't offer you a seat because you won't be stoppin'.'

Charlie produced his notebook. 'How well do you know your neighbours, Mr McFadyen? In particular, the Gibsons on the fifteenth floor?'

McFadyen snorted. 'I don't have any truck with the neighbours. I keep myself to myself and mind my own business.'

'I'm sure you do. However, could you tell me if you've seen either Mr or Mrs Gibson during the past fortnight?'

'Gibsons, you say? Fifteenth floor? Is that their name? Wouldn't know them from Adam. Doubt if I've clapped eyes on them in my life. If you want to know anythin' about the neighbours, you should ask the caretaker. He's a nosy wee bachle.'

'Do you know the Leslies on the second floor?'

'The only ones I even know exist are those noisy buggers upstairs. If they ever make a racket like that again, you'll be hearin' from me, an' no mistake. I'll be filin' a complaint.'

Charlie's fingers slackened on his pencil. He couldn't control the surprise in his voice. 'Who on earth are you talking about?'

'I don't know what they're called. You'd have to ask the caretaker. All I know is that they had one hell of a barney one night last week. Whit a shirrackin'. Both of them at it. Right above my bedroom it was too. It sounded like he was giein' her laldy. He was shouting the odds and she was screamin' blue murder – while I was trying to have a kip. I'm tellin' you, I'm no' goany stand for it. Any more of that nonsense and I want your lot round here smartish to sort them out. I paid a bloody fortune for this place and I'm no' gauny have my peace and quiet ruined by those yobs.'

'Do you remember which night this was?'

'I'm no' sure. Tuesday or Wednesday, I think.'

'Had you heard any noise from upstairs previously?'

'Only when they flitted in two or three weeks ago. Not a lot of noise then. Just furniture being shoved around – that kind of thing.'

'And after the shouting and screaming last Tuesday or Wednesday – have you heard anything since?' McFadyen shook his head. 'Did you mention this to the police officer who came to take your statement?'

'No. Why should I?'

'Did he not ask you about it?'

'He asked me if I'd seen or heard anything suspicious. Rowdy neighbours are a bloody nuisance, but hardly what you would call 'suspicious'.'

Charlie put away his notebook. 'I think that's all for now, Mr McFadyen. Thanks for your time.'

'Before you go, leave me your phone number. I'm goany call you if I get any more trouble from that lot. I want your personal number, mind. I don't want to get fobbed off with some spotty-faced kid hardly out o' short breeks.'

Charlie handed across his card. 'That'll get you straight through to my office.'

'Right. Thanks,' he said, thrusting the card deep into his dressing gown pocket. Charlie stood back while McFadyen undid the locks and bolts on the front door. The lift was still at the thirteenth floor. He descended to ground level and pressed Harry's door bell.

'Any joy, Inspector? Did auld misery-guts let you in?'

'Why didn't you tell me someone had moved into number 14, Harry?'

'Number 14? That's rubbish. There's nobody in number 14. Nobody's even looked round that flat since I've been here.'

'Old misery-guts swears blind that someone moved in two or three weeks ago and that there was a barney in the flat last Tuesday or Wednesday. He's threatening to have them done for breach of the peace. You said you've got keys for all the flats?'

'Yes.'

'Get the key for number 14. You and I are going up to have a look around.'

Harry bustled to his wall safe, dialled the combination and took out the key for flat 14. He tapped in the security code at the connecting door and they rode up in the lift to the fourteenth floor. When Harry inserted the key into the lock, he started to frown.

'Something's no' right here.'

'What's wrong?

'The key won't turn.'

'Is it stiff? Let me try.'

'It's no' stiff. These locks are never stiff. The key's just no' turnin'.'

'Then you must've picked up the wrong key. Go back down and get the right one.'

Harry shook his head. 'I never make a mistake with keys,' he protested. 'When I was the janitor at the school I had lots of keys to look after and I never misplaced one in my life. I'm tellin' you, I took this key from hook 14.'

Charlie was getting fractious. It showed in his voice. 'Harry, is that, or is that not, the key for this apartment?'

Harry was flustered. 'It must be. I checked the keys the day I started. They all worked perfectly. I've no idea what could've happened. Ah!' Harry snapped his fingers. 'The serial number! I've got a list of the serial numbers of all the keys and the corresponding apartment numbers. I can soon find out if this is the right key or not.'

When they arrived at the ground floor, Harry unlocked his front door and hurried to his desk. He pulled out a single sheet of paper and ran his finger down the column, stopping when he reached flat 14. He screwed up his eyes to read the serial number on the key. 'It's the wrong key, Inspector. In fact,' he said, referring back to the serial number list. 'This is a key for flat 15.'

'Then you've mixed the keys up, man. You've put the key for flat 15 on hook 14 and vice versa.'

'That's not possible. I use the key on hook 15 every day to go up and feed the Gibsons' cat.' Harry opened up his wall safe and took the key from hook 15 to study the serial number. 'This is also a key for flat 15. I've got two keys for flat 15, but none for flat 14.'

Charlie shook his head in frustration. 'You said all the keys worked perfectly when you first arrived. Are you sure you opened up flat 14?'

'Definitely. There's no doubt about that.'

Five minutes later Harry had painstakingly checked off all the keys in his safe against the list of serial numbers. Everything else matched. He confirmed he had two keys for flat 15, but none for flat 14.

'I want to get into flat 14 – pronto. How can we get another key?'

'I'd have to get in touch with the estate agency.'

'Which one is it?'

'Viewpark. Their office is in Hope Street. That's where Mr Chalmers works.'

'You have his number?'

'I've got his office number. But he'll not be there on a Sunday.

I have his mobile as well, but I've been told to use that only in an emergency.'

'Give me his number,' Charlie said, pulling out his phone.

Jason Chalmers answered the call.

'Sorry to disturb you on a Sunday morning, Mr Chalmers. This is DCI Anderson, Glasgow CID. I'm calling from Dalgleish Tower – from the caretaker's flat. I want to have a look round flat 14, but for some reason the key seems to be missing. I believe you have a spare set?'

'In the office, yes. But it's not convenient right now. I'm just about to set off for the golf club. Can't it wait until tomorrow?'

'No, it can't.'

'Could Kennedy not show you round one of the other flats? Apart from the view, they're all identical.'

'Mr Chalmers, I think we may be at cross purposes. I'm not thinking of buying a flat. I'm conducting an investigation and I specifically need to get into flat 14.'

'This really is terribly inconvenient,' he said stiffly.

'I don't have time to debate this with you. I'll have someone meet you at your Hope Street office in fifteen minutes to collect the key. And if you're not there, I'll arrange to have flat 14 opened. And it will not be subtle. We'll blow the door off its fucking hinges.' Charlie snapped his phone shut. 'I think I might have upset your boss, Harry.'

Charlie called O'Sullivan's mobile. 'Urgent job for you, Tony. Go across to the Viewpark Estate Agency in Hope Street straight away. A bloke called Chalmers will meet you there in fifteen minutes and give you a key. Bring it to me at Dalgleish Tower. I'll be with the caretaker.'

Charlie sat down on Harry's sofa. 'Let's try to unravel this mystery. You definitely had a key for flat 14, but now it's missing – and in its place is a key for flat 15. Right?' Harry nodded. 'Has anyone ever tried to borrow the key for flat 14?'

'No. Anyway, I'm not allowed to lend out keys.'

'Then someone nicked it.'

Harry shook his head. 'That's not possible. I keep that safe locked at all times. No one else knows the combination.'

'Has anyone ever been in here while the safe was open?'

Harry furrowed his brow. 'Anyone in here when the safe was open?' he repeated the question as he tugged hard at his moustache. 'I opened the safe to get a key out when Mr and Mrs Moore came to look round number 10, but they hardly crossed my threshold. Mrs Gibson left her key at her bridge club one day and I opened up the safe to get her spare key to let her into her flat,' he added. 'I can't think of any other time.'

'Mrs Gibson? Think very carefully now, Harry. Did you leave Mrs Gibson alone in here while the safe was open – even for a short time? Could she have switched keys while your back was turned?'

Harry sucked hard on his bottom lip. 'I remember she had a headache. She asked me for a glass of water so she could take a pill.'

'When you went to get the water, was the safe open or closed?'

Harry sucked even harder on his lip, then shook his head. 'I honestly can't remember.'

Charlie paced up and down outside the building while waiting impatiently for O'Sullivan to arrive. He ran down the steps when he saw his car approaching. 'Have you got it?' he shouted. O'Sullivan waved the key out of the window as he pulled up. 'Come upstairs with us, Tony. I've no idea what we're going to find, but it could prove interesting.'

'I must say,' O'Sullivan said as they were riding up in the lift. 'You seem to have upset Mr Chalmers. He said you swore at him. He told me to let you know that he's playing golf with Niggle today and he's going to report your behaviour.' O'Sullivan could barely conceal his grin.

'Sod Chalmers. If I get any snash out of him,' Charlie growled, 'I'll stick his putter where it hurts most.'

Harry took the key from O'Sullivan and unlocked the door to flat 14. The three of them stepped inside. The hall was empty. All the rooms were empty. 'I told you McFadyen was a nutter,' Harry stated with obvious satisfaction. 'Nobody's moved in here.'

Charlie led the way to the main bedroom. Noticing a slight scratch on the parquet flooring, he dropped to his knees. He saw a few more small indentations. 'I reckon there's been furniture in here recently, Tony. Check out the rest of the apartment.'

O'Sullivan found a scratch on the floor in the hall. Apart from that, nothing. 'What do you reckon?' he asked.

'This bedroom and the hall have been furnished and now they're empty. I reckon we're standing in the room where Anne Gibson was murdered.'

TWENTY-SEVEN

Not wanting to switch on his mobile in case it was being traced, Michael Gibson went into a telephone booth in Dumbarton Road to call McGurk. He recognised Bernie's voice. 'Do you have anything for me?'

'Good mornin', Mr Gibson. I think I may be able to help you. I believe the punter you're looking for is stayin' in Turnberry Road. Do you know where that is?'

'Off Hyndland Road? Near Clarence Drive?'

'That's the one. Your friend's dossin' down at Larry Robertson's place. He's got one of those swanky detached houses near the top of the street, not far from the junction with Hyndland Road. But you wouldn't be wantin' to go near the place. There are CCTV cameras everywhere.

'However, tomorrow mornin' at ten o'clock your man is goin' to meet some of his pals in a flat in Great Western Road. It's less than a mile from where he's stayin' an' it's odds-on he'll walk. He likes walkin' – and I'm told the weather forecast for tomorrow is good.' McGurk chuckled. 'Which means you could probably bump into him in Hyndland Road sometime between half-past nine and ten o'clock, if that suits your purpose?'

'Thanks, Bernie. I'll send an envelope across as soon as I can.'

'Thanks very much, Mr Gibson.'

When Charlie got back to the office there was an urgent message waiting for him, asking him to call Sheila Thompson

'Miss Thompson? This is Inspector Anderson. I believe you were trying to get in touch with me?'

'It's about Michael Gibson, Inspector. I saw him yesterday.' Sheila sounded extremely agitated. 'He came round here,' she blurted out, omitting to mention that he had been in the flat during Anderson's visit.

'Do you know where he is now?'

'No. But I'm worried about him. He's gone looking for Jack McFarlane – he says he's going to kill him.'

'Jesus Christ!'

'You've got to find him before he gets to McFarlane, Inspector. He's been drinking. He needs help.'

Philippa Scott pulled two heavy bags of groceries from the boot of her car. Sunday shopping suited her because by the time she got out of the office on weekdays, she never felt like going to a supermarket. She was slightly out of breath by the time she'd climbed to the third floor landing. She dropped her groceries onto the doormat and fumbled in her bag for her key to unlock the door.

'I'll get those.' The voice from behind startled her and when she spun round she saw Michael Gibson sweep up the groceries and carry them ahead of her into the apartment.

'Michael! What are you doing here?'

'Where do you want these?' he said, ignoring her consternation. 'In the kitchen, I suppose.' He walked down the hall and dumped the bags on the kitchen table.

'You're crazy! You shouldn't have come here. The police have been round looking for you, questioning me about you and Anne. For all I know they might be watching the building.'

'They are. There's in an unmarked car out front. I spotted it. I climbed over the wall and came across the back court. I was worried for a minute that the entry code for the back door might've been changed, but it hasn't.'

‘Why have you come here?’

‘I had to see you. I had to find out why you’ve been avoiding me. Why didn’t you return any of my calls or answer my texts? You don’t know how much I’ve missed you, Pippa.’ He put his arms around her and pulled her close, running his fingers through her long hair. She didn’t respond, her body remaining rigid, her arms by her side.

‘It’s no use,’ she said steadily. ‘It’s too late for this. In any case, I’m seeing someone else.’

Michael released her from his grip and took a step back, his face turning scarlet, his eyes rolling in their sockets. He felt the room start to spin. He made a grab for her arm to steady himself, but his legs crumpled beneath him and he crashed to the floor in a dead faint.

When Michael came round, he was lying on his back on the kitchen floor with a pillow propped beneath his head. Philippa, kneeling by his side, was dabbing at his burning forehead with a damp sponge. ‘What happened? Where am I?’

‘You fainted. You’re on my kitchen floor. I couldn’t lift you.’

‘How long have I been out?’ He tried to sit up but felt nauseous as soon as his head left the pillow. He sank back down.

‘Only a few minutes. Lie still. Don’t try to move. I’ll call a doctor.’

He grabbed her by the arm. ‘No doctor. I’ll be all right. I only need to rest for a while. And don’t call the police either,’ he implored. ‘Trust me. I just need twenty-four hours.’

Philippa continued to dab at his forehead with the sponge. ‘This cut looks septic – there’s dirt and gravel in the wound. And you’re shivering. I’ll fetch a blanket.’

Michael closed his eyes to try to stop the room spinning.

Philippa fetched a woollen blanket and draped it over him, tucking it in at the sides. She cleaned out the weeping wound with surgical spirit and dressed it. His shivering got worse.

'You shouldn't be lying on cold linoleum. I can't lift you. Do you think you could make it as far as the bedroom?'

Michael raised his head tentatively from the pillow. The worst of the nausea seemed to have passed. 'I'll try.' He pulled himself to his feet, steadying himself against the kitchen table. Philippa supported him by the arm as she led him to the bedroom. He was sweating profusely. He lay down on the bed and she pulled the duvet over him. 'You've got a fever. Why won't you let me call a doctor?'

'I just need to rest,' he insisted.

'When was the last time you had something to eat?'

'I don't remember.' His eyelids fluttered briefly, then closed as he sank into a troubled sleep.

Charlie summoned O'Sullivan and Renton to his office.

'Forensics told me I'd have the results from flat 14 within thirty minutes,' Charlie complained to O'Sullivan when he arrived. 'That was an hour ago. What the hell's keeping them? We might as well start to – ' Eddie McLaughlin's rap on the office door interrupted Charlie's flow. 'What have you got for us, Eddie?' he demanded.

'The scratches in the parquet flooring in the bedroom and the hall are consistent with furniture having been there recently. There are small holes in the bedroom wall that look as if they were made by picture hooks and there were some minute stains on the floor in which we found traces of vomit and blood.'

'Anne Gibson's blood?'

'A mixture. Anne Gibson's blood – and sheep's blood.'

'For Christ's sake, Eddie. What the hell's been going on?'

Charlie phoned home. 'I'm not going to make it back for lunch, Kay. There have been developments.'

'I'll see you when I see you.' There was resignation in Kay's voice.

Charlie pulled the flipchart stand to the middle of the office and picked up a blue marker pen. 'Right, boys. Let's take it from the top and sort out what we've got.' He started writing on the flipchart:

FACTS

- **Anne Gibson was the only person who had the opportunity to steal the key for flat 14 from Harry Kennedy's wall safe.**
- **She almost certainly faked her suicide in flat 14 on Wednesday 9th March. Motive unknown.**
- **She hid out at her parents' house from 10th to 15th March.**
- **She was murdered in flat 14 on Tuesday 15th March (traces of her blood, and sheep's blood, were found on the floor).**

Charlie put down his marker pen and stepped back from the board. 'Let's assume, for the sake of argument, that Michael Gibson didn't murder his wife. In that case, he got out of the lift on the fourteenth floor on the evening of March 15th and found her dead body.'

'Why would he get out at the fourteenth floor?' O'Sullivan asked. 'That doesn't make any sense.'

'He thought he was on the fifteenth floor?' Renton suggested.

'You mean he pressed the wrong button in the lift?' O'Sullivan said.

'That's so improbable it's not even worth considering,' Charlie chipped in.

'Then what could have happened?' Renton insisted.

Charlie scratched at his bald head as he paced up and down the room. 'The only conceivable way that could've happened is if the lift had been tampered with to make it stop at floor 14 when Gibson pressed the button for floor 15.'

'Is that possible?' O'Sullivan asked.

'I haven't the remotest idea. But nothing else fits, so let's give it a whirl.'

Charlie called Harry Kennedy. 'Harry, what are you supposed to do if something goes wrong with the lift?'

'There's a maintenance contract with the firm that installed it. If the lift breaks down, I phone them and they guarantee to have an engineer here within an hour.'

'Call them right now and report a breakdown. I'll be there to meet the engineer.'

Charlie turned back to the flipchart board. 'What the hell's this sheep's blood nonsense all about?'

'If we rule out satanic rites and bestiality for the moment,' Renton said, 'we can only assume the murderer took a container of sheep's blood up to the flat for some reason.'

'To pour over the corpse? To make the murder look as gory as possible?' O'Sullivan suggested.

'Seems really weird,' Renton said, shaking his head.

'Worth checking out,' Charlie said. 'If the murderer wanted to get his hands on sheep's blood, for whatever perverted reason, I assume he'd go to an abattoir or a butcher's – unless he gets his kicks by wandering into fields and slitting sheep's throats. Check out everywhere you can think of, Colin. Ask around if anyone has tried to get their hands on animal blood recently. Tony, you come with me to Dalgleish Tower.'

Tom Simpson was not at all pleased when he discovered there was nothing wrong with the lift. 'I was in the middle of my dinner,' he complained bitterly to Harry. 'That phone number's only supposed to be used for an emergency breakdown.'

'No point in shoutin' the odds at me, pal. I was just doing' what I was telt. The cops'll be here in a minute. You can moan all you like at them.'

'Don't worry. I will.'

When Anderson and O'Sullivan arrived at Dalgleish Tower, Simpson was waiting outside the building to confront them. 'What's this all about?' he demanded. 'I get called out in the middle of my dinner, only to find the lift's working perfectly. I'm going to report this to Mr Chalmers.'

Charlie adopted a conciliatory tone. 'I'm very sorry about that, Mr… Mr…?'

'Simpson. Tom Simpson.'

'Don't blame Mr Kennedy. It was entirely my fault. However, this isn't a false alarm. I had to get you here. I'm conducting a murder investigation and I need your expertise.'

'Well… if it's really that important… I suppose…'

'It is. Your knowledge could be the vital factor in solving a murder.' Putting his arm around Simpson's shoulder, Charlie led him up the steps and into the building. When they reached the internal door, Simpson tapped in a code.

'How did you do that?' Harry demanded, scuttling across. 'How did you know the code? I didn't give it to you.'

'Whenever one of our lifts is installed, we're given a master code that works on all the secure doors in the building. We need that in case there's an emergency and there's no one around who knows the code the user has assigned.'

'Nobody telt me about that,' Harry grumbled.

'This lift looks like a pretty complicated bit of equipment,' Charlie said, stroking Simpson's ego. 'There can't be many people who understand how it works.'

'It's the latest technology.'

'Tell me, suppose you wanted to make the lift stop at a different floor from the one indicated on the buttons. Would that be possible? For example, if you wanted to make the lift stop at floor 14 when you pressed button 15. Could that be done?'

Simpson furrowed his brow. 'That wouldn't be too difficult. When you press a button, it transmits a signal to the lift motor via a printed circuit card that sits behind the control panel in the lift. If you wanted to make the lift stop at a different floor, you would just have to cross the wires on the circuit board. Piece of piss for someone who knew what they were doing.'

'Show me how you'd go about it.'

Simpson summoned the lift and stepped inside, flicking the

switch to hold the doors open. He took a screwdriver from his bag and undid the retaining screws that held the control panel in place. Having eased the panel away from the wall, he unclipped the circuit board and lifted it out. 'This is what controls the movement of the lift,' he explained, showing the printed circuit to Charlie. 'If you wanted to change the floor all you would have to do would be – Hey!' Simpson broke off as he examined the card. 'Someone has been buggering about with this.'

'What is it?'

'Look at the card. Somebody's tampered with it.' Simpson studied the board carefully. 'The connection from button 15 has been cut and an extra wire, with a clip on the end, has been soldered on in its place. It's a neat bit of work.' He nodded admiringly. 'Right now, the clip's connected normally. But by moving this clip to a different position on the card, you could make the lift stop at any floor you wanted when somebody pressed button 15. Let me show you.' He switched the clip to position 3 on the circuit board and replaced the card in the control panel, then released the switch that held open the doors. 'Press number 15.' Charlie pressed the button and the lift started to climb. When the indicator panel showed they had arrived at the fifteenth floor, the lift doors slid open and Charlie gazed out at the number '3' on the apartment door opposite.

He whistled softly. 'As simple as that, eh?' Simpson took the lift back to the ground floor, removed the circuit board and reconnected the wire to the correct position before screwing the panel back in place. 'Mr Simpson, I can't thank you enough.' Charlie pumped his hand enthusiastically. 'You've been of great assistance. Once again, please accept my apologies for dragging you away from your lunch, but we could never have got to the bottom of this without your help. I'll make sure Mr Chalmers gets to hear how cooperative you've been.'

'Glad to have been of assistance. Anyway – getting dragged away from my dinner wasn't that much of a hardship,' he confided. 'The wife's mother was there.'

Charlie and Tony O'Sullivan drove back in convoy to Pitt Street. As usual on a Sunday afternoon, the city centre roads were quiet. When he got to his office, Charlie pulled off his jacket, rolled up his shirt sleeves and went back to the flipchart board. 'Now we're getting somewhere, Tony. Find Renton and tell him to join us. Let's see where this leads us.'

As Renton entered the office, Charlie was adding to his list of 'facts' on the flipchart:

- **The lift in Dalgleish Tower was tampered with by person or persons unknown.**

'Before we go on,' Renton said. 'The red Ferrari belongs to a bloke called Jonathan Sharp – he's a partner in Colesell and Sharp – the law firm where Philippa Scott works now.'

'A partner? Interesting. First Gibson and now Sharp. Our Miss Scott doesn't mess about with hoi polloi.' Charlie turned back to study his flipchart. 'Some bits of the jigsaw are beginning to fall into place, but there are still a lot of unanswered questions.

'Let's start with Anne Gibson's fake suicide on 9th March. She steals the key for flat 14 from Kennedy's safe. Harry can't remember the date precisely, but it was sometime early in March. She sends Harry to the kitchen to fetch a glass of water and while he's out of the room she swaps her own door key with the one for flat 14. Harry's not likely to notice the switch. He's got no reason to try to use the key for flat 14 and, superficially, all the keys look the same.

'The next step is to furnish the hall and the master bedroom in flat 14 so they look identical to number 15. That's no easy matter in itself. There can't be many suppliers of that type of furniture in Glasgow – and they can't get too many orders for Charles Rennie Mackintosh reproduction bedroom suites. Get onto that first thing in the morning, Tony. Find out who supplies the stuff and what orders they've taken in the past few weeks.

'The next problem is to work out how she got the furniture into the building. Kennedy never said anything about a furniture van making a delivery to Dalgleish Tower, but check with him in case it slipped his mind.

'The more you delve into this, the more you realise how well this fake suicide was planned – though I still don't understand her motive. The apartment door being wide open when Gibson got out of the lift was beautiful. It would instantly engender a sense of panic, which may have been part of the plan. And, of course, it was necessary to have the front door open because Gibson's key wouldn't have unlocked it.

'And the phone line being dead. Effective – and yet so simple. Again, it adds to the tension and all she needed to do was get a handset that had never been connected. That's something else to check out, Tony. Get in touch with the telephone company and find out if the line to flat 15 was out of order at any time on either the 9th or the 15th of March. I'm prepared to bet it wasn't.'

'What about his mobile?' Renton asked. 'Why was that not working?'

'Maybe his wife managed to jam the signal to their flat,' O'Sullivan offered. 'You can buy gadgets that will do that.'

'Can mobile phone companies tell if their signal was jammed at a particular location at a particular time?' Charlie asked.

'I've no idea,' O'Sullivan said.

'Talk to his service provider and see if they can give us anything on that,' Charlie said. 'I remember Gibson telling Doctor McCartney,' Charlie added, 'that when he found his wife's body, the bedroom curtains were drawn. Another important detail. Even a slight change in the angle of the view might have registered in Gibson's subconscious. And what about the cat? That was a master stroke. Anne took her cat downstairs with her. He'd be unsettled. No matter how similar flat 14 looked, the smells would be wrong. The cat would know this wasn't his house, so he'd complain loud and long. Another way to build up tension for Gibson.'

'Wasn't she taking a bit of a risk?' interjected O'Sullivan. 'What if Gibson had gone to one of the other rooms in the flat and found it empty?'

'In that case, the scam would've been blown sky-high,' Renton said. 'But when you think about it, how likely was that? When you find what you think is a dead body, the instinctive reaction is to grab the phone and dial '999'. If the phone doesn't work, I think most people would react as Gibson did – run out of the apartment and try to get help.'

Charlie shook his head. 'That's too much of a gamble. Gibson might well have gone to another room – the lounge, perhaps, to try to phone from there, or even to get a drink.'

'So do you think she had a contingency plan to deal with that possibility?'

'Probably. But we'll come back to that later. For now, let's stick with what did happen. Gibson runs out of the flat and as soon as he's gone, all she has to do is pop the cat back upstairs and rewire the lift to its correct setting. In fact, she might well have been still hiding in flat 14 when I returned to Dalgleish Tower with Gibson. She might even have spent the night there. The next morning, she takes the train to Aberdeen and does her disappearing trick. But what's her motive, boys?' Charlie mused. 'What the hell was she trying to achieve with all this palaver?'

'Let's consider what she did achieve,' O'Sullivan said. 'She caused her husband to start doubting his sanity – though it's not immediately apparent what she stood to gain from that. Something's just struck me,' he added with a glint in his eye. 'Let's move on to March 15th – the day she came back down from Aberdeen – the day she was murdered.'

'Yes?'

'Let's suppose her objective *was* to make her husband flip his lid. What would be the next step? To make him go through the nightmare again. To make him believe he was hallucinating. But not exactly the same scenario. If she replayed the suicide routine, he might well react differently. He might try to revive her or, as you said, he might go to the lounge to try to phone from there, or get a drink, or whatever. No, this time it would have to be more dramatic. This time, she would act out a violent murder – and if you're going to enact a gory murder, you'd want to get your hands on some blood, wouldn't you? Maybe sheep's blood?'

'I like it!' Charlie clapped his hands enthusiastically. 'You're on to something. Keep going.'

'She sets up a murder scene. The same rigmarole with the lift and the cat and all that. Then she pours sheep's blood over herself. But here's the twist. Something goes horribly wrong. Gibson somehow rumbles the con and decides to give it to her for real. He ties her to the bed, gets his razor and slashes her throat to pieces. He throws up when he realises what he's done, then he runs off to tell you he's found his wife's corpse. What do you think of that?'

Charlie scratched at his chin. 'Ten out of ten for ingenuity. But too many holes. For a start – who reset the lift before I got to Dalgleish Tower? Who took the cat back upstairs? Who removed the corpse, disposed of the furniture and tidied up the flat?'

O'Sullivan shrugged. 'Over to you, sir.' He winked at Renton. 'Give us your theory.'

'Try this one on for size,' Charlie said. 'Anne Gibson is indeed planning to act out a murder scenario. But she has an accomplice. His job – assuming for the moment the accomplice is male – is to hide in the lounge and invoke the back-up plan, whatever that might happen to be, if Gibson tries to go to any other room in the flat. But before Gibson arrives, Anne and the accomplice fall out over something – I don't know what. He ties her to the bed, slits her throat for real, then pours the sheep's blood over her for good measure and leaves the body for Gibson to find. When Gibson runs off, he takes the cat upstairs and re-programmes the lift before I get there. Later, when the coast's clear, he ships her body out to the Gleniffer Braes, cleans up flat 14 and disposes of the furniture.'

O'Sullivan nodded in admiration. 'Not bad, sir. Not bad at all. And who do you have marked down as the accomplice?'

'I haven't a clue.'

'I sniff a boyfriend in the frame,' Renton offered knowingly.

'That's not impossible,' Charlie conceded.

'Don't forget one thing,' O'Sullivan said. 'Jack McFarlane got out of a taxi at Dalgleish Tower around six o'clock that evening.'

Charlie groaned and threw up his hands. 'Jack McFarlane, the demon lover. In the name of the wee man! Give me a break, lads. Give me a fucking break!'

TWENTY-EIGHT

Monday 21 March

Michael Gibson was wakened by the sun's rays piercing his closed eyelids. He blinked several times as he slowly regained consciousness. His gaze travelled round the room, but he didn't recognise his surroundings. He felt his heartbeat quicken. Everything was blurred. When he tried to sit up in bed, the room began to spin. He immediately lay back down, breathing heavily. He rested for a few moments before raising his head gingerly from the pillow. The room was no longer going round, though he still felt queasy. As his eyes came into focus, he realised it wasn't the first time he'd seen that pink, floral wallpaper. The leather bench seat in front of the dressing table was also familiar. It slowly dawned on him that he was in Philippa's bedroom – in her bed. It looked totally different in the early morning sunshine. He'd only ever been here in the afternoons.

'Pippa!' His shout caused a sharp stab behind his eyes. He waited for the pain to subside before calling out again. 'Are you there, Pippa?' There was no reply. He eased his legs over the side of the bed. He was still fully dressed. He walked unsteadily through to the kitchen where he saw a sheet of paper propped up against a packet of cereal in the middle of the table. He unfolded the note.

> *'I had to go to work. I decided to leave you to sleep for as long as possible. When you get up, make sure you have something to eat. There's cereal on the table. You'll find eggs, orange juice, milk, butter, etc in the fridge and there's a loaf in the bread-bin. I'll come home at lunchtime to see how you are. Pippa.'*

Michael crumpled the paper in his fist and dropped it onto the floor.He opened the fridge and poured himself a glass of orange juice, sitting down at the kitchen table while he sipped at the cold liquid. The taste felt bitter on his tongue. As he pushed the glass to one side his eye caught the time on the kitchen clock. 'Half-past nine!' he exclaimed, scrambling to his feet.

He took the tenement stairs two at time, staggering to a halt on the bottom landing when he remembered the police car in the street outside. He raced out the back entrance and stumbled across the courtyard. He scrambled over the wall. He was confused and disoriented. He didn't know in what direction he was running. He pounded along the pavement as fast as he could, head down, rocking unsteadily from side to side. When he rounded a corner he saw the brake lights of a taxi pulling up at a set of traffic lights. He ran into the middle of the road and waved his arms up and down, yelling at the top of his voice until the pain in his skull became unbearable.

When the lights changed, the taxi made a tight U-turn and drove back towards him. 'Where to, mate?' the driver asked, leaning back to fling open the rear door.

'Junction of Great Western Road and Hyndland Road – as fast as you can.' As the taxi sped off Michael checked his watch. Almost twenty to ten. Was he going to be in time? He fumbled anxiously in his jacket pocket, seeking the reassuring feel of the pistol. He stroked the smooth, cold barrel as he struggled to make some kind of plan. McFarlane would be walking along Hyndland Road towards Great Western Road. Should he wait at the corner for him? Not a good spot – busy traffic lights – too many witnesses. Better to head back up Hyndland Road and meet him as he came towards him. It would have been so much better if he could have hidden near the squash club, as he'd planned. That stretch of the road was much quieter. But it was too late for that now. He'd have to gun him down in the middle of the street.

The traffic was dense as the taxi crossed the city centre. When they pulled up at the traffic lights opposite the Botanic Gardens,

Michael sat forward on the edge of his seat, willing the lights to change. It seemed an eternity before they flicked through amber to green. Only a couple of hundred yards to go. He glanced at his watch. Five to ten. Had McFarlane passed by already? He threw open the taxi door before the cab had come to a complete halt. As he scrambled out he thrust a ten-pound note through the driver's open window.

'Keep the change.'

'Thanks, pal.'

He stared along Hyndland Road, scanning both sides of the pavement for any sign of McFarlane. There was a stream of traffic coming towards him. As the cars whipped past, the sun reflected off their windscreens into his eyes – a succession of blinding flashes. He cupped his hands over his eyes to try to shield them. He could make out two women walking towards him on the far pavement, about fifty yards away. They were pushing a pram. There were no other pedestrians in sight. Was he too late? Had McFarlane decided to drive rather than walk? Had McGurk's information been wrong?

He cursed and kicked at the base of the traffic lights. Tears of frustration welled in his eyes and ran down his cheeks. He leaned back against a lamp post, closed his eyes and breathed in and out slowly, attempting to slow his racing heartbeat while trying to figure out what to do. Would McFarlane come back this way later on? If so, at what time? Should he wait for him?

When he opened his eyes again, his heart skipped a beat. He saw a figure, wearing a black anorak, hurrying along the pavement on the other side of the road. Could this be him? He'd just overtaken the two women with the pram. He tried to make out the man's features, but the sun was hurting his eyes – he couldn't focus. He stumbled off the kerb and dodged between the moving cars as he lurched across the road. Tyres screeched. Horns blared. When he reached the far pavement he steadied himself, slipping his hand into his jacket pocket and releasing the safety catch. His fingers tightened round the butt of the pistol. If it was McFarlane, he was late for his meeting, so he'd be hurrying. The dizziness returned. The sun's rays were reflecting off car windscreens as they sped past – successive flashes of dazzling light stinging his eyes – like running alongside railings. He held his left arm up in front of his face to shield his vision as he tried desperately to make out the features of the person hurrying towards him.

He hesitated – doubt and confusion filling his brain. His fingers slackened on the gun butt. Had he made a mistake? He didn't recognise the shaved head. Then he saw it – the unmistakable jagged scar that had haunted his dreams for the past twelve years. He tried desperately to lick some moisture into his swollen lips. How he'd waited for this moment. He'd only get one shot. He mustn't miss. Wait until he gets right up to you, he told himself.

McFarlane was twenty yards away and closing fast. Michael's heart was thumping against his ribcage – his head spinning. He could see the piercing, cold, blue eyes. For once, they weren't locked onto his. Ten yards away. He clenched the pistol butt tightly and tugged the gun from his pocket. Five yards. Streaks of purple light filled his vision. The veins on the side of his neck bulged. His tongue seemed to be expanding and filling his mouth. He was choking. His heart felt as if it was about to explode inside his chest.

Michael Gibson keeled over and collapsed, face down, on the pavement.

Jack McFarlane threw a glance over his shoulder as he hurried past. He saw the tramp fall down in the street, but he didn't have time to stop. He was late for his meeting.

Tony O'Sullivan walked into Charlie's office just after ten o'clock. 'How are things?' he asked.

'As well as can be expected after spending the last half hour listening to Niggle rabbiting on. I thought he'd be pleased with the progress we'd made over the weekend, but he was more interested in tearing a strip off me because I swore at his golf partner.' Charlie shook his head in exasperation. 'What've you got?'

'I spoke to Harry Kennedy. There have definitely been no furniture deliveries to Dalgleish Tower in the past few weeks – and also the phone company confirmed there were no problems with the Gibsons' phone line on either of the dates in question.'

'As expected.'

'With regard to the furniture, there appear to be only two suppliers of that make of Charles Rennie Mackintosh reproductions in the Glasgow area.'

'And?'

'And one of them took an order, on the fourth of March, for a bed, a dressing table, two bedside tables, a Victorian reproduction hallstand and a grandfather clock.'

'Who placed the order?'

'Gordon Parker.'

'Who?'

'Parker. The bloke who was killed in Paul Gibson's flat.'

'Are you sure?'

'That was the name the secretary found in the order book. The salesman who took the order wasn't there when I phoned. He'll be in at half-past ten. I'm going across to talk to him. Do you want to come?'

Charlie was already pulling on his jacket before O'Sullivan had finished the question.

They parked in the large car park in front of the furniture showroom and as they entered the building a salesman walked across to greet them.

'Good morning, gentlemen. What can I interest you in today?' O'Sullivan flashed his I.D. 'Has Mr Churchill arrived? When I phoned earlier I was told he'd be in at half-past ten.'

'He's in the office. I'll let him know you're here.'

William Churchill came trotting down the stairs. He was in his fifties, a heavily-built, round-faced man wearing cord trousers and a loud-checked sports jacket. 'How can I help you, gentlemen?'

'Do you remember taking an order recently, Mr Churchill?'

O'Sullivan asked. 'On the fourth of March to be precise. For a bedroom suite of Charles Rennie Mackintosh reproduction furniture as well as a Victorian hallstand and a grandfather clock?'

'Indeed I do.'

'What can you tell me about the buyer?'

'A young lad. Early twenties, I would say. He had long hair, tied back in a ponytail, but quite well-spoken nevertheless.'

'Do you remember his name?'

'Not offhand. But if you come up to the office I'll pull out the file copy of the order.' Charlie and Tony followed him up the narrow stairs to the cluttered den that served as an office.

'Did he know what he wanted, or did he look around?' Charlie asked as Churchill was searching through his filing cabinet.

'He knew exactly what he wanted. It was the easiest sale I've ever made.' He smiled at the recollection. 'He had a list with a full description of everything he wanted to buy – dimensions, colours, etc. It was just a matter of flicking through the catalogue to find the items and filling out the order forms. He didn't even try to haggle over the price. I only wish I could make commission as easily as that every day.' Churchill pulled out an order book and thumbed through it. 'Fourth of March, you said? Here it is. Gordon Parker. That was his name.'

'How did he pay for it?' Tony asked.

'Slightly strange. There was a woman waiting outside in a black Volvo. She didn't put in an appearance until after we'd completed the paperwork, then she came in and paid for the lot by credit card.'

'Do you have her name?'

'It'll be in the file. Here it is. Anne Gibson.'

Charlie exchanged a glance with O'Sullivan. 'Where was the furniture delivered to?' O'Sullivan asked.

'Another strange one. We didn't deliver.'

'What do you mean?'

'For that size of order, we provide a free delivery service anywhere within a fifty mile radius. But Mr Parker didn't want that. The order arrived on the seventh of March, that was a Monday, and he asked us to hold it here, saying he would collect it, as he did, bit by bit, over the following couple of days. This type of furniture is shipped to us from the manufacturer in kits and normally we would assemble it for the customer before we deliver. However, Mr Parker specifically asked us to give it to him in kit form because he wanted to assemble it himself.'

'Did you see how he collected it?'

'Of course. I helped him load it into his van. He had a Ford transit with a logo painted on the side.'

'Which was?'

'Something to do with a band, I think. 'Popular Band'? 'People's Band'? Something like that.'

"Citizens Band'?'

'Yes, I think that was it.'

'The plot thickens,' Charlie said when they got back to their car. 'So Parker was aiding and abetting Anne Gibson. Kennedy told me the 'Citizens Band' van often used to turn up at Dalgleish Tower, but only when Michael Gibson was at work. Was it Paul Gibson visiting his mother? Or was it Gordon Parker delivering furniture? There would've been nothing to stop Mrs Gibson giving Parker the key to flat 14 and lending him her remote control so he could set up the bedroom for her 'suicide' and her 'murder'.'

'What was his angle?'

'Toy boy, perhaps? That was Renton's hunch.'

'Do you really think Mrs Gibson was the type to have a toy boy?'

'It's not impossible. Anyone capable of putting together this elaborate little scheme must've been a very dark horse indeed.'

'There's an urgent message, sir,' Pauline said when Charlie got back to Pitt Street. 'Colin Renton phoned it in.' She handed across the single sheet of paper.

'Monday 21st March – 11.00 am,' Charlie read, 'Michael Gibson collapsed in Hyndland Road an hour ago. An ambulance was called and took him to the Western. I'm going across there now. I'll wait with him until I hear from you. Colin Renton.'

Charlie handed the note to O'Sullivan. 'Gibson's in the Western and Renton's gone across there. Call him and find out if he's got any more information about what happened.'

Charlie had his feet up on his desk with his eyes closed, deep in thought, when O'Sullivan returned. His discreet cough caused Charlie's feet to slide off the desk and drop to the floor with a bang.

'Didn't mean to startle you, sir. I've spoken to Renton and to a Dr McCormick. There's no more information about what happened to Gibson, apart from the fact he was clutching a gun when he collapsed.'

'A gun?'

'He keeled over in Hyndland Road with a pistol clenched in his fist. A passer-by called an ambulance. Dr McCormick told me Gibson's condition is serious but stable, though he reckons he hasn't eaten for days – it seems he's been getting all his calories out of a whisky bottle. And before you ask,' O'Sullivan added. 'The doc said Gibson needs complete rest and can't be questioned for at least twenty-four hours.'

Charlie grimaced. 'So you can read my mind, now? Definitely time I was put out to pasture. Okay, nothing we can do on that front for the time being, but I want to be informed the minute the quacks will let me near him.'

'I'll see to it.'

'Before you go, Tony, sit down and help me think something through.' Charlie rocked back on his chair and swung his feet back up on the desk. 'While you were on the phone to the hospital, I was thinking about this Parker bloke. I was wondering how deeply he was in this with Anne Gibson. I mean, you don't get involved in clandestine furniture removals without having some idea about what's going on. Perhaps Parker was involved in staging the fake suicide and murder.'

'If he was in it to that extent, could he have been the accomplice? In fact, could he have killed her? You surmised that he might've been her toy boy. Did a lovers' tiff develop into an argument, causing him to switch from assisting with a fake murder to participating in a real one?'

'I suppose he then suffered from such pangs of remorse that he contrived to tie his own hands behind his back before somehow managing to slit his throat and swallowing the razor to conceal the suicide weapon?'

O'Sullivan shrugged. 'Give me your theory.'

'Let's assume Parker was the accomplice and that he was in the flat at the time of the murder. If he was hiding in one of the other rooms when the killer struck, he would know who murdered her… Michael Gibson? Jack McFarlane? Whoever. The killer somehow finds out that Parker had witnessed the murder, so he goes after him. Which raises the interesting possibility that Parker's murder might not have been a case of mistaken identity for Paul Gibson after all. Perhaps Parker was the killer's intended victim all along.'

'This gets weirder and weirder.'

Charlie dropped his feet to the floor. 'Where is Paul now?'

'Still in Traquair House, the clinic Dr McCartney took him to. I left instructions that I was to be informed if he tried to check himself out.'

'I think I'll mosey over there and have a word with him. Perhaps he can cast some light on the relationship between his mother and Parker.'

Bernie McGurk, perched on a high stool at the end of the bar, ordered another large whisky. He added a splash of water to his drink and returned to studying the form, underlining his selection for the one-thirty at Pontefract. He glanced up at the clock behind the bar and saw it was twenty-past one. Taking a betting-slip from his hip pocket, he filled in his selection and his stake, then threw back his drink and climbed down from the barstool.

'I'll be back in a wee while, Sammy,' he called to the barman. 'I'm off to the bookies. Do you want me to put on a bet for you?'

'No thanks, Bernie. I put my line on this morning.'

Whistling cheerfully, Bernie walked out of the pub, blinking to adjust his eyes to the spring sunshine as he shuffled down the road towards the bookies. He hadn't gone twenty yards when a white Rover pulled up at the kerb beside him, the rear-seat passenger getting out and standing in his way. Bernie muttered under his breath as he moved to dodge round him, but the man stepped across to block his path.

'Drinking at lunch-time, Bernie?' said a voice from behind, the voice of the man who had followed him out of the pub. 'Large whiskies, as well. I don't know how you manage to afford it. Have you come into some money recently?'

Bernie spun round. 'Who the hell are you? What do you want?'

'Someone would like a wee chat with you. In private. Get your arse into the car.'

'No!'

'I'm asking you nice this time, Bernie. I won't be asking nice again. Get your arse into the fuckin' car.'

'Goany gie's a break, pal.' Bernie looked round in panic, but before he could make any attempt to escape he was grabbed by the scruff of the neck and bundled into the back seat of the Rover, wedged tightly between the two men. As the car pulled away from the kerb, Bernie's hands were pinned behind his back and fastened with rope. 'What do you want with me,' he whimpered. 'I've no' done nothin'.'

A strip of tape was rammed across Bernie's mouth and a blindfold was tied round his eyes. He felt a sudden, sharp pain as something heavy crashed into the base of his skull.

TWENTY-NINE

Charlie Anderson arrived at the reception desk in Traquair House and asked to see Dr Glen. He was ushered into a plush office.

'Good afternoon, Inspector,' Mike Glen said. 'What can I do for you?'

'If it's possible, I'd like to have a word with Paul Gibson. I realise the lad's been hit with a lot in the past few days, but I do need to ask him some questions.'

'You can speak to him, as long as you realise he's still in traumatic shock. He's on very heavy tranquillisers and he's going to find it difficult to talk about the murders.'

'I'll be as gentle – and as quick, as I can.'

Charlie was shown into a spacious lounge where Paul was sitting in front of a computer screen. He was pale and drawn. Charlie couldn't help noticing how thin he looked. He was playing a game that involved twisting and guiding bricks cascading down from the top of the screen into gaps in a wall. Charlie had seen the game before but it was years since he'd seen anyone play it. He couldn't remember what it was called. Paul was so engrossed in the spinning shapes that he didn't hear Charlie come in. Without interrupting him, Charlie sat on the chair beside the door and watched. As the bricks fell faster and faster, Paul's fingers danced around the keyboard, his body arching in the direction he was willing the bricks to twist. He eventually lost control and the screen rapidly filled up with jagged shapes.

'Hello, Paul.'

Paul turned round with a start. 'I didn't hear you come in.'

'You were engrossed in your game. Do you remember me?'

'It's Inspector Anderson, isn't it? We met in my father's office a while back.'

'So we did.'

'How long have you been sitting there?'

'Only a few minutes. I didn't want to disturb you in the middle of your game.'

Paul looked embarrassed. 'I'm no good at Tetris. Apparently it's a very old game, but it's the first time I've played it. I'm just beginning to get the hang of it.'

'How are they treating you here?'

'Everyone's very friendly – and they've got an amazing selection of computer games.' He paused. 'I suppose you want to talk to me about the murders?'

'I would like to ask you a few questions, but only if you feel up to it.'

Paul nodded grimly. 'I'll do anything I can to help you catch whoever murdered my mother and Gordon.'

Charlie pulled out his notebook and his propelling pencil. 'Do you know that your mother chose to 'disappear' last week, Paul? That she was hiding out at your grandparents' place in Aberdeen?'

Paul nodded. 'Dr McCartney told me.'

'Do you have any idea why she would do that?'

'None whatsoever.'

'When was the last time you saw your mother?'

'A few days before she disappeared. I went round to her flat one morning for a coffee.'

'Did you go to Dalgleish Tower at all during the time your mother was missing?'

'A couple of times. But only when I was sure my father wouldn't be there. I went there to make sure Brutus was all right. He's Mum's cat. He needs a lot of t.l.c. Mum idolised him, but if it was left to my Dad he'd be lucky if he didn't starve.'

Charlie paused while he rolled down the lead in his pencil. 'Last Thursday – the night Gordon Parker was killed – where were you?' Charlie noticed tears welling up in the corners of Paul's eyes, but he displayed no other sign of emotion. His voice was steady.

'I was through in Edinburgh with Tommy and Dave. We were rehearsing our next gig.'

'Was Gordon a member of your group?'

'He was the lead singer.'

'But he wasn't at the rehearsal last Thursday?'

'He was supposed to be going, but he had a sore throat and had to call off.'

'How did you go through to Edinburgh?'

'I took the train. Gordon wanted the van.'

'The 'Citizens Band' van?'

'Yes.'

'Is the van yours, or Gordon's?'

'Technically, it's mine. It's registered in my name. But we split the cost between us and we both used it whenever we wanted. The arrangement worked out fine. There was never any hassle about whose turn it was.'

'Do you know why Gordon wanted the van last Thursday?'

'He didn't say.'

'How long had your mother and Gordon known each other?'

'Mum and Gordon?' Paul looked surprised at the question. 'About fourteen years, I suppose. Ever since Gordon and I became friends at primary school. We must've been six or seven at the time.'

'Did she like him?'

'Of course. She often invited him to come up to Aberdeen with us, to my grandparents' house, during the Easter holidays. She liked his sense of humour.'

'Did Gordon get on well with her?'

'He thought she was terrific. He used to go on about how lucky I was to have a mother like her. Gordon's father died when he was quite young. While he was at University he stayed at home with his mother and sister, but that was only because he couldn't afford a flat. He rarely spoke about his mother. They didn't get on.

'Where is this all leading?' Paul asked in a perplexed tone. 'Are you trying to establish some sort of connection between Gordon and my mother?' He got to his feet, a little shakily. 'You're not trying to imply that Gordon had anything to do with my mother's death, I hope? What kind of a sick – ?'

'Don't get worked up, Paul. I'm not trying to imply anything. To be frank, I'm just trying to uncover anything that might help me find out who killed your mother.'

'And Gordon. Don't forget about Gordon. The poor guy's dead as well. On account of me, probably. If I'd been in the flat that night, Gordon might still be alive today.'

Paul broke down and wept openly. Charlie stood up and put a comforting arm around his shoulders. 'I think that's enough for today.' Putting away his notebook, he took a packet of tissues from his pocket and unfolded one, handing it across. Paul took the tissue and blew his nose hard.

'Sorry, I didn't mean to lose control.'

'It's understandable.'

'I thought I was beyond losing control. I've always prided myself on that.' Paul managed a haggard smile as he wiped his nose. 'But it looks as if I need to let myself go as much as the next man.'

As he came round slowly, Bernie McGurk lifted his throbbing head, but when he tried to open his eyes, everything remained black. He realised he was still blindfolded. His attempt to stand up got him nowhere as he was bound by his wrists and ankles to an upright chair. He couldn't even open his mouth.

When he heard approaching footsteps, he let his chin fall limply back onto his chest, feigning unconsciousness. The footsteps rang out louder, then stopped. Bernie sensed someone was standing directly in front of him. He remained motionless. Suddenly his head was jerked up and the tape was ripped unceremoniously from his mouth. His lips stung fiercely. When a glass of ice-cold water was thrown into his face, he squealed involuntarily and started to struggle.

'You're wasting your time, Bernie.' He heard the footsteps move round behind him and he blinked as his blindfold fell away. Looking up, he saw he was in an empty warehouse, the faint echo of his cry still reverberating from the high ceiling. 'You can shout your head off in here,' the voice behind him said. 'Nobody's going to hear you. And nobody's going to help you.' It wasn't the voice of either of the men who'd grabbed him in the street. A much deeper voice.

Bernie watched out of the corner of his eye as his captor walked round to face him. He saw the purple, jagged scar before he could focus on the rest of his features. Recognising McFarlane, he started twisting feverishly against his bonds.

'No point in struggling, Bernie. It won't get you anywhere,' McFarlane said, pulling across a wooden chair and straddling it. He took a packet of cigarettes from his jacket pocket and lit up, blowing a large smoke ring which he watched in silence as it drifted upwards, almost intact, towards the high roof.

'Would you like a fag?' Bernie nodded nervously. 'In a minute, then. First, you're going to answer a couple of questions.'

'Who are you, mister? What do you want with me?'

'You don't know who I am?' McFarlane asked, feigning incredulity. 'Really? I don't think I believe you, Bernie. In fact, a wee birdie told me you were being very nosy – asking all sorts of questions about me. Why did you do that? Who was paying for the information?'

Perspiration rolled down Bernie's face. 'I don't know what you're talking about, mister. I've no idea who you are.'

'You said you wanted a fag?'

When Bernie nodded again, McFarlane took a long drag on his cigarette until the end glowed red hot, then he leaned forward and crushed the burning tip into the middle of Bernie's forehead. Bernie let out a blood-curdling scream as the cigarette sizzled and seared his skin, the acrid smell of his scorched flesh filling his nostrils and making him want to vomit. 'You're a fucking bastard, McFarlane!' he yelled.

McFarlane dropped the cigarette onto the ground and crushed it under his heel. His face broke out in a broad grin. 'There you go. You were just teasin' me, you fly wee bugger. You knew all along who I was. All you needed was a wee memory jog.'

Taking a fresh cigarette from his packet, McFarlane lit up. 'You can see why they say fags are bad for your health, can't you, Bernie?' He chuckled. 'Now we're going to try the question again.' He blew another smoke ring and followed its languid progress as it spiralled upwards. 'But no more joshin'. Because if I don't get a proper answer this time, this fag's goin' into your eye.'

'Oh, for fucksake, McFarlane,' Bernie whimpered. 'Screw the fuckin' nut.'

THIRTY

Tuesday 22 March

On his way to work Charlie Anderson stopped off at the Western Infirmary and asked at reception for Dr McCormick. Taking the lift to the second floor, he was approaching his office when he saw a tall, athletic-looking man about to close the door. 'Dr McCormick?' Charlie enquired.

'How can I help you?'

'DCI Anderson, Glasgow CID,' he said, showing his warrant card. 'I was told I'd be able to talk to Michael Gibson this morning.'

'If it really is necessary.' Charlie detected a slight Lancashire accent in the dubious assent. 'Come with me. I'm on my way to see another patient on the same ward.'

Charlie fell into step as they strode along the wide corridor.

'Do you know what caused Michael Gibson to collapse?' Charlie asked.

'Apart from his dietary deficiency, he's suffering from angina pectoris.' Charlie raised an enquiring eyebrow. 'It's a condition characterised by paroxysmal attacks of extreme pain,' McCormick explained, 'often associated with a sense of apprehension or fear. Such attacks are usually precipitated by severe physical or emotional strain. That probably sounds rather horrific but the condition is controllable and the pain can be alleviated by rest and administration of small doses of nitroglycerine.'

Charlie stopped in his tracks and placed a restraining hand on McCormick's arm. 'Did I hear you right? Did you say nitroglycerine?'

'It does have uses other than blowing open safes, Inspector. It's a vasodilator – it widens the lumen of blood vessels.'

Charlie removed his hand and they resumed walking. 'Do me a favour, Doc. Keep the lid on that. The last thing I need is for word to get out in Easterhouse that nitro is available on prescription.'

'Our secret,' McCormick said, pushing open the swing doors leading to the ward.

'Where is Gibson?' Charlie asked.

'Third bed on the left. But remember, he's still very weak. Five minutes maximum – and nothing stressful.'

Charlie looked down the open plan ward of some twenty beds, all of which were occupied. He saw Michael Gibson propped up on several pillows, dozing, a drip attached to his forearm. When he heard the visitor's chair being pulled from under his bed, Michael slowly opened his eyes. He nodded in recognition.

'So, what've you been up to since the last time I saw you, Michael? Which, if I recall correctly, was when you stepped out of the lift in the Marriott.'

'Sorry about that.' Michael managed a weak grin.

'You'd think I'd have known better. It's definitely time I packed it in and headed off to potter about in my allotment.'

'I've got some information for you, Charlie.' Michael's whisper was urgent. 'I know where McFarlane's hiding out.'

'Where?'

'He's staying at Larry Robertson's place at the top of Turnberry Road.'

'How do you know that?'

'Bernie McGurk found out for me.'

'McGurk?'

'You must know Bernie. He's the best source of information in Glasgow.'

Charlie let out a low sigh. 'That explains it.'

'Explains what?'

Charlie pulled The Herald from his coat pocket and tugged his reading glasses from his shirt pocket. Putting on his spectacles, he flicked through the paper until he found the article he was looking for. He read aloud:

> *A man's body was recovered from the River Clyde late last night, near the weir in Glasgow Green. He has been identified as fifty-eight year old Bernard McGurk.*

Mindful of Michael's condition, Charlie skipped over the paragraph describing the fact that McGurk had been blinded in both eyes before being shot by a single bullet through the temple.

> *The police are appealing for anyone who saw McGurk within the past twenty-four hours to come forward, etc, etc.*

Charlie pulled off his glasses. He folded the newspaper and stuffed it back into his pocket. 'A pound to a pinch of shit McFarlane got wind of the fact that Bernie was asking questions about him,' Charlie said, shaking his head. 'I doubt very much if he'll go anywhere near Robertson's place now.' Michael felt a knot in the pit of his stomach. 'I'm told you were carrying a gun when you collapsed in the street. What in the name of God was that all about?'

'I was going to kill McFarlane. It's the only way of dealing with him.'

'You have got to leave these things to us,' Charlie snapped. 'You can't take the law into your own hands and wander round Glasgow brandishing a gun. You're descending to his level.'

Michael struggled to sit up straight. 'He murdered Anne. He tried to kill Paul. Now it's him or me.'

'For Christ's sake, Michael. Spare me the B-movie melodrama. You're talking about going after one of the most ruthless bastards ever to walk the streets of Glasgow. Leave it alone, for God's sake.'

Dr McCormick strode down the ward towards the bed. 'What's all this commotion about?' he hissed. 'Do I need to remind you, Inspector, that Mr Gibson needs complete rest. Shouting and arguing is not conducive to his recovery, to say nothing of the disturbance you're causing to the other patients on the ward.'

'I'll be the one having a coronary if I can't talk sense into this pig-headed idiot.'

McCormick glared at Charlie. 'I'll have to ask you to leave.'

Charlie took a deep breath, then exhaled slowly. 'Sorry, doctor,' he said getting to his feet and holding up a hand in apology. He turned back to Michael and spoke quietly. 'If McFarlane murdered Anne, we'll find him – and we'll deal with him. Trust me.'

As soon he got back to Pitt Street, Charlie summoned O'Sullivan. 'It appears that McFarlane was staying at Larry Robertson's place in Turnberry Road. I don't have the address, but it'll be on file. He'll almost certainly have shot the crow by now but check it out anyway.'

After a light lunch, Michael Gibson had been given his second nitroglycerine treatment. For the first time in months, his headache was almost gone, even when he lifted his head from the pillow. A plan was forming in his mind. He tugged open the locker beside his bed to check his clothes were inside, then he picked up his watch from the bedside table and timed the two nurses who were busying themselves collecting lunch trays. They were nearing the far end of the ward, six beds to go. He reckoned it would be about two minutes before they would turn round and come back down the ward. He looked around to make sure no one was paying any attention to him. Most of the patients were settling down for an after-lunch nap. Snatches of snoring were already in evidence.

Pulling the adhesive tape from his forearm, he eased out the drip needle and got out of bed. He tucked his clothes and shoes under his arm and walked as steadily and as confidently as he could towards the top of the ward.

As soon as he got to the toilets, he stepped out of his hospital pyjamas and pulled on his clothes. Glancing back up the ward, he saw the nurses stacking the last of the trays. He headed for the wide staircase and gripped the banister tightly as he made his way down.

It was dusk by the time Philippa Scott left her office. Balancing her briefcase on her head to protect her hair from the light drizzle, she trotted as fast as her tight mini-skirt would allow, across Bath Street, towards her parked car, cursing when she saw the folded plastic envelope sticking out from under the Peugeot's windscreen wiper. 'Not another bloody ticket! I'm barely ten minutes over the time, for God's sake.' She snatched the envelope from under the wiper.

Unlocking the car door, she threw her briefcase onto the passenger seat and got in. 'How much this time?' As she was taking the sheet of paper out of the envelope, she realised it wasn't a parking ticket. She recognised Michael's handwriting. She started to read:

> *Pippa, I have to see you. It's a matter of life and death. I know who killed Anne and Gordon Parker but I need your help to prove it. I can't risk going to your place. Meet me in Dalgleish Tower tonight at seven o'clock. Whatever you do, don't mention a word of this to anyone, especially not the police. You have got to trust me. I'll explain everything when I see you. Michael.*

Philippa's mind was in turmoil. What should she do? Should she go to meet him? She checked her watch – ten past six – she had half an hour to make up her mind. She stuffed the note into her handbag and got out of the car. She hurried along the street as far as the nearest pub and ordered a gin and tonic at the bar. Having re-read the note, she decided to call Jonathan. He would give her sensible advice, maybe even come with her to Dalgleish Tower. She took her mobile phone from her bag and clicked onto his number, but only reached his messaging service. She clicked onto another number.

'This is Philippa Scott,' she said to Jonathan Sharp's secretary. 'Would it be possible for me to talk to Mr Sharp? It is rather urgent.'

'I'm sorry, Miss Scott, but he's still in the board meeting. It was scheduled to finish at six but they're running late. I don't know how long they'll be. Can I take a message?'

'No message. Thanks.'

Charlie Anderson paced up and down his office. The pieces of the jigsaw didn't fit. Something was nagging at the back of his mind, something significant. He sensed it, but he couldn't put his finger on it. He needed help to get his thoughts straight. He buzzed through on his intercom. 'Pauline, find out if O'Sullivan is still in the building.'

A few moments later Pauline was back on the line. 'He'll be with you in a couple of minutes, sir.'

'Thanks. I need peace and quiet to do some thinking, Pauline. Hold any calls. I don't want to be disturbed for the next hour.'

'Close the door and grab a seat,' Charlie said when O'Sullivan walked into the office. Taking his propelling pencil from his jacket pocket, Charlie wound down the lead. He opened the top drawer of his desk and took out a blank sheet of paper. 'I need your help to get everything down in writing, Tony,' he said. 'Dates, times, places, people. It's a slog, but it's the only way to find *The Key Question*.' Referring to his notebook, he started to compile a chronological list of events.

Philippa depressed the button on the remote control and waited while the doors shuddered open before driving down the steep ramp to the underground garage in Dalgleish Tower. Michael's Mercedes and Anne's Volvo were sitting in their usual parking bays, both covered in a thin film of dust. She drew up alongside the cars. Her high-heels clicked on the stone floor as she hurried across towards the control panel to tap in the security code. As she was riding up in the lift to the fifteenth floor she rummaged in her handbag for her key.

When she unlocked the apartment door, she saw the hall was in darkness, except for a pool of light seeping from under the closed door of the master bedroom. She shut the front door as quietly as she could and tiptoed towards the bedroom. 'Michael!' she called out in a hoarse whisper. 'Are you in there?'

She could feel her heartbeat flutter as she turned the handle and eased open the door. The top light was on and the curtains were drawn. 'Michael, where are you, for God's sake?' She pushed the door open wide and stepped inside, then squealed in fright when the bedroom door slammed behind her.

Spinning round, she saw a tall figure standing with his back against the door, blocking her escape. He was dressed from head to toe in black with a woollen hood covering his face and neck. Wild eyes stared at her through narrow slits. He was brandishing an ivory-handled, cut-throat razor. 'I see you found my note,' the muffled voice whispered. 'Thanks for coming.'

Philippa's scream was throttled as he grabbed her by the hair and yanked her to the floor. He dropped to his knees behind her and held her neck in a vice-like grip in the crook of his arm, the blade poised – inches from her eyes. 'Shut up!' he commanded. 'Or I'll slit your throat. Do you understand?'

Choking back her scream, Philippa tried to nod her head. 'You're choking me,' she gasped, struggling to twist from his grasp.

Without warning, her assailant sprang to his feet, his arm still locked around her throat. She was dragged up by him. He dropped the razor onto the floor and spun her round to deliver a sickening punch to her solar plexus. She folded in two and collapsed in a crumpled heap, groaning and clutching at the pit of her stomach.

Yanking her up by the hair, he threw her violently on her back onto the bed. He grabbed her right arm and, before she realised what was happening, he'd pulled her wrist through a loop of white rope that was already attached to the bedpost. He tugged the noose closed. He went quickly to the other side of the bed and grabbed her other wrist. When she glanced over her shoulder she saw another noose waiting. She struggled to pull her arm back, but she was no match for his strength. Inch by inch, he dragged her wrist towards the rope and forced her hand through the loop, pulling the noose tight. He grabbed her left ankle and flicked off her shoe. Looking down, she saw the ropes attached to the bottom of the bed. She kicked out frantically with both legs, catching him a glancing blow on the side of the head and forcing him to release his grip.

'You little bitch!' he cursed hoarsely as he took a step back, massaging his bruised jaw through the hood. He swept the razor up from the floor and held it under her chin. She looked down in terror. Her eyes couldn't focus on the blade but she could feel the cold steel pressing against her throat. 'You do exactly as I say, or I'll cut you.' She froze. 'Stretch your legs out towards the corners of the bed,' he demanded. She didn't move. 'Do it!' he yelled applying pressure to the blade. The razor stung painfully as it bit into Philippa's flesh and she felt a trickle of warm blood running down her neck. 'I said – do it!' he screamed in her face. 'Now!'

Slowly, she stretched out her legs as he had commanded. He went to the bottom of the bed and grabbed her left ankle to pull it through a noose, then he stretched her right leg to the other corner of the bed and flicked off her shoe before fastening her ankle securely, her leather mini-skirt riding up her thighs as she lay, spread-eagled, gasping for breath. He paced up and down beside the bed, peering closely at his victim, a stalking lion examining his prey. He picked up a roll of brown adhesive tape from the bedside table and sliced off a length with the razor. Philippa's mind started racing. Desperately, she tried to recall what she could remember about such situations – theories she'd read about in magazines, never dreaming she'd ever have to put them into practice. Jumbled phrases came flooding into her brain – 'even if you're physically overpowered, don't concede the mental initiative' – 'never show fear' – 'stay calm' – 'talk to him' – 'discuss and debate' – 'try to win his confidence' – 'most important of all, make him talk to you – and keep him talking'.

She realised that if she allowed him to gag her, she was finished. She had to communicate with him. She had to get him talking. As he stretched across the bed to fasten the tape over her mouth, she made a superhuman effort to keep her voice steady. 'You don't need to do that.' She spoke as calmly and as confidently as she could. 'I'm all right now. I'm not going to scream.' Cramp was seizing the calf muscles in her left leg. She mustn't let the pain show in her face – he might interpret it as fear. She was in agony as she looked him straight in the eye. How was he was going to react? He stared back at her. She tried not to blink. Before, she'd thought the glaring eyes were those of a maniac. Now they just looked cold and cruel.

'You promise not to scream?'

'I promise.'

'You wouldn't lie to me?'

'No.' She summoned all the willpower she could muster to keep her voice steady. 'I wouldn't lie to you.' He gazed at her in silence for a full minute – to Philippa, it seemed like an eternity – then he crumpled the tape in his fist and dropped it onto the floor. She swallowed hard. At least there was a vestige of hope. Get him talking, her brain screamed at her. Communicate with him.

'Who are you? Why are you doing this?' She pressed the sole of her left foot against the bed post and tensed her ankle as best she could to try to control the cramp. Thankfully, the pain was easing.

'You really don't know who I am?' His laughter was muffled by the hood. 'Well, you might as well know, because it won't make the slightest bit of difference. You won't be leaving here alive.'

He tugged the hood from his head.

THIRTY-ONE

Charlie Anderson rocked back in his chair and put his feet up on the desk. He lifted up the sheet of paper and studied what he'd written:

> **At the start of March**: Anne Gibson switches her key to flat 15 for the key to flat 14 in Harry Kennedy's safe.
>
> **Friday, March 4**: Anne Gibson and Gordon Parker order a duplicate set of Charles Rennie Mackintosh furniture.
>
> **Wednesday, March 9**: McFarlane travels from London to Glasgow (gives O'Sullivan the slip) / Michael Gibson reports his wife's 'suicide' in Dalgleish Tower / Anne Gibson disappears (and hides out in Aberdeen).
>
> **Tuesday, March 15**: Anne Gibson returns to Glasgow from Aberdeen / McFarlane takes a taxi to Dalgleish Tower / Michael Gibson reports his wife's murder (which happened in flat 14).
>
> **Thursday, March 17**: Anne Gibson's body is found in the Gleniffer Braes / Michael Gibson absconds from the Marriott.
>
> **Friday, March 18**: Gordon Parker found murdered in Paul Gibson's flat.

Charlie scanned the page several times, his eye finally settling on the first line. 'Okay, Tony, let's see what we've got here,' he said. 'Anne Gibson switches keys. That's logical enough, she needs access to flat 14 to set up the suicide and murder scams. However, that means that, from then on, she no longer has a key for her own flat – she had to leave her key in Harry Kennedy's safe when she did the swap. She didn't order a replacement – Harry would certainly have mentioned if she had.'

'But she continues to go in and out of her flat during the following week,' O'Sullivan said, 'so she must have had a key.'

Harry told me there were only four issued,' Charlie said. 'Michael had his – and she'd hardly ask Philippa Scott if she could borrow hers. Ergo, she must have borrowed Paul's. Funny, he didn't say anything about that.'

Furrowing his brow, Charlie leaned across his desk and picked up his notebook, thumbing through the pages until he came to the shorthand notes of his interview with Paul in Traquair House. He read them out loud:

> *'When was the last time you saw your mother?'*
>
> *'A few days before she disappeared. I went round to the flat one morning for a coffee.'*
>
> *'Did you go to Dalgleish Tower at all during the time your mother was missing?'*
>
> *'A couple of times. But only when I was sure my father wouldn't be there. I went there to make sure Brutus was all right. He's Mum's cat. He needs a lot of t.l.c.. Mum idolised him, but if it was left to Dad, he'd be lucky if he didn't starve.'*

Charlie's eyes flicked back to the top of the page. He drew a circle round the first question and answer:

> *'When was the last time you saw your mother?'*
>
> *'A few days before she disappeared. I went round to the flat one morning for a coffee.'*

'Eureka, Tony! That's *The Key Question.*' Charlie slammed his fist into the palm of his hand. 'Paul Gibson told me that the last time he saw his mother was '*a few days before she disappeared*'. That was a lie. He must have seen her on the day she left – and he must have known she was leaving – because she had to give him back his key so he could get into the flat to take care of the cat.' Charlie allowed himself a wry smile. '*The Key Question.* Quite literally. I must remember to include that in the next graduate seminar.'

Charlie's train of thought was broken by the ring of his phone.

'Sorry to interrupt you, sir,' said Pauline. 'I know you said you weren't to be disturbed, but there's a girl on the line who insists she has to talk to you straight away. She says she knows who killed Gordon Parker, but she won't speak to anyone but you.'

'Put her through.'

'Is that Inspector Anderson?' the hesitant voice was trembling.

'Yes.'

'My name's Maureen Donnelly – Gordon Parker's girlfriend. I know who did it. I know who killed Gordon.'

'Where are you calling from, Miss Donnelly?'

'I'm not saying. If he finds me he'll kill me too.'

'Try to stay calm. No one's going to kill you.'

'You don't know what he's like. He's insane.'

'Who's insane?'

'Paul,' she whispered. 'Paul Gibson.'

Charlie's fingers tightened around the receiver. 'What makes you think Paul Gibson killed your boyfriend?'

Maureen's voice went even quieter. 'I was with Gordon the night he was murdered.' Charlie clamped the phone to his ear, straining to make out her words. 'I'd planned to go out with a girlfriend because Gordon was supposed to be rehearsing with his group in Edinburgh, but he phoned me at the last minute and asked me to meet him at Paul's flat. He said he'd something important to tell me.

'When I got there he was on a high. He'd been smoking pot all afternoon. As soon as I walked through the door, he picked me up and waltzed me round the room. He asked me to marry him. I laughed. I told him he was being ridiculous. I reminded him that we were both stony broke, but he said he was about to come into a lot of money. I didn't believe him.

'Then he blurted out the whole story – how he and Paul were going to help Anne Gibson fake her murder and arrange for her husband to find 'the body'. The idea was to drive Michael Gibson insane so Anne would get control of his estate. Gordon told me he was going to be paid handsomely for his contribution so we could afford to get married.' Maureen was speeding up, scarcely pausing for breath. 'I didn't like the sound of it – I begged him not to get involved. But Gordon laughed it off and said I was being silly. He told me about the 'murder' plan – how Paul was going to tie Anne to the bed and pretend to slash her throat, then cover her body in sheep's blood he'd got from an abattoir.

'Later, when Sergeant O'Sullivan broke the news to me that Gordon had been murdered, I asked him how he'd died. When he told me he'd been tied up and his throat had been slashed, I knew it had to be Paul who'd killed him. I was terrified he'd suspect that Gordon had told me about the plan and that he'd come after me, so I ran away.'

'Tell me where you are and I'll send someone to collect you. We'll give you protection.'

'I'm not coming back. I'm not telling anyone where I am. Not until that maniac is locked up.'

'But Miss Donnelly...'

The phone went dead in Charlie's hand.

'Tony, go across to Traquair House straight away and bring in Paul.'

Philippa gasped when he tugged the hood from his head.

'Paul! What are you playing at?'

'You really didn't know, did you? None of them did. They're all so stupid.' His eyes glazed over as he stared down at her, his look gaunt and feverish – like a consumptive.

'Why are you doing this?'

'To make sure the money comes to me. I'm entitled to it. You're not.'

'I don't know what you're talking about, Paul. You're not making any sense!'

Laughing inanely, he took a small white pill from his pocket and popped it into his mouth. 'You know – those are the very words my mother used, just before I slit her throat.' Philippa gasped and started to struggle violently, straining against the ropes, frantically trying to pull herself free. Paul made no move to stop her. He stood by the side of the bed with a smile quivering on his lips as he watched her thrash about helplessly. 'You can struggle. You can struggle all you want. But you mustn't scream. You promised. Remember?'

Philippa exhausted herself within moments, having made no impression on her bonds, succeeding only in tightening the nooses around her wrists and ankles. She lay still – gulping for air. Tears welled up in her eyes but she forced them back. She had to keep him talking. 'Why did you do that, Paul? Why did you kill your own mother?'

'You really want to know?'

'Yes.'

'Why shouldn't I tell you?' His smile was cold and distant. 'You'll appreciate it. It's really neat.' He sat down on the bed beside her.

'You know Dad wanted to dump Mum? Of course you do. It was so he could shack up with you, wasn't it? But there was no way she was ever going to allow that to happen. She was desperately hoping to be able to patch up their marriage. She knew he couldn't walk out on her because she had a hold over him. When I went round to the flat one day for a coffee, she told me about it. She knew her paragon of a husband had shagged Saoirse when she was underage and she was threatening to spill the beans if he tried to leave her. But despite everything, she wanted him back. Can you believe that? Once you had ditched him, she was hoping they could start over. I couldn't stomach the idea of Mum taking him back – you have no idea how much I hate the bastard – so I told her about Carole. That totally freaked her out.'

Paul leaned across to wipe the beads of perspiration from Philippa's glistening forehead. He smoothed away her hair and ran his fingertips down the side of her face, gently caressing her cheek. She made no attempt to turn her head away. She had no idea who Saoirse and Carole were, but the only thing that mattered right now was to keep him talking.

'What freaked your Mum out, Paul?'

Paul blinked twice, then carried on rapidly. 'I hadn't said a word about it to her in twelve years – not in twelve fucking years! Not to save his miserable skin, of course. Nothing would have given me greater pleasure than to see his face when Mum confronted him with it. But I couldn't tell her, could I?' Paul paused.

'Why couldn't you tell her, Paul?' Philippa prompted.

Paul sprang to his feet and strode to the bottom of the bed. 'I knew she'd be devastated if she found out about Carole.' He spun back round to face Philippa. 'But I had to tell her – you can see that, can't you?' he shouted. 'Otherwise she was going to take him back, for fuck's sake! She broke down in tears. I knew she would. Then she started ranting and raving. 'How could the bastard have shagged my sister?' she screamed. There wasn't any question of patching up the marriage after that, I can tell you!' Paul chortled.

'When she eventually calmed down, the only thing on her mind was revenge. And who could blame her, after the way he'd treated her? I needed money desperately – my dealer was threatening to cut off more than my supply if I didn't pay up. I suddenly thought of an idea. 'What if we could get him committed, Mum?' I suggested. 'That way we could get our hands on all his money. He's pretty unstable at the best of times. It wouldn't take too much pressure to push him over the edge.'

'She thought that was a brilliant idea. Mum came up with the plan of a fake suicide, followed by a fake murder. She had the acting ability, the make-up expertise and the production skills to make it all happen – and she was confident she could carry it off. She promised me half the money if I helped her with it. She planned everything meticulously. She got her inspiration from a black comedy her amateur dramatic society put on a couple of years back. It was a spoof thriller about a stiff that disappeared mysteriously from inside a locked room. It was called *Rigor Mortice* – get it?' He chuckled. 'As she was planning to make her corpse disappear twice, I christened our plan *Double Mortice*. We needed a codename to use when we discussed the arrangements over the phone – you never know who might be listening in. So, *Double Mortice* it was. Phase I for the 'suicide', Phase II for the 'murder'.

'It was her twisted Catholic logic, you see. Having your husband certified as insane is more acceptable than him leaving you.' Paul grinned broadly.

'Having Mum tied to the bed, spread-eagled, for the murder routine was my idea. I knew that would drive him crazy. Oh yes, I knew that all right. Mum didn't want to go along with that at first. She couldn't see the point. But she didn't take a lot of convincing when I reminded her about Carole.'

Paul's eyes positively sparkled. 'We started with Phase I – the suicide ploy. What a scheme! Mum nicked the key to flat 14 from the caretaker's safe, then I went with her and we bought the duplicate bedroom furniture.'

Philippa was getting more confused by the minute. 'Flat 14' and 'duplicate bedroom furniture' meant nothing to her, but as long as he was talking there was a glimmer of hope. Perhaps someone might find her before it was too late? At all costs, she had to keep him talking.

'Why did you buy duplicate bedroom furniture?'

Paul continued as if he hadn't heard the question, rattling on in a world of his own. 'I ordered the furniture in Gordon Parker's name so it couldn't be traced back to me, then I picked the stuff up in my van, a bit at a time, and brought it round here and assembled it in flat 14 while Dad was at work. Mum went to great lengths to ensure everything looked identical. She ordered a duplicate set of curtains for the bedroom; she had a new number '15' made in gold letters to replace the number '14' on the front door; she even had copies made of the Rennie Mackintosh paintings on the bedroom wall.'

Paul paused to swallow another pill before continuing at high speed. 'We let Gordon Parker in on the act because we needed his expertise to fix the lift. He was magic with anything electronic. He came round one day and re-wired the control panel. Just like that!' he shouted, letting out a manic Tommy Cooper chuckle. 'Gordon showed us how we could switch the lift to stop at floor 14 any time we wanted. He also got a mobile phone jammer on the Internet and set it up for us. With just a flick of a switch we could block all mobile phone communications, in and out of the flat. Good old Gordon. He was desperate to get his hands on enough cash so he and Maureen could get hitched and Mum promised to see him all right as soon as she got control of Dad's estate.

'Everything went like a dream. I was hiding in the kitchen, nursing my baseball bat. You don't know about my bat, do you? That's it over there.' He pointed towards it lying on the dressing table. 'It's a very special bat – a present from my old man, would you believe?

'If, by any chance, Dad had gone to the kitchen or the lounge, the game would've been up. In that case we were going to switch to plan B. I'd smash him over the head with the baseball bat and we'd tip his body over the bedroom balcony and make it look like suicide.

'Mum didn't want to resort to killing him unless it was absolutely necessary. She just wanted to drive him mad. But me,' he whispered hoarsely, 'I wanted to use the bat on him.' His eyes hardened as he spoke. 'It would've been the ultimate poetic justice – using that particular bat to smash his skull to smithereens.

'All my life I've had to suffer his patronising crap; how grateful I should be that he gave me a job in the firm; how I was wasting my time on a brain-dead rock group. My God, you don't know how much I hate the smug bastard. But tonight,' he whispered. 'Tonight

– I am going to use the bat on him. I'll show him who's brain-dead.' Paul suddenly fell silent and stared at the wall. Taking another pill from his pocket, he slipped it between his teeth.

Don't let him stop talking! You must keep him talking! 'What happened after that?'

Paul switched his gaze back to her, studying her face. 'When Dad arrived at the flat, Mum was lying on the bed doing her suicide act. She almost blew it when he held a mirror to her lips – we hadn't reckoned on that. But she managed to hold her breath just long enough. Nice going, that. Then she disappeared off to Aberdeen. She told her parents that Dad had beaten her up and that she was terrified of what he might do to her next. She even gave herself a few fake bruises with theatrical make-up; a special skill of hers – very handy. She was establishing her rationale for going into hiding. After she'd got Dad committed, she planned to reappear as the terrified, battered wife who'd run away to escape from the violent, sadistic monster.

'Clever, eh? After the suicide scenario, we decided to wait until Dad went back to work before enacting the murder. I went past his office every morning to check if his car was there. The following Tuesday, I saw it, and I phoned Aberdeen straight away. Grandad answered the phone so I used a high-pitched voice to ask for Mum. *Double Mortice – Phase II – We have lift-off*. That was all I had to say; the pre-arranged signal for Mum to come back to Glasgow. I'm not boring you, am I?'

'No, Paul. Go on. Tell me what happened next.'

Paul furrowed his brow. 'Mum was in a foul mood when I picked her up at Queen Street station. Apparently Gordon Parker had written to her while she was in Aberdeen. The idiot had told her he was worried about me because I was messing about with hard drugs and he thought she should know. The stupid pillock. As if I couldn't handle it. As soon as she got off the train, she started giving me a hard time. She said she wasn't going to give me any more money unless I promised to give up drugs. She went on and on about it all the way back to the flat. Eventually I had to promise – just to shut her up.

'When I finally got her off that subject we set up the 'murder'. I'd got hold of a container of sheep's blood from an abattoir outside Edinburgh – I told them it was for the final scene in Hamlet in a school play. We switched the lift so it would stop at the fourteenth floor and we jammed the mobile phone signal. I nicked Dad's razor from his bathroom and brought Brutus down to flat 14, leaving the apartment door wide open. Mum applied theatrical make-up to her throat to give it the appearance of having been slit – black lines and jagged red weals. She even managed a sort of 3-D effect – it was amazingly realistic. It almost convinced me. Then I tied her to the bed. She was stretched out, just like you are.' Paul closed his eyes. 'Just like Carole,' he added in a hoarse whisper.

Paul's eyes flicked open and his gaze travelled the length of Philippa's body, coming to rest on the shallow rise and fall of her breasts. He was breathing heavily.

'The plan was that I would watch at the window for Dad's car and when I saw it coming I was to pour the sheep's blood over Mum's throat. I went to the en suite bathroom – that's where you get the best view of the road. It was really exciting. I knew we could pull it off – and I might even get the opportunity to smash the bastard's head in with my bat.' Philippa saw his eyes dance at the prospect. 'Suddenly I had a craving for a hit. I had a needle and a speedball in my jacket. I'd been planning to save it for the evening but I felt an overwhelming need for a fix right there and then. Although Mum was only a few yards away, she couldn't see into the bathroom. It was magic. What a rush. The best high I've ever experienced. The adrenaline and the speedball mixed beautifully. I was ecstatic.

'Then, even lying tied to the bed, Mum started nagging me again, droning on and on about how worried she was that I was messing about with hard drugs, especially heroin. How it must be very serious if nosy-bloody-Parker felt he had to write to tell her about it. How she'd never give me another penny if I ever touched hard drugs again.

'She was ruining everything. I was freaking out – and she was spoiling it. I shouted to her to shut up. She told me to stop shouting. I went into the bedroom and screamed at her. She looked at me – she knew I'd had a hit – I could tell by her eyes – she could tell by mine – we knew each other's eyes, Mum and me. She ordered me to untie her immediately. She said the game was over; that we weren't going to go through with it.

'But I couldn't allow that, could I? I desperately needed my share of the money. Speedballs are expensive. I already owed my dealer a fortune. He was leaning on me to pay up. You only get one warning, and I'd had that. He was threatening to cut off more than my supply. 'I can't untie you, mother', I explained. 'If I untie you, you won't give me any money'. Then I suddenly thought of a way to get all the money for myself. I picked up Dad's razor. 'But you are right, Mum – the game is over. We're playing for real now.'

'Paul, you're not making any sense!' she shouted. I slashed at her throat and she went berserk, twisting and struggling like a maniac. I cut strips of tape and fastened them across her mouth to shut her up. Still, she twisted and struggled. I slashed again and again.

'Eventually she stopped moving – just an occasional reflex jerk. Jesus, I felt great. I went back to the bathroom window to watch for Dad's car. It wasn't long before I saw him arrive. There was already blood everywhere but I poured the sheep's blood over her for good measure – a high budget production. The effect was brilliant. Then I hid in the kitchen.

'When Dad found her body he was sick as a dog, then he ran off. I took Brutus back upstairs, re-set the lift and unblocked the mobile phone signal. All going according to plan. I was well on top of it. I went back down to flat 14 and watched from the window. I saw the cops arrive and I heard them go upstairs. I waited until I saw them leave with my Dad in a squad car, then I wrapped Mum's corpse in a sheet and took it down to my van. I drove to a quiet spot in the hills and I tied her body to four trees to make it look as if the murder had taken place there. The following day I waited till the caretaker had gone to the pub at lunchtime, then I went back to flat 14 to clean up the floor, dismantle the furniture and load it into my van. I even went to the trouble of smashing it to smithereens and dropping bits off at several different rubbish tips around the city. That's the way to do it.' He nodded, relishing his ingenuity.

'Of course, that left me with the problem of what to do about Parker,' he continued. 'I hadn't told him that we'd triggered Phase II but I knew that as soon as the news broke about Mum's murder, he'd realise I'd killed her and he'd run whimpering to the police.

'I went through to Edinburgh for a rehearsal last Thursday and I came back to Glasgow on an early train on Friday morning. I'd given Parker a key to my flat so he could shack up with Maureen. I knew she was on the early shift, so I waited outside the apartment until I saw her leave, then I went upstairs and let myself in quietly. Gordon was fast asleep. I had his hands tied behind his back before he'd properly wakened up. I grabbed his feet and tied them too. I told him I'd had to kill my mother and it was all his fault because of that stupid fucking letter. The wimp had never done heroin in his life – he'd never got beyond smoking pot and dropping a few tabs – and he was trying to lecture me on what I should and shouldn't use? For Christ's sake!

'I decided to let him experience a *real* high. I gave myself a hit and then I pumped a speedball into his arm. He went berserk. Totally lost his cool. Can you believe it? I gave him few more jabs. He was screaming like a stuck pig, just like my mother, so I had to gag him. But you don't scream, Philippa, do you?' He smiled at her coldly.

'I don't scream.' Her voice was trembling.

'Then I slit his throat. He'd left me no option. He knew too much. It's not so difficult when you have the knack – and I've certainly got the knack,' he giggled. 'I got a screwdriver and burst the lock on the front door of the flat to make it look as if it had been forced from the outside. You're a lawyer, Philippa. You can see how it all fits together.'

Her mouth was dry. She was struggling to swallow. She could barely speak. 'I … I suppose so.'

Almost absent-mindedly, his hand moved down her neck and slipped inside her jacket, coming to rest on her breast. She wasn't wearing a bra. She didn't flinch as he fondled her through her blouse. 'You're very like Carole, you know. I must say, I have to give my old man credit for his taste in women, if for precious little else.'

'Who's Carole?'

He didn't reply, but continued to massage her breast.

'Would you like to make love to me, Paul?'

He eyed her up and down. 'You are a sexy little minx.' His breathing was becoming laboured.

'Untie me – and let me show you just how sexy I can be,' she whispered.

He looked at her in mock amazement. 'You don't realise, do you? I can't untie you. I have to screw you tied to the bed. It's all part of the plan.'

Philippa's heart skipped a beat. 'What plan?' Again he ignored her question as he teased her nipple through the thin material. 'Don't you like doing it this way? Tied to the bed? Carole did. Isn't this the way you used to do it with my old man?'

He picked up the razor and flicked his thumb across the edge of the blade, testing the sharpness. Philippa's whole body tensed as he tugged her blouse from the waistband of her skirt and started slicing it up towards her neck, the blade coming to rest just below her chin. Folding her jacket and her tattered blouse away from her breasts, he leaned across her body and took her nipple in his mouth.

Philippa felt something brush against the inside of her thigh. She flinched when she realised it was the razor. Her skirt was already riding up around her waist and she could feel the cold steel as the blade travelled slowly up her leg, grazing her bare flesh, then she gasped involuntarily when she felt it slide inside her pants. She heard a rending sound as the blade sliced through the flimsy material. Paul's mouth was still clamped firmly to her breast, his tongue pressing down hard on her nipple.

'Paul,' she pleaded desperately. 'Why don't you untie me so we can do this properly?'

He lifted his mouth from her breast and sat up straight. 'How many times do I have to tell you?' He spoke in a matter-of-fact tone. 'I have to screw you tied to the bed. It's all part of the plan.'

'What plan?'

'You really want to know? Then listen carefully. This is good.' He sprang to his feet. 'The only way I can be sure of getting my hands on my father's money is if he's dead. But if he's murdered, that will cause all kinds of complications – it might take years to get things straightened out through the courts. Everything would be so much simpler if he committed suicide. But for that to happen, he would need a reason. And what better reason than remorse after he's raped you and killed you? So, I'm going to screw you, Philippa, then I'm going to slit your throat,' he stated casually. Philippa let out an involuntary squeal. 'After I've done that, I'm going to call lover boy and tell him you're here and that you're in danger. He'll come galloping across like a knight in shining armour – nothing in this world is more certain – and when he gets here I'm going to smash his head in with the baseball bat. Then I'm going to daub his clothes with your blood and tip his body over the balcony. Beautiful, isn't it?

'The police will find the evidence. The message he left on your windscreen enticing you here – painstaking work, that was, forging his handwriting. I don't think you'll have destroyed the note. The police will probably find it in your handbag or in your car. Even if they don't, what does it matter? They'll deduce that he lured you here, overpowered you, tied you to the bed, raped you and slashed your throat. Then, in a fit of remorse, he leaped from the balcony.'

Philippa's pulse was racing out of control – the nightmare overwhelming her. It was all she could do to hold back the scream that threatened to burst forth.

'I've thought of everything. The autopsy will conclude that the blow from the baseball bat was sustained during the fall. And look at this.' He produced a packet of condoms from his trouser pocket and held it triumphantly in front of her eyes. 'I'm going to wear one of these when I screw you so there'll be no DNA evidence available from my sperm. And there's an upside too – no risk of AIDS – and no risk of you getting pregnant.' He spluttered with laughter.

'And there's something else,' he continued eagerly. 'You're really going to enjoy this.' He ran to his jacket, which was hanging on the back of the bedroom door. He pulled a slim packet from the inside pocket and unfolded it carefully on the mattress, taking out two syringes. 'Look what I've got. One for each of us.'

'No Paul! No! I don't use that stuff. I don't need it.'

'Now, now, Pippa. Don't fib. I bet you've snorted a few lines of coke in your time. Probably tried a bit of smack as well, eh? But this is the combo to beat them all,' he said, lovingly caressing one of the syringes.

He rolled up his shirt sleeve and slipped the belt from the waistband of his trousers, looping it round his left arm, just below the elbow. He pulled it tight, gripping the loose end of the belt with his teeth and tugging on it until the veins on his forearm stood proud. He selected a bulging vein and lanced it with the needle, then closed his eyes as he pumped the plunger. His head arched back and he gave a long, low moan. He slackened his jaw and the belt fell loose. 'You fucking beauty! There's nothing to touch it, I promise you. Your turn now.'

'No, Paul!' He slid Philippa's jacket up her arm and unbuttoned the sleeve of her blouse, rolling it beyond the elbow. She thrashed wildly when he applied his belt as a tourniquet. 'For Christ's sake! I don't want that!'

Impervious to her pleading, he started whistling the Dambusters' theme, smirking as he primed the second syringe. 'Bombs away!' Philippa felt a sharp stab of pain as the needle pierced her skin, then the liquid started pumping, coursing into her veins. It was really happening to her. She twisted and jerked violently, her arms and legs flailing against their restraining bonds. Rivulets of perspiration oozed from every pore. All her restraint dissolved as the nightmare imploded. She screamed at the top of her voice, a long shuddering wail that seemed to fly from her body and hover like a mantle round the head of the crazed creature sitting by her side.

Paul went berserk, slapping her across the face and splitting open her bottom lip. 'Shut up, you stupid bitch! Stop screaming! You promised!' Another scream, cracked and half-whimpering, filled the room.

Paul grabbed the roll of adhesive tape from the bedside table and picked up the razor to cut off a strip. He slammed the palm of his hand under Philippa's chin to force her jaws closed, then stretched the tape across her mouth. Slicing off several more strips, he used them to criss-cross her mouth before collapsing onto the edge of the bed, panting from the effort. 'That wasn't right. You're spoiling everything. You promised not to scream. Why did you lie to me?' He fixed her with a wild-eyed glare. 'Why does everybody lie to me?'

Within seconds, the speedball started to take effect. Philippa felt wave after wave of hot flushes and the room started to swim crazily, the backs of her eyes throbbing and her brain filling with scrambled images. She was running through a black void, plummeting head-over-heels into a bottomless pit, her body twisting and turning – spinning and falling. She managed to pull herself out of the vertical dive and was now floating face-up in gravity-free space, her mouth gaping, her limbs dangling limply. Her eyelids grew incredibly heavy and she was consumed by an irresistible drowsiness as she struggled to blink away the sweat from her forehead, which was stinging her eyes.

She heard him speak. She could make out the words but the voice was detached from his body. It seemed to be coming from another room, another universe. 'Speedballs are great before sex. They heighten everything.'

She looked towards him. He was standing by the side of the bed, stripping off his clothes. His body was gaunt and white – a spectre. She thought this cackling, emaciated creature was ogling her but she couldn't focus – his features were twisted and blurred, his face zooming rapidly towards her then receding at an alarming rate. He climbed onto the bed and lay on top of her. She felt his bare flesh pressing against hers. She watched helplessly as her left nipple stood proud in response to his touch when he rolled it firmly between thumb and forefinger. He clamped his mouth to her breast and started teasing her hardened nipple with his tongue. She could feel his hand creeping up the inside of her thigh, fingernails scratching gently at her flesh.

THIRTY-TWO

Philippa couldn't control the cough building up in her lungs. With no release of air possible through her mouth, she gagged when the cough exploded in the back of her throat. Lathered in sweat from the effects of the speedball, light-headed from lack of oxygen, she was on the verge of vomiting as she struggled to exhale through her nose. Tears of despair streamed down her bulging cheeks.

Paul was totally indifferent to her agony as he knelt between her outstretched thighs, fumbling with the wrapping on the contraceptive. He winked at her as he dangled the condom in front of her terrified eyes, then he leered malevolently as he slowly unrolled it down the length of his erect penis. Stretching to the top of the bed for a pillow, he plumped it up and thrust it under her hips.

Philippa imagined she heard a noise – some kind of metallic click. She couldn't make out what it was or where it had come from. Was she hallucinating? It sounded like a key turning in a lock. Her heart skipped a beat. She realised she hadn't imagined it – Paul had heard it too. Springing from the bed, he grabbed the razor and moved silently across the room, standing stock still behind the closed bedroom door.

When Paul saw the door handle start to turn, he flicked off the top light, plunging the room into darkness. He crouched behind the door, razor poised. The door was slowly eased open. Philippa stared across. Through her blurred vision, she thought she could discern the shadowy image of a figure standing in the doorway.

She wanted to cry out a warning. She tried desperately to push her tongue through her teeth, striving to burst through the gagging tape, but to no avail. She blinked hard, attempting to focus. If she could only warn him with her eyes… Could he see her eyes? Could he see her at all? Looking straight towards him, then switching her gaze to behind the door, she pleaded with her eyes that he might understand. He's behind the door! He's behind the door! She switched her gaze back and forth as rapidly as she could – again and again. Her head was reeling. The nausea was overpowering. She passed out in a dead faint.

As soon as the figure took a step inside the room, Paul launched himself round the side of the door, striking out blindly, stabbing at head height – going for the face. Charlie Anderson had only a split second in which to react. Instinctively, he turned side-on and threw up his arm, grunting as he felt the searing pain of the razor plunging into his shoulder. Letting out a roar like a bull elephant, he crashed into the door, sending Paul rolling and tumbling across the bedroom floor. Charlie winced as he eased the blade from his shoulder.

Paul scrambled to his feet and crouched, naked, wild-eyed, searching frantically for a way to escape. Charlie didn't move, his frame blocking the doorway, blood dripping from his shoulder onto the floor. He flicked on the light switch.

'Take it easy, Paul.' Charlie dropped the razor and clasped his hand to his shoulder to stem the flow of blood. 'It's all over. Put on your clothes and come with me.' Like a cornered animal, Paul's eyes darted round the room. He yanked aside the curtain and tugged at the handle of the sliding patio doors, leading to the balcony. Dashing outside, he rammed the door closed behind him. 'Come back!' Charlie shouted. 'You can't go anywhere from there.'

Paul swung his legs over the railing and slid down as he far as he could, facing inwards, gripping the base of the concrete balcony with his fingertips. He knew there was an identical balcony on the floor below. Charlie wrenched open the patio door. 'Don't try it,

Paul!' he yelled. 'You can't get down that way.' Paul swung back and forth several times to build momentum, then with one final outward lunge of his legs, he released his grip as he started to arch inwards. 'I can fly!' he cried triumphantly.

His clawing fingers bounced off the railings of the balcony of the floor below and he made no further sound as his body spiralled downwards, arms and legs flailing like a rag doll. His spinning body crashed onto the paving stones then rolled, as if in slow motion, down the gentle embankment, coming to rest, face up, by the river's edge.

Charlie stepped out onto the balcony and gazed down at the crumpled figure – naked – spread-eagled – silent.

Wednesday 23 March

Kay Anderson carried a steaming bowl of porridge across to the kitchen table. 'Would you like me to pour milk on for you?'

'I'm not a complete cripple. I can manage some things by myself. Anyway, I don't need this damned sling. I'm going to take it off.'

'The doctor said you had to keep it on for a week to give the wound a chance to heal.'

'I don't need it. It's just – '

'You're worse than a bairn,' Kay interrupted forcibly. 'If the doctor said a week, he meant a week – not one night.'

'I hardly slept a wink. I can't sleep lying on my back.'

'I suppose you'd be better off lying on your side and opening up the wound?'

'It's just a scratch. I don't know what all the fuss is about.'

'A week,' she repeated firmly.

'But Kay, I – ' His attempt at further protest was interrupted by the toot of a car horn outside. 'That'll be my driver. I'd better be going.'

'He can wait until you've had your breakfast. I'll let him know you'll be out in a few minutes.'

When Charlie had finished his porridge, Kay held up his jacket while he slid his right arm into the sleeve. She tugged the left sleeve over his shoulder. 'I'll try to get away early tonight, love. Maybe we could have something for dinner that I could eat one-handed?'

'You wouldn't be thinking of shepherd's pie, by any chance?'

He grinned and gave her a peck on the cheek before hurrying out to the waiting car. When he saw Charlie coming, the driver jumped out and held open the passenger door.

'Been in the wars, I hear, sir.'

'It's nothing, Phil. Just a flesh wound, as they say in the movies. Sorry I had to drag you all the way over here, but the quack won't let me drive for a week. It's a bloody nuisance.'

'No problem.'

'Would you stop off at the Western on the way? I want to visit one of the patients.'

Charlie got Philippa's ward number from the reception desk, then took the lift. He went to the office at the top of the ward where a nursing sister was seated at an oval desk, studying a patient's chart. Her lapel badge identified her as Sister Tate.

'DCI Anderson,' Charlie announced, tugging out his I.D. 'Could you tell me how Philippa Scott is, please? She's the young lady who was brought into casualty last night.'

Sister Tate put down the chart. 'She had a disturbed night. I don't know the full story but I'm told she was attacked and forcibly injected with drugs, which is probably the truth. Although her blood shows a high concentration of heroin and cocaine, there's only one puncture mark in her arm. I don't think she's an addict.'

'I'm aware of the circumstances. I was involved in the incident last night. Would it be possible for me to talk to her?'

'Yes, but please be brief. She needs rest. She's in the first bed on the right.'

When Charlie approached the bed, Philippa was lying on her back staring at the ceiling, her long, auburn hair splayed across the pillow. Her complexion was ashen, her cheeks gaunt and her jaws were blotched with angry red weals where the gagging tape had adhered to her skin. Her eyes, sunken and red-rimmed, had none of their natural sparkle; the cornea cloudy and dull, the pupils dilated.

Charlie lowered himself onto the bedside chair. 'How are you feeling this morning, Miss Scott?'

Philippa turned her head on the pillow and blinked as she adjusted focus. Slowly, she recognised Charlie. 'Pretty groggy,' she mumbled. 'But I'll survive. This makes it a bit awkward to talk.' She fingered the stitches in her lower lip gingerly. 'How's your arm?' she asked, staring at his sling.

'It's my shoulder. Nothing much wrong with it,' he said dismissively. 'Just a zealous doctor over-reacting.'

Philippa attempted a smile. 'I'm told I have you to thank for saving my life.'

Charlie felt himself blush. 'I wouldn't go that far.'

'I would. Paul would have killed me for sure if you hadn't turned up. I can still scarcely believe it. I used to see him around the office, you know.' She paused. 'Is he…?'

Charlie nodded grimly. 'He didn't survive the fall. Broke his neck.' Philippa shivered and looked away. 'I realise you're supposed to be resting, but do you feel up to answering a couple of questions?' She nodded. 'Why did you go to Dalgleish Tower last night?'

'Would you get my handbag?' She struggled to sit up in bed. 'It's in the locker.' She produced the note from her bag. 'I found this on my car windscreen when I came out of the office last night. You probably don't know Michael Gibson's handwriting, but I can assure you, this is a very good imitation.'

Charlie struggled, one-handed, to pull his spectacles from their case. Putting them on, he squinted at the note, then peered over the top of his glasses. 'You should've called us as soon as you got this.'

'I realise that now. But at the time I thought I was helping Michael. Despite our bust up, I was feeling guilty about the way I'd abandoned him. He'd left God knows how many phone messages and texts asking me to get in touch with him, but I'd ignored them all. To be honest,' she continued, 'for a while I thought he had killed Anne because she wouldn't let him have his freedom. It's a terrible thing to say, but I actually believed he'd done it. That's why I lied to you and your men when you asked if he'd been in contact with me. I didn't want to get implicated – mess up my career and all that jazz…' Her voice tailed off. 'Then the guilty feelings started – and I had some serious doubts about whether Michael was capable of doing anything like that. When I read in the papers that the killer had struck again, I knew for sure it couldn't be him. I tried to get in touch with him yesterday. I must have called his number a dozen times but there was no reply. When I got this note, I thought it would give me a chance to make amends and help him. Or at least listen to what he had to say.'

'Do you know why Paul tried to kill you?'

'I guess so. I got his whole life story last night. As far as I could make out he was using me as a decoy to entice his father to Dalgleish Tower. He was planning to kill him and make it look like suicide so he would get his hands on his money. Pretty crazy stuff. He also regaled me with the sordid details of how and why he murdered his mother and Gordon Parker.'

'I'll get a full statement from you later. I'm not supposed to overtire you this morning. And on that score,' he added in a confidential whisper, 'my standing in this hospital isn't all it might be.' Charlie winked and nodded towards Doctor McCormick who was striding down the ward. 'Okay if I hang onto this?' he asked, holding up the note.

'Of course.'

'Last night was a very harrowing experience for you. Are you sure you're going to be able to handle it?'

'I'm not at all sure. But deep down I'm a tough cookie. There's a counsellor coming to see me this afternoon. If necessary, I'll keep on with her.' She smiled wryly. 'At least this will give me a personal insight into the problems of some of my abused clients.' Charlie wrestled with his spectacles. 'Let me help you with those.' Folding Charlie's glasses, she slipped them into their case and popped it into his top pocket.

'Thanks. Try to get some rest. I'll come back and see you later.'

THIRTY-THREE

Monday 28 March

Six days had passed since Paul Gibson's death and Charlie had spent most of that time in his office, writing reports and clearing a never-ending backlog of correspondence. It was late in the afternoon when he heard a rap on his office door. He put down his pen when he saw who it was.

'Come on in.'

Michael Gibson stretched across the desk to shake his hand. 'Stephen McCartney came to see me in hospital. He told me what happened.'

'I tried to visit you, but Dr McCormick wasn't having any of it.'

Michael managed a weak smile. 'How's the shoulder?'

'It's fine. I can get rid of the sling tomorrow. I'm only glad it wasn't my right arm, otherwise I'd have to have spent all week writing reports left-handed.'

'About Paul,' Michael began hesitantly. 'I don't know what to say.'

'Say nothing.'

'I'm told he tried to kill you.'

'He didn't know what he was doing. He was high on drugs. He just struck out blindly. But what about you? What's all this nonsense I hear about you trying to check yourself out of the hospital?'

Michael reddened with embarrassment. 'Not too clever, eh? Actually, it wasn't long after you came to see me. I was feeling really good – the headaches had gone – and I decided to go after McFarlane again. I wanted to settle the score on behalf of Bernie McGurk, as well as myself.

'But I didn't get very far. The ward sister noticed my bed was empty and she'd informed main reception before I'd even got to the bottom of the stairs. Two orderlies were waiting for me. The last thing I remember was arguing with them and insisting I was well enough to check myself out. I'm told I collapsed. The next thing I knew I was back on the ward with a drip in my arm. They didn't allow me out until this morning.'

'Have to learn everything the hard way.' Charlie shook his head. 'Anyway, it's good to see you up and about. How are you coping?'

'There's no easy answer to that. In some ways, surprisingly well. The old ticker seems to be hanging in there. Dr McCormick tells me there's no reason I shouldn't make a complete recovery, provided I stick to a sensible diet and lay off the booze. And the medication he's got me on seems to be controlling the headaches. I only wish I'd gone to see him months ago. Other than that, I'm still in a bit of a daze. It's scarcely believable. I've lost... everyone...'

'I'd recommend you continue seeing Stephen McCartney, Michael. He could be a real lifeline.'

'I intend to.' Michael paused. 'Do you have any news of Philippa?'

'She's in the Western too, didn't you know? You were practically neighbours.'

'I didn't realise that. I'd have gone to see her if I'd known. How is she?'

'They kept her in for observation, but they'll be letting her out soon. McCartney and I have been to see her a few times. Physically, she's over the worst of the effects of the drugs. Emotionally, she's still badly shaken, but Stephen's confident there won't be any long-term psychological damage. In any case, she's talking things over with a counsellor.

'What about you and her?' Charlie asked. 'Any chance of you getting back together?'

Michael shook his head. 'That's over.'

'What are your plans?'

'To try to get some order back into my life. I haven't been back to the flat yet, but I'm going to have to face up to that sooner or later. I called Sheila Thompson yesterday and told her I'd come into the office tomorrow morning. I don't know if I'll be able to contribute much, but anything's better than moping around feeling sorry for myself. Sheila's been marvellous. She's organised everything for me, including booking me in for therapy sessions with Dr McCartney.

'By the way,' Michael added. 'I've found a new home for Anne's cat. Harry Kennedy phoned me in hospital and asked if it would be all right if he kept Brutus down in his flat for the time being. He said it was a drag going upstairs twice a day to feed him and change his litter. It sounded like an excuse. The way Harry goes on about the beast, I don't think there would be much chance of me getting him back, even if I wanted to. But tell me. How did you know to go to Dalgleish Tower that evening?'

'We've got Harry to thank for that. When Maureen Donnelly called me and told me about Paul and Gordon Parker, I sent O'Sullivan across to Traquair House straight away to bring Paul in for questioning. Tony had no sooner left the office when Harry called me to tell me he'd just seen 'Mr Gibson's bit of stuff', as he so elegantly put it, driving into the garage at Dalgleish Tower. He thought I might be interested. I phoned Dr Glen at Traquair House to make sure Paul was there and he told me Paul had asked for permission to go across to his flat to pick up a few things. Glen had agreed. Paul had left Traquair House around lunchtime and hadn't come back. I put two and two together and raced over to Dalgleish Tower. I got the apartment key from Harry and – as they say in the movies – you know the rest.' Michael nodded grimly. 'By the way, we arrested Jack McFarlane last night,' Charlie added.

'Where?'

'In a warehouse in Cumbernauld. We nabbed him red-handed with Larry Robertson and the Routledge brothers as they were sharing out the proceeds of the Bothwell Street bank robbery. They were all in on it. I'd a hunch at the time that Robertson was involved, but McFarlane was the only one we could prove anything against. It transpires that McFarlane was the only one who knew where the loot was stashed and he did a deal with Robertson that he would get a double share if he didn't shop any of the others while he was inside. Honour among thieves and all that crap.'

'How did you manage to nail them?'

'We got a tip-off about where and when the share-out was going to take place. From Francie McGurk, actually – Bernie's brother. He wouldn't take any reward for the information. He said he was doing it for Bernie.'

'I owed Bernie some money,' Michael said. 'If I leave it with you, could you make sure it gets to Francie?'

'Sure.'

'Will you be charging McFarlane with Bernie's murder?'

'No chance. Bernie walked out of a pub last Monday and wasn't seen again until his body was fished out of the Clyde. Even though I'm one hundred percent certain McFarlane killed him, I couldn't begin to build a case. No evidence – no witnesses. I'm afraid Bernie will become one more unsolved murder statistic, much to Superintendent Hamilton's chagrin. Talking about McFarlane, you're probably not even aware that he was hanging around Dalgleish Tower the night Anne was killed.'

Michael looked incredulous. 'What in the name of God was he doing there?'

'When I asked him about that, he laughed like a drain. It's hard to credit it, but it seems he was intent on winding us up. When he gave us the slip, he was on his way to Larry Robertson's place in Turnberry Road. Naturally, he wasn't going to give Robertson's address to a taxi driver as he knew we'd question every cabbie in Paisley.

'Apparently his threat to take revenge on you and your family had just been an emotional outburst when he got sentenced. He'd forgotten all about it until I triggered his memory when we picked him up. His lawyer, Frank Morrison, had told him that you'd moved to Dalgleish Tower, so he thought it would be a bit of a giggle to get out of the taxi there, just to put the wind up us, and walk from there to Robertson's place. He thought that if he could convince us he'd come back to Glasgow to get his revenge on you, it might deflect us from cottoning on to the real reason for him being here. The bastard has an extremely sick sense of humour. He even went to the trouble of going back to Dalgleish Tower later that same evening, just to catch a taxi into the city centre.'

After Michael had left, Charlie spent another hour clearing his backlog of paperwork. He was about to leave for the night when his intercom buzzed. He flicked across the switch.

'Yes, Pauline?'

'Superintendent Hamilton would like to see you in his office straight away, sir. He's just received the year-to-date figures for violent crime and he wants to discuss them with you.'

Charlie barely hesitated. 'You just missed me, Pauline, I – '

'I know, sir,' Pauline interrupted. 'Five minutes ago...'

Tuesday 29 March

Just after nine o'clock, Michael Gibson pulled up in his private parking bay, then walked up the stairs to his office. Sheila waved across when she saw him come through the door.

'The young lady is waiting for you in your office,' she said.

'What young lady?'

'She said you were expecting her, Mr Gibson. She told me she's joining the firm next month.'

Michael's brow furrowed. 'There must be some mistake. I don't know anything about a new member of staff. I hope Peter Davies hasn't hired someone without consulting me?'

Sheila looked bemused. 'But she told me you'd recruited her personally, Mr Gibson. Her name is – ' Sheila broke off to refer to her notepad. 'Saoirse MacBride.'